Barbara,
Enjoy my b
for the encouragement!
Carol Selick

Beyond the Song

© 2021 Carol Selick

To request permissions, contact: carolselickmusic.com

ISBN 978-1-09838-369-5
eBook ISBN 978-1-09838-370-1

Library of Congress Cataloging-in-Publication Data

Printed in the United States of America

BEYOND
the SONG

CAROL SELICK

ACKNOWLEDGMENTS

To *Nina, Stevie, Dani, Marsha, as well as Melanie and Bonnie,* who left us too soon, thank you for your friendship.

A beyond enormous thank you to my incredibly skilled editor Gayle Wurst, Princeton International Agency for the Arts, LLC, who guided me through this project with patience and vision.

A big thank you to my dear departed friend Gail Shapiro-Scott who loved to read and was one of my biggest supporters. I will always be grateful for your enthusiastic encouragement.

Thank you to songwriter Rose Marie McCoy, whose spirit I felt guiding me during this project. I will always treasure the time we spent together, writing songs at 1650 Broadway. Thank you for sharing your talent, your laughter, and above all your friendship.

A big thank you to my aunt, Marion Crosby, whose book *I Will Fear No Evil,* gave me invaluable insights into my family history.

Appreciation and gratitude to my parents who stood by me during my growing pains and whose love never wavered.

Love and gratitude to the two men who encouraged and believed in my creativity - my dear departed husband, Wally Selick, and my present husband, Gordon James.

Imbedded in my memory, deep within my soul
Are feelings coming out of me, I buried long ago
Tunes rewinding endlessly on vinyl plates of gold
Timeless, ageless feelings neither young nor old
Hidden dreams awaken me like an old forgotten song
And images so vivid, invite me to sing along
Lovers beg, "Please dance with me. Let's give love one more try."
But I can still remember why I had to say goodbye
I need to find some meaning for the steps I dared to take
And have trust that my journey was not a big mistake
Changes came so quickly, now I turn around
My life has come full circle, and what was lost is found

TABLE OF CONTENTS

1
NEW YORK CITY, 1971

When I was just a little girl, my Daddy said to me,
"A man's gonna come and love you some,
That's your Daddy's prophecy."
But it keeps on a-worryin' me,
Oh Lord, it keeps on a-worryin' me.

I stood on the corner of 72nd and Columbus Avenue feeling like a human want-ad. I had a copy of the *Village Voice* in one hand and an unlit cigarette in the other. I was out of matches. And then I heard a voice behind me. "Looking for an apartment?"

I turned around. He was older than me and definitely not my type with his professional, straight look and short brown hair. But he had a sweet smile and his round, wire-rimmed glasses revealed soft blue eyes.

"How did you know?"

"I saw the paper. Do you need a place to make some calls? I live right up the street."

"Why not?"

It wasn't the first time I'd gone with a stranger to his place, and the July heat of the city was getting to me.

We exchanged names on the way to his apartment. Marvin Silverman—lawyer, liberal, almost thirty, and climbing. Carol Marks—hippie, singer, twenty-two, and drifting.

"Far out, you have a nice place!" It was on the third floor of a classic brownstone very close to Central Park.

"Thanks. It's small, but I like the neighborhood."

I walked toward the bay windows in the living room where a telescope was mounted on a tripod. There were no curtains or blinds. I wondered what that was about, but didn't want to ask.

"What's that building across the street?"

"That's the Dakota. A lot of famous people live there like John and Yoko."

"I *love* New York! I can't *wait* to move here!"

"Where do you live? On the Island?"

"No *way*! I live in Jersey with my parents, but *that's* only temporary."

I fumbled in my bag for a cigarette and started to feel nervous.

He was pretending to be hipper than he really was. He probably got stoned on the weekend and came to work on Monday wearing a three-piece suit. It's as if he climbed to thirty and didn't know whether to lead those behind him or follow those in front. I was glad that *I* didn't have an identity problem. I *did* have an apartment problem, though, and couldn't get sidetracked by this weekend hippie.

Ten calls and five lewd propositions later, I was still without a place. I thanked Marvin for the use of his phone.

"Next time you're in the city, give me a call. Maybe we can do something."

"Sounds good, Marvin." I knew what "do something" meant. I threw his business card in my bag, the purple woven one I'd bought from a street vendor in Berkeley the day I'd left California, and ran down the stairs to meet my friend. I hoped she'd had better luck than me finding a place.

I rushed to catch the Broadway uptown bus, and by the time I got off at 86th Street, Marvin Silverman had completely left my mind.

I was meeting Nina at Professors, a typical uptown neighborhood bar. People dressed down and the prices climbed up. Its inhabitants were considered native New Yorkers. That meant they'd lived in the city for at least one year, but not necessarily in the same apartment.

"Any luck?" I asked Nina. I knew what her answer would be by her tired look and the pile of cigarette butts in the ashtray. Even her curly red hair looked droopy.

We'd been friends since eighth grade and had managed to stay in touch throughout college. We'd rebelled in different ways. Nina was very serious when it came to politics. She sometimes asked her friends, "Are you political?" If someone answered, "a little," she would ask, "Can you be a little pregnant?"

Nina also had a fun side and we laughed a lot. Like the time we were hanging out in my bedroom at my parents' house and my father knocked on the door. He walked in wearing my mother's blue and green paisley tent dress. It was 1968, and bell-bottoms were all the rage. "Do you see how silly you girls look wearing bell bottoms?" Dad asked with a straight face. "Just as silly as I look wearing a dress." Nina and I were hysterical. In a couple of years, Dad would change his mind about bell-bottoms and the Vietnam War.

Three rounds of sodas and one heaping ashtray later, Nina and I headed out of the bar to Port Authority. Sitting on the downtown bus, I remembered meeting Marvin.

"I met a really nice guy today," I informed Nina.

"Oh *yeah*?" she kidded me.

"No really, he let me use his apartment to make phone calls."

"I bet that's not *all* you made."

"You have a *dirty mind*! Look! He gave me his card and asked me to call him the next time I was in the city." I started digging around in my bag. "I can't find it!" I exclaimed hopelessly, looking up at Nina sitting by the window, skeptically arching her eyebrow at me. "Hey, wait! This is his street! Let's get off the bus—let me run up and say hi."

I recognized the brownstone and ran up the steps leaving Nina waiting on the sidewalk. Why was I even bothering? Was I flattered that an older man had shown interest in me?

When I rang the doorbell Marvin opened the door wearing a half-buttoned shirt and a confused look on his face.

"Gee Marv, I didn't mean to bother you. It's just that I lost your card and I was passing by and—"

"Yeah kid, that's okay. I just can't talk to you now. Give me your number. I'll call you up sometime."

I scribbled my number on the back of a matchbook and caught up with Nina who was already halfway down the block.

"I'll probably never hear from him again. He wasn't my type anyway, too straight," I told her but I secretly wanted him to call.

It seemed like Nina and I were spending most of our time in Port Authority. It was the dirtiest gate to the city, a haven for every degenerate and vagabond. I took a deep breath and boarded the Suburban Transit bus back to the burbs.

I was twenty-two, had dropped out of college, moved to California, run out of money, and moved back home. I hated riding on any kind of public transportation. It was sort of a phobia. I had a lot of fears, like being stuck in an elevator—or worse, a subway. Sometimes I had trouble eating in restaurants. But *nothing* was going to stop me from living in the city. My one goal was to make it in the music business and New York was *the* place to be. I was taking my music seriously, practicing my songs every day on the French Provincial piano at my parents' house that I'd unfortunately branded with a cigarette burn. Carole King, Laura Nyro, and Carly Simon were my idols and I was determined to follow in their footsteps.

My mother, a junior high social studies teacher, described my life as "the Perils of Pauline." My father, a self-made businessman, just thought I was lazy. Both were relieved I hadn't found an apartment in the city. They were waiting for the day when I would wake up and come to my senses. They told the relatives that I was finding myself and wondered when they had lost me. They'd told me many times that I was a follower and that my friends were the reason I'd dropped out of college, wore bell bottoms, smoked cigarettes, and wanted to live in the city with no cross-ventilation in the middle of July.

"Carol! Telephone!" I heard my mother shout the next evening. She put her hand over the receiver and whispered, "It's a boy."

"Carol, this is Marvin. You know, we met on the corner of 72nd Street?"

"You really did call! I thought you were just giving me the brush."

"I wouldn't do that—I'm a lawyer, remember? We always keep our word. What are you doing Friday night? You want to go to dinner and a movie?"

"Are you asking me on a *date*?"

"No. I don't go on them anymore. I'm being spontaneous."

"Far out, Marvin! I'll be there."

He was my first older man and I was ready for him! I'd always been drawn to stories like *My Fair Lady*, *Pygmalion*, and *Gigi*, where older, more worldly men influenced younger, naïve women and then they fell in love.

Getting ready to go to Marvin's, I looked in the mirror and ran my fingers through my hair. Nearly black, contrasting sharply with my light, freckled skin, it was long and wavy in winter, but frizzy in summer. I'd given up trying to straighten it and just let it go à *la* Janis Joplin. I'd read that she ironed her hair on an ironing board. Since I rarely ironed my clothes, I decided that wasn't an option.

It was liberating not to worry about my hair, and so was not wearing a bra. Liberated women everywhere were giving them up and burning them. Besides, I was thin enough to get away with it. The Indian print tops I wore with my jeans looked fine without one. I felt perky, sexy, and hip.

I checked myself out in the mirror. My lips were small and I never bothered with lipstick. I picked up my eyeliner, the one makeup I always used and underlined my hazel-green eyes with black pencil on the lower lids. One of my college boyfriends had described my eyes as sideways exclamation points. Of course, he was stoned at the time.

"This is the first apartment in New York that hasn't given me claustrophobia," I announced, sitting on the couch at Marvin's. The kitchen was small, but the living room was large with high ceilings and two bay windows. I hadn't seen the bedroom yet. The telescope was still pointed towards the undraped windows. I had to ask.

"What's with the telescope, Marv? Are you into astronomy?"

"You might say I'm into sociology. I like to check out the people in the apartments across the street. Everyone does it in New York."

"Oh. So you let them study you, too? There are no drapes on your windows."

"Sometimes. It doesn't matter. No one knows who I am."

I tried to hide my nervousness. I was in a strange man's apartment in the middle of a strange city. I reminded myself it was nothing compared to all the hitchhiking I'd done in California a couple of years ago, back when the Manson murderers were still on the loose.

"I really should be a good boy tonight, Carol."

"What do you mean, Marv? I thought *you* were a *man*."

"I should take you out to dinner and a movie." And then he kissed me.

What happened next was every girl's fantasy from the first time she practices kissing her favorite movie star's face in her pillow. The faces change and the movie stars become rock stars and radicals. But the plot is the same and every Gothic novel describes the hero and heroine's all-consuming passion.

The speed of our attraction felt like two magnets rushing without question to be one. Of course, in Gothic novels, it always took at least half an hour to get your clothes off, thanks to laced corsets and rows and rows of buttons. But it was 1971 and women went braless, men wore no jockey shorts under their jeans, and clothes were meant to be thrown on the floor.

"Oh, Marvin!" I screamed and Marvin exploded in a fit of laughter. We were positioned like two trapeze artists getting ready for the final jump. The bed was not very high but the risk of falling was tremendous.

"Why did you start laughing? I was almost there!" I couldn't decide if I was hurt or angry.

"That voice! It was so loud it startled me."

"I *told* you I was a singer. And I always bring my voice to bed with me."

"Sorry, Carol."

But this was no time for talking. We both remounted our imaginary trapezes, took a few low rides, and started pumping.

I could hardly wait to tell my friends all about it. "Nina, it was the best! And he couldn't believe I'd been celibate for four whole months! I think it did something to his male ego. He's definitely not my type, but he's got money and he wants to show me around the city—if we ever get out of bed!"

We were hanging out at our friend Stevie's college apartment in New Brunswick. Stevie wasn't her real name, Marilyn was. I never asked her why she picked Stevie for a nickname instead of Mary, but there were a lot of things I didn't understand about her. Like why she called her latest painting "Early Morning Blues Sculpture." I never could figure out why she had stopped seeing her cute astrologer boyfriend, the one who told me that I had *divine discontent,* to be with a married, forty-something professor. Maybe she liked the challenge, or maybe she'd just listened to too much Janis Joplin. With her platinum blonde Marilyn Monroe haircut and blue-violet eyes, she certainly didn't have any problem attracting men.

I stopped to take a gulp of coffee. This wasn't the first time I'd sat at Stevie's old Formica kitchen table swapping stories about the night before. Instead of housewives trading recipes, we were independent women sharing our sex lives. Women our age all over the country were holding their own roundtable discussions. The men we slept with would have blushed if they knew how thoroughly we scrutinized their sex techniques, no pubic hair left unturned.

After a couple of months, our "morning after" coffee klatches started to influence the "night before." Nina confessed that the last time she'd had sex with her boyfriend she thought she'd heard the sound of coffee percolating. At first, she thought Daniel, an ex-acid rock guitarist who had found peace by playing country music, had the hiccups. Then she realized her mind had started editing, rewriting a blow-by-blow account of the evening's events. She vividly reenacted how Daniel had screamed her name at the crucial moment. Afterward, he denied it, blaming his questionable utterance on a sore throat from smoking too much pot. He said two people had to be very serious before they called out to each other in bed and he was positive that married people stopped using each other's names after the first year of marriage. By then they were too busy fantasizing.

"He was just getting scared," I told Nina. I secretly envied her ability to hold on to men for longer than six months. My record was three months, but who was counting?

Marvin and I were meeting spontaneously on a regular basis. We went to the movies and tried going out to dinner, but I was having trouble eating in restaurants again. Most of the time, we ordered Chinese take-out.

Sex was still exciting and he had gotten used to the sound of my orgasm voice. Sometimes we would stand nude together in front of the living room windows and give the neighbors a show. Then one night we were sitting on the couch and he popped the question.

"I'm thinking of taking a few months off and going to California. Do you want to sublet my apartment?"

"Making the pilgrimage to paradise? If I'd found a job there, I would still be in Berkeley."

"So, do you want the apartment or not?"

"Yes!"

Nina and I still hadn't found a place and this was the answer to our prayers. I couldn't wait to tell her the good news.

"Oh, and Carol—you know your eating thing? I have a friend who could help you with that." Marvin offered. "He's the best shrink in the city. Here's his number. When I get back from California, I'm taking you out to dinner."

"Thanks, Marv. Maybe I'll give him a call."

My father packed up his station wagon with Nina's and my things and reluctantly drove us into the city. It was a sweltering hot Sunday in July and no one felt like talking. I knew my father wasn't happy about the move, but I was twenty-two and desperately seeking my independence. I'd saved enough money working temp jobs to pay my share of the rent for the next few months. By then, I hoped to have a job in the city. Even if I had to work a day job in an office

We miraculously found a parking spot right in front of the apartment. Everything was going smoothly until I handed my father the key to the front door of the building.

"Are you sure this is the right key, Carol? It won't open." Before I could answer, he yelled, "It's stuck! I think I broke the key!"

I didn't need a shrink to figure out the symbolism of my father breaking the key that opened the door to my freedom.

I went down to the corner phone booth and called Marvin. He was staying with his mother in Jersey until he left for California the next day. He said he could get to us in under an hour.

When he arrived, Marvin was a perfect gentleman. He managed to get the old key out of the lock and used his spare to unlock the door. He even helped bring some of our things up to the apartment. Before he left, he told my father in his most serious lawyer voice, "I want you to know, Mr. Marks, that I was never 'romantically involved' with your daughter" (code for "I never slept with her"). "We just went out a few times."

My father grabbed his hand and thanked him.

Just before my father left, he handed me an envelope. Inside was a hundred dollars in cash and a handwritten note:

Carol,

Boys must play and grow

Before they fall in love and know

The beauty and the longing theme

Of a girl's aching heart and dream.

So, my dear Carol, until then,

Until boys learn to be men,

Please accept a father's love

That's as old as you and a true love.

2
THERAPY

Time has come to stop believing
In fairy tales that never can come true.
You held them close, swore you'd never leave them,
But you knew you would, 'cause you understood
Grown-up children can't survive.

I'd been seeing Marvin's therapist friend for about three weeks. Twice a week I took a crosstown bus to his Eastside office on 75th between Madison and Park. He said he could help me get over my phobias about eating in restaurants and riding the subway. I'd also been experiencing anxiety attacks. It was a free-floating, almost paralyzing fear that came on suddenly. Sometimes it would happen when I was crossing a busy street. My legs felt like jelly and I prayed I would make it to the other side.

I sat in his small waiting room on the sixth floor and stared at the Gustave Klimt print hanging on the wall. The one of a handsome dark-haired man kissing a beautiful woman. I smoothed down my untamable summer hair and waited for Bruce to open the door to his office. I was curious to see if one of his clients would walk out of his inner sanctum, but so far, I'd never seen one. I assumed he timed it that way for privacy reasons. I didn't understand what the big deal was about seeing a shrink. It seemed like everyone in the city bragged about being in analysis and was just as eager to give out their analyst's number as they were their hairdresser's.

Bruce Pasternak was no ordinary therapist. Although he was the same age as Marvin he seemed more adult. He had a calmness about him and a good sense of humor. He was the most caring man I'd ever met—and also the most handsome. With his thick, dark hair and large hazel eyes, he sort of looked like the man in the Klimpt painting.

The first time I walked into his office I was hooked. One of the earliest songs I wrote in college was "I'm a Girl/Woman, I Need a Boy/Man." I was still a girl/woman but Bruce was definitely all man. He was the first person who accepted me unconditionally and the feeling was intoxicating!

During my very first session, I'd asked him what sign he was and he replied "positive!"

"Oh, come on, let me guess! I bet you're a Virgo." He smiled in spite of himself.

"I knew it! That's a very analytical sign. Perfect for a shrink!"

I knew a few other things about him from Marvin. He was divorced, introspective, and slow to make decisions. Marvin said when he had brunch at Bruce's apartment, his soon-to-be ex-wife asked him how he wanted his eggs cooked, and it took Bruce a few minutes to decide.

He was a hardcore Freudian psychologist, so I wasn't surprised when he asked, "How did you feel when your father got the key stuck in the door, Carol?"

"Hmm . . ." I took a long drag on my cigarette. We were sitting face-to-face. There was a sofa in the office, but Bruce hadn't asked me to lie on it yet.

"I don't know. Maybe he didn't want me to start a new life?"

"Dig deeper, Carol. Think about the shape of the key."

"Are you saying it's a phallic symbol?" I wasn't completely clueless about Freudian analysis. I had taken Psychology 101 in college.

"Did it remind you of any other times in your life?"

"I was too young to remember, but my father told me that one night my mother cut her hand in the kitchen and he had to rush her to the hospital. He left me alone in the apartment and when he got back someone had tampered with the lock. I must have been frightened, but like I said, I don't remember."

Bruce blew a smoke ring from his cigar. A deliberate smokescreen to create a barrier between us. But it couldn't hide the thick sexual tension in the air. I didn't need a textbook to figure that out.

"Oh, wait, there was another time in college when I locked the keys in the car on moving day. It was when Melanie and I were moving into our apartment at George Washington University."

"Do you see a pattern regarding moving and being on your own? From what you've told me, your parents were overly protective. Can you tell me more about them?"

"Well, my father came to this country from Poland right before the Nazis killed his family."

"Your father lost his entire family?"

"Yeah, except for one brother who survived."

"That could explain why he was so overly protective. Let's talk more about this in a future session. Tell me about your mother."

"She didn't have it easy growing up either. Her parents came from Russia and owned a dry-cleaning store in Brooklyn. They lived in an apartment above the store and she and her brother were left on their own a lot. Oh, and she grew up during the Depression."

"Sounds like a hard life."

I stopped for a minute and tried to think objectively about my mother. Betty Marks was an attractive, petite woman, with short, frosted, permed hair and a flair for fashion. She liked shopping at Loehmann's and was perfectly capable of picking out her own clothes, but wouldn't think of buying anything without my father's approval. Even though she contributed to half of our family income, my father was clearly the boss. Theirs was a great love, and sometimes I thought they would've been a lot happier if I hadn't come along. They had a tight system that worked for them, based on a mutual fear of germs, Germans, messes, and non-conformity.

I found the courage to look directly into Bruce's eyes and asked, "How can talking about my parents' lives get rid of my phobias and anxiety attacks?"

"From what you told me so far, your parents were overly protective. They didn't want you to grow up."

"Why not? Why wouldn't parents want their child to grow up?"

"Control. You and your father had an unconscious agreement. You made a mess and he cleaned it up."

"Hmm, I never thought about it that way. My mother hated messes too, but more the spilled milk and mud on the floor kind. I guess they *could* be afraid for me to be on my own."

"Everyone grows old, Carol, but not everyone grows up. Seeing your parents as people with their own challenges and flaws is a good first step."

I nodded, but my head was deep into my favorite daydream. The one where Bruce puts down his cigar takes my hand and throws me on the couch. I can feel his strong body on top of mine and he's kissing me behind my ears, whispering, *this is what you really need, Carol.*

"Carol? Did you hear me?"

"Sorry, I guess I spaced out there for a minute." My face felt flushed. If he knew what I'd been imagining, I'd be mortified! I knew that transference was common between a patient and a therapist, but I was sure I could feel his attraction to me, too. If only he weren't so incredibly handsome, kind, funny, and accepting! He was everything I wanted in a man. The only thing missing was he wasn't a musician, but I could live with that.

Bruce was my oasis in a world that I didn't understand, and that never understood me either, from the time I was a child. A world that I was trying to make sense out of and find a place in. I couldn't risk telling him how I really felt. I was searching for transcendence, not transference. That was a label I wasn't willing to accept.

As I sat on the crosstown bus, the line *Everyone grows old, but not everyone grows up* echoed in my mind. By the time I climbed the stairs to my third-floor apartment, I'd come up with the title for a song: "Grown-Up Children Can't Survive." I grabbed a pen and a paper bag lying on the coffee table, sat at my rented piano, and played around with some chords. The verses poured out of me, or maybe it was through me. I scribbled them down and finished the entire song in twenty minutes. It was the fastest one I'd ever written and, I felt, the most meaningful.

> *And time has come to stop your grieving*
> *About your parents' love that seemed to pass you by.*
> *You'll understand, that you can't make reasons*
> *For the love you lost, when you paid the cost to see things as they are*
> *'Cause grown-up children can't survive.*
> *And time will come when you'll start believing*
> *In your own strength, the way that people do.*
> *You're so afraid 'cause the child is leaving,*
> *But you fight your fear, 'cause you know 'round here*
> *Grown-up children can't survive.*

3
COLLEGE DAZE

All my life I was waiting for someone to start me,
Sitting like a wind-up doll, looking outside for the key.
On my shelf, I was feeling kinda lonely and dusty,
Ain't nothing or anyone around gonna help me live my life.

Flashback: 1968, sophomore year. I'd transferred from boring, sub-urban Rider College in New Jersey to George Washington University in DC. When the Dean of Women at Rider asked me why I was transferring, I made up something about wanting to be in a more cosmopolitan environment. I couldn't tell her the real reasons: that I wanted to be with hipper people, protest against the war, smoke dope, and stay out past my 9:00 p.m. curfew. It wasn't any of her business, I thought, as I stared into her middle-aged patrician face. She looked like she was born old. She could never understand what it was like to be young and free. As I proudly handed her my letter of acceptance from George Washington, she just smiled and wished me luck. Even *she* couldn't deny that I was moving up in the world!

Imagine my disappointment, when I got to GWU and found myself sharing a dorm suite with five straight-laced women who all knew each other from Freshman year. I felt like I was back at Rider. What were the odds, in a building that was so large, they called it Super Dorm, of rooming with five women who'd never heard one electrifying guitar riff from groups like Cream and Procol Harem? I was mortified later to hear that on the first day, they'd gone through my Indian print tops and bell-bottom jeans and labeled me their token hippie.

Although, *one* of my new roommates was her *own* kind of crazy. Randy Messinger came from a poor section of Philly and was on a full scholarship. She was very smart, but for extra money, she managed a nightclub downtown. She also belonged to a sorority and barely had time to sleep. Her short, red, pixie-cut hair drew attention to the ever-present dark circles under her eyes. Randy's schedule was so erratic, she got to sleep in the only single room in the suite that was cordoned off by two wooden glass-paned doors. Some nights she got back from the club at 2:00 a.m. and fell asleep in her clothes and makeup. The next day she woke up early, washed her face, and went to class, then piled on the mascara and went back to work at the club that night. I started to question why I'd bothered to transfer.

That changed the day Melanie Bloom moved next door. A few weeks into the semester, I was rushing down the hall, late for my European Lit class, when I noticed that the door to the room next to mine was slightly open. I glanced in and saw a girl with long brown wavy hair sitting at the edge of the bed, staring out the window. She looked almost doll-like, sitting perfectly still and expressionless, although I sensed a feeling of sadness. When I came back from class, I knocked on the sad girl's door and asked if I could come in. We bonded instantly probably because we both felt like outsiders.

Melanie told me she'd left her sorority because she couldn't take the phoniness of the other girls and that quitting was a turning point in her life. She no longer wanted to be the "popular girl" and depend on friends and family to make her feel good. She wanted to take an inner journey. Like me, she wasn't going to college to get her MRS. Degree and she definitely wasn't a JAP—a Jewish American Princess. There were plenty of those at GWU. You could see them sitting in front of the dorm on a warm day, holding their shiny aluminum sun reflectors under their hopeful faces.

A few days later, she waved me into her room and read me one of her poems. I was blown away. She wasn't rhyming *moon* and *June*, she was pouring out her pain. It was deep and symbolic and profound, *not* the ramblings of a superficial sorority girl!

> *I want to be in the pink-red rose womb of warm bloody cushions*
> *To keep me from cold winds, cold money, cold people's arrowed spears.*
> *I want the world to love my insides, no matter how messy and frightened they are.*

There were things we could learn from each other. I was an experienced hippie, but she was an experienced woman, having lost her virginity in high school. It was easy to see why, with her almond-shaped brown eyes, perfect nose, and pouty lips. She was petite but her C cups were too big to go braless. No doubt about it—Melanie Bloom was a fox and men were drawn to her wherever we went. That was the downside of hanging out with her, but I had found my first friend at GWU and I was willing to risk it.

"I almost did it first-semester last year," I confessed to her one Friday night. We were lounging in her dorm room making plans for the weekend.

"He was a senior and one of the few cool guys. He looked like Woody Allen and everyone called him Woody, including me." I stopped to light a cigarette. That was another thing Melanie and I had in common, we both smoked Tareytons.

"He asked me to go away with him for the weekend to his best friend's place in Bayonne. It was the first time we'd spent the night together. We were down to our underwear when I pushed his hand away. That's when he played the love card. *If we loved each other, blah, blah, blah.* I don't know what stopped me, but I just wasn't ready. The next day we were history. He just cared about the sex."

"What a jerk! Obviously, he wasn't the right one."

"Yeah, but I'm tired of waiting."

Two days later, Melanie came up with a bright idea. "Let's go on a double date," she said. It was more of a statement than a question.

Three weeks had gone by since I'd first knocked on her door and we were now officially best friends. Melanie was getting hipper and we'd even shared a joint that she'd scored from one of her ex-boyfriends.

"Far out! Who are they?" I asked.

"It could be weird, but I met this cute Navy guy when I was studying by the Washington Monument, and he asked me if I had a friend."

That Friday night I peeked over the second-floor balcony to check out our sailors down in the lobby. I spotted them right away. They looked out of place with their bright white sailor uniforms in a sea of blue denim, but they were cute enough to make me want to go downstairs. Bill was tall and blond and from the Midwest. He kissed Melanie on the cheek and introduced us both to Jerry. He was more my type, medium height, and build with dark wavy hair. He looked me up and down but not in a creepy way.

"Let's go to Georgetown!" Jerry suggested.

"Yeah, let's have some fun!" Bill chimed in, then turned to Melanie and me. "It's our last weekend. We're shipping out to Vietnam," he informed us with a serious look.

I wondered if it was true or just a line to get us into bed. I started to feel uptight. I'd never met anyone in the military. Everyone I knew was against the war and afraid of getting drafted. They were thinking up clever ways to get rejected from the army. One popular idea was to stay up for an entire week, never shower, and drop acid the night before the physical. The idea of *wanting* to fight in a war was way too heavy.

We drove to Georgetown in their rented Volkswagen and found a parking spot in the middle of the action. As we walked along the quaint, narrow cobblestone streets it reminded me of Greenwich Village, but pricier. Jerry took my hand and we maneuvered through the usual weekend crowd of students, tourists, and hippies.

Melanie peered into the window of a trendy boutique and suggested, "Let's go in this shop.'"

"Cool," I said as we walked in the door. A light tan dress immediately caught my eye. It was suede and had beads and fringe on the bottom. "Look at that!"

"Try it on, Carol!" Jerry said. There was a devilish twinkle in his eyes.

"I don't know. I couldn't afford it. I guess I could try it just for fun."

Jerry's eyes lit up as I walked out of the dressing room.

"I'm buying you that dress!"

As hard as I tried to talk him out of it, I had to admit it was my style. No man had ever bought me a dress before. I let him buy it but worried that the fringe on the bottom might not be the only strings attached.

We ended up in an overpriced Italian restaurant. Melanie sat up against Bill in the booth and he curled his arm around her. I couldn't tell if she was into him or just being polite, but I doubted she was taking him seriously. I picked at my Fettuccine Alfredo, thinking it was just a fancy word for pasta and cheese, and hoped no one noticed how little I was eating. All I could think about was what was going to happen *after* dinner. Meanwhile, Bill and Jerry ate as if it were their last meal, and joked around as if they hadn't a care in the world. Were they that naïve about going to war? Or had they made the whole thing up just to get some weekend action?

On the ride to the dorm, Jerry and I sat in the back again. He pulled me towards him and stared deep into my eyes with such intensity I knew this was the moment I'd been dreading.

"Stay with me tonight, baby," he whispered.

How could I say no to a sailor who was going to war the next day?

"Jerry, you are *so* sweet, but I hardly know you." I shook my head and started to cry.

I couldn't tell him the truth. That my first time wasn't going to be with a lonely sailor. It was too cliché. We would both have to be brave.

I promised to pray for him whenever I wore the suede dress.

Two weeks later, I got the chance to make good on that promise. Randy asked me to fill in for the hostess at her nightclub. It was another Saturday night without a date and I thought it might be a fun way to get out and even make some extra money.

As soon as I walked into the club Randy came running over to me.

"Great! You made it! *Nice dress*. It'll be perfect for dancing!" she exclaimed, a little out of breath.

"*Dancing*? You said I was gonna be a hostess. I'm not a dancer."

"Look, all you have to do is stand in that cage." My eyes followed her finger as she pointed to the elevated platform at the head of the crowded room. I must have looked shocked, because she quickly added, "Just keep changing the records and move a little to the music. That dress is perfect with all the fringe and beads. You'll be great. I'm really in a bind."

"Okay, but just for tonight." I couldn't believe I'd agreed to be a go-go dancer!

Randy's bar was called The Attic. It was located above a seedy lingerie shop right in the heart of DC. By day, the neighborhood diners and mom-and-pop stores bustled with office workers looking for a quick, cheap lunch. By night, the streets were deserted except for the patrons of the many clubs and bars, who were also hunting for something quick and cheap. The Attic attracted businessmen, traveling salesmen, and low-level politicians. That's how Randy described them, anyway. The ratio of men to women was three-to-one and the women looked like they were "working."

The place was dark and smoky. I made my way past rows of packed-in tables and self-consciously mounted the stairs to the platform. I took a deep breath, stepped into the cage, and started flipping through the stack of 45s piled up next to the turntable. *You can't get out of this now*, I figured, *so you might as well make the best of it*. I started with "Light My Fire"—a sexy, mid-tempo song—and worked my way up to "Jumpin' Jack Flash" and on to "Dance to the Music" by Sly and the Family Stone. With the strobe lights blinking on and off, I could barely see the top of the dancers' heads as they gyrated to the music. I swayed along with them and felt the fringe of my dress caressing my knees. As I spun around, I pictured my younger self as a star-struck little girl, dancing and singing to the records from the Broadway musicals my parents took me to.

Sitting in the balcony as a child, I always wanted to jump on stage and be the star. At home, I played my parents' records from every Broadway hit we saw: *My Fair Lady, Camelot, Golden Boy*—until I knew every lyric by heart. I imagined the day when I would be famous and newspapers would say how I always loved singing and dancing as a child. I could already see my name on the marquee—Carol Marks! Was I ready to set the room on fire tonight? I wasn't sure, but if not, I'd better be able to fake it.

As the night wore on, I gradually relaxed and got into my part as a sexy, aloof nightclub dancer. I thought about the "Sock It to Me" girl on *Laugh-In*. The wide-eyed, beautiful young woman who danced and pretended to be dumb. I was being viewed as a sex object, nothing but window dressing. A pulsating image like the staccato rhythm of the strobe lights. A flash of temptation to tease one's senses. I could be anyone I wanted to be. By the end of the night, I knew I'd played the part well. Some men wanted more than a song but I turned them down. One gave me a twenty-dollar tip anyway.

The dress had gotten me through. True to my word, I said a prayer for Jerry the sailor as I rode the elevator from The Attic down to the street. Back at the dorm, I counted my money with a sense of satisfaction. I'd worked hard for it, but I'd never do it again. It wasn't my scene.

And unlike Randy, I didn't have to work my way through school. According to my parents, I had two jobs: to get good grades and stay out of trouble. Getting good grades was easy, but staying out of trouble was getting harder and harder.

4
CROSSING THE LINE

Too many people are dealing in pain,
Selling it over and over again.
Sometimes I think I'm the one who's insane,
Or too damn dumb to get out of the rain.

Ho, Ho, Ho Chi Minh! The NLF is gonna win! The chanting grew louder as I walked through Lafayette Park on my way to fencing class, ten blocks from the main campus, on a cold but sunny November afternoon. My curiosity got the better of me, so I took a detour to check out the crowd. About fifty protestors had gathered on the sidewalk in front of the White House, carrying signs. BETTER RED THAN DEAD! NO MORE—STOP THE WAR!

I moved in a little closer and joined in the chorus. *Hell no, we won't go! Hell no, we won't go!* I chanted, caught up in their energy. Fencing class would have to wait until next week. Besides, I'd had enough of aggressive girls lunging at me with fake swords as I stood there barely trying to defend myself. This was way more important - there was a *real* war going on and soldiers were dying.

Still on the edge of the action, I peered through the bars of the black, wrought iron fence and caught a glimpse of the White House looking unapproachable and virginal. Then, without warning, a blast from a bull horn assaulted my eardrums. *Disperse Now!* Swat Team pigs wearing helmets were surrounding us raising their billy clubs. The demonstrators just kept chanting, *Hell no, we won't go! Hell no, we won't go!*

I was getting jostled by the crowd and knew I had to get out of there when I heard the sickening sound of wood hitting an innocent skull. I felt dizzy and scared and turned to make my escape when out of the corner of my eyes, I saw a guy with a Dylan afro get clobbered and topple to the ground. Blood splattered everywhere, staining the sidewalk in front of a White House that already had blood on its hands. I ran back to the safety of my dorm feeling scared and shaken. There was a line that I wasn't willing to cross. I was still playing it safe.

The room was quiet, my industrious roommates all in class. I collapsed on my bed, freaked out, yet grateful to be safe. *Whatever happened to free speech? How did I get so involved in politics, anyway?* I thought back to the summer after high school. My girlfriends and I were hanging out at Rutgers, going to frat parties and dances at the student center. The guys labeled us "Townies," but we didn't care. We were having fun! I became friends with Art Berman, a half-Chinese, half-Jewish history major who liked to dance, but whose true passion was politics. He was a Senior and President of SDS, Students for a Democratic Society. When I got to Rider, we kept up through letters until he wrote that it was too dangerous to contact him. "The revolution is coming," he warned.

Was this what Art meant? Was the war between protestors and the government just as dangerous as the war in Vietnam? Last summer, I'd watched the Democratic Convention in Chicago turn into a war zone on tv. The news showed shocking footage of police attacking protestors with clubs in front of the Hilton and Grant Park. Then the National Guard rushed in, bayonets fixed on the crowd. All hell broke loose. One reporter described the chaos as "a sea of tear gas and billy clubs". Reportedly, Mayor Daley had given the pigs permission to shoot to kill.

Not until the next semester was I ready to dip into political waters again. The first thing I did was volunteer to help at the Counter-In-Hog-aural Ball, in protest of Nixon's inauguration. The flyer said:

Now is the time to let Nixon know what the people expect him to do.

The National Mobilization Committee to End the War in Vietnam

is calling on Americans to come to Washington—

on January 18-20 in a peaceful affirmation

of the country's true priorities and needs.

Box seats & Orchestra seats (For the People) — $2.00

Outer Rim & Back Row seats (For Republicans,

Regular Democrats & Such Folk) — $35.00

I was proud to be one of "the people."

Nixon had gotten elected by a slim margin, running on a "Law and Order" platform, and he was using the violence at the Democratic National Convention to instill fear in Middle America. He also lied about his intention to stop the war, calling it, "Peace with honor," but there would be no peace and he was far from honorable. Even Walter Cronkite admitted that the only way out of the war was by negotiation, not victory. Young soldiers were still being slaughtered every day in Viet Nam and pictures of their dead bodies were plastered all over the front page of every newspaper.

On Saturday there was no *real* job for me to do other than showing up, so I stood around in a muddy circus tent listening to Phil Ochs and The Fugs. I'd tried convincing Melanie to go with me, but she was studying Buddhism in her Comparative Religion class and didn't want to "cause any ripples," as she put it. I respected her choice but I *wanted* to make some waves.

Eventually, the crowd started marching toward Pennsylvania Avenue. I kept looking around, feeling alone, hoping to find a kindred spirit, but I was too shy to approach anyone. There were freaks, hippies, and protestors from SDS and other student organizations. They were carrying the usual signs and some I'd never seen before: ABOLISH the DRAFT, FREE POLITICAL PRISONERS, BRING the BOYS HOME, STOP EATING GRAPES, DEFEAT IMPERIALISM. Others were playing kazoos, and a guerrilla theater group in green camouflage jungle fatigues and gas masks was staging fake ambushes on the onlookers. The whole scene was a rainbow of color and energy.

As we approached the museum on the National Mall where Vice President Agnew's Inaugural Ball was being held, women in ball gowns and men in tuxedos were lining up at the entrance, protected by a line of police on horseback. Suddenly, a gun fired! No, a firecracker—purposely thrown at the line of mounted police. A horse reared up amid the screams, and a policeman hit the sidewalk. "Grab some horse shit!" a protestor yelled from the front. He threw down his sign, scooped up a fistful of steaming manure, and walloped a woman in an elegant white evening gown. It landed in a big gob on the front of her white silk gown, just above the knees. After a moment of silence, the "shit hit the fan" and other protesters tossed their signs and started hurling horse manure. I could feel my stomach churning. I'd reached my limit. Once again, this was a line I wasn't willing to cross, and I ran back to the safety of my room.

I may have been closer to the political action, but I was still no closer to becoming a real woman. Melanie and I were sitting on her bed with the window open, smoking a joint and bitching about how bored we were. Second semester was flying by and it was another dateless, depressing Friday night. Melanie had scored the weed from a frat boy she knew from her "former life," as she liked to call it, as a sorority girl.

"Paul still thinks there's a chance I might sleep with him," she said, giggling as she passed the joint.

"Yeah? Keep him guessing as long as you can. This weed is pretty good!" I said and winked as I took another toke. We both started to laugh. We were stoned enough for everything to sound funny.

"Last semester this guy Stu, from my psyche class asked me out for coffee and he wanted to know if I was a virgin! Just came right out with it!

When I said yes, he looked surprised!" I told her, trying to balance the last of the joint in the tweezers we used as a roach clip.

"What an ass!"

"God, can you believe it? But dig this, it gets worse! A few times after class he walked with me and asked if "things" had changed. I guess he didn't want to be my first! I'd rather stay a virgin *forever* than sleep with *him*!"

"Geesh!"

After another burst of giggling, Melanie got a bright idea. "Maybe it's time to expand our territory! We're spending *waaay* too many Friday nights like this."

"Yeah! I know! Let's go to California this summer!" I jumped up and almost overturned the full ashtray precariously balanced on the edge of the bed.

"San Francisco *is* where it's all happening: communes, free love, Flower Children, Haight Ashbury. Hell, yeah! You could lose your virginity there for sure!"

"Far out! Let's do it!"

It was my "geographic cure." Change the scenery and change my life. Only problem was, I had to convince my parents.

"Everyone's going to California and I've never even been on a plane." I was pleading with my father during one of our Sunday night phone calls. I knew my mother would go along with whatever he decided.

"Melanie's aunt is a travel agent and she can arrange everything."

"Ca-rol!" When my father said my name like that, chills ran up my spine. This was the sign he was on the verge of getting angry. "Why do you need so much excitement? You already moved to Washington. Don't you want to rest this summer so you can do well Junior year?"

"I'll be okay, *I promise*. I'll work for a month and use that money for the trip. I *really* want to see California!"

"I guess you've made up my mind for me." There was a long, torturous pause as I held my breath waiting to hear his decision.

"Okay, as long as the trip doesn't interfere with your Junior year."

I got a temp job for a few weeks and saved some money. After a month spent typing labels eight hours a day feeling like a fucking machine, I had my trip money and on July 5th, my father drove me to meet Melanie at Newark Airport. I knew he wasn't happy about the trip and my whole hippie thing, but I'd kept my part of the bargain.

We pulled up to the airport entrance and my father got my suitcase, knapsack, and guitar out of his trusty station wagon. As he hugged me goodbye, he whispered, "Have fun, but think for yourself, Carol!" His comment didn't surprise me. He'd said many times that he thought my rebellious ways were due to my friends' influence. I had to admit he was partially right. I *was* attracted to older men like Woody, my first boyfriend at Rider, and my activist friend Art. Maybe that's why I found *My Fair Lady*, a play based on Pygmalion, about an older experienced man transforming a young, naïve woman so romantic.

Melanie was already at the gate. We both had on army jackets, black t-shirts, and blue jeans. As we boarded the plane I asked to sit in the aisle seat. My claustrophobia was kicking in and I didn't know what to expect. I fastened my seatbelt and prepared for takeoff by popping a couple of Dramamine—there was no turning back now. I didn't dare look out the window the whole trip! After the Dramamine, a few cigarettes, lots of prayers, and some white-knuckling, my fear turned into excitement as we landed in Chicago, home of the blues.

We got into the city and headed for the YWCA, where we settled into a small, bare room with a shared toilet down the hall. We unpacked and took a walk along Michigan Avenue near the lake. There were tons of tourists in Bermuda shorts carrying cameras and shopping bags, and conservatively well-dressed businessmen walking in groups, eyeing us up and down as they passed. I felt bummed-out and started to question why we came to Chicago in the first place.

"Looks like a bunch of suits, Mel. I don't like the way they're looking at us!"

"They're probably convention guys searching for some action. Yuck!"

"There's got to be more to the city. This isn't our scene!"

We sat down on a park bench, and Melanie pulled out the map of Chicago we'd picked up at the Y.

"According to this map, we can take the "L" to Old Town. That's supposed to be a happening place. It shouldn't take very long to get there."

Fifteen minutes later, we were in Old Town. It was Sunday, and the sidewalk was teeming with hippies, gays, and excitement. There were head shops, boutiques and plenty of bars. We spotted a neon sign for a club called The Blues Cellar and went to check it out.

"What time does the music start?" I asked the sexy guy at the front door. He was dressed in tight black jeans, a white t-shirt, and a black leather vest. His thick black hair was pulled back in a long ponytail. But it was his hands that caught my eye. He had long slender fingers with four silver rings on each hand. I couldn't stop staring at them.

"In about an hour," he said.

"Are they any good?"

"I think so." His mood changed and he cracked a slight smile as he opened the club door.

We ordered some burgers and fries and waited for the music to start. About an hour later, the lights dimmed and five musicians took to the small stage.

"Carol, check out the guitar player. Isn't he the guy we talked to at the door?"

"Cool. No wonder he said the group was good."

I was instantly blown away by the tightness of the group, which reminded me of the Paul Butterfield Electric Blues Band. But most of all, I was drawn to the soulful energy of the guitar player. I could not take my eyes off him. After an amazing first set, he and the bass player sauntered over to our table.

The guitar player placed his hands on my shoulders and leaned over. "So, how did you girls like the music?" he asked in a soft, sexy voice. My whole body felt an electric current zap through it. I couldn't believe he remembered talking to us! I didn't want to let on how I was feeling, so I stiffened, turned around, and smiled.

"Incredible! You didn't tell us you were in the band," I answered in my best flirty voice.

They sat down and introduced themselves. Carlos played guitar and Conway played bass. I moved my head towards Carlos and caught Melanie's glance. She picked up on my signal. "You're not from Chicago?" Conway asked, but it was more of a statement.

"Is it *that* obvious?" Melanie turned to ask him. I could feel her kicking me under the table. I'd have to ask her what that was supposed to mean later.

"Well, your New York accents kinda gave it away. Would you like us to show you around tomorrow?"

"Cool!" Melanie and I said together.

The next day Carlos and Conway pulled up in front of the Y in an old, beat-up, white station wagon. Carlos motioned to me to sit next to him in the back seat. I looked in his eyes and smiled. He smiled back, but something was missing. His eyes looked tired, one-dimensional. He touched my hand very gently and I felt a spark. That's where his magic is, I thought, in those long sensitive fingers that make his guitar come alive. I wondered how old these two musician/guides were. They looked older than us, their faces thin and gaunt. Probably the late hours, I thought.

We ended up in The Old Town Ale House, which Carlos said was famous for bringing well-known folk singers to Chicago. He and Conway ordered some beers and Melanie had a glass of wine. I wasn't into drinking, so I just had a Coke while we made small talk waiting for the music. A singer-songwriter whose name I'd never heard of was announced. A young woman about my age with long, straight, medium brown hair and bangs covering her eyebrows took a seat on a bar stool on stage and picked up her guitar. As soon as she began to sing, goosebumps ran up my arms. I was struck by the power she commanded with just her voice and guitar, singing the words of her own songs. I'd written some poems in high school and my English teacher had encouraged me to continue.

I'd taught myself to play some chords on the guitar, but the only things I ever played were from the Joan Baez or Judy Collins songbooks. I was getting tired of singing "Someday Soon" every time someone asked to hear something. The more I listened, the more I felt the desire to share my feelings, frustrations, and longings with an audience. It wasn't a "star thing"—I just wanted to express myself and maybe strike a chord with others who felt the same way.

Why couldn't I set my ideas to music and write my own songs, too? I knew with all my being that was what I had to do. As I walked out of the club that night, my life felt like a blank canvas waiting to be painted in wide, colorful strokes. But as time went on, I would discover that it was the gray, dark colors that changed me the most.

On the ride back to the Y, Conway invited us to their gig the following night.

"We're catching a plane to Montana tomorrow. From there we're going to California," Melanie informed him.

"Bummer," Carlos muttered and pulled me closer.

"Why don't you guys meet us in San Francisco?" I asked.

"You have your whole life ahead of you, babe. There's no future left for us," he whispered in my ear.

"What do you mean? You're not *that* much older?"

"We're into some heavy shit. Can't just break free." He rolled up his sleeve and showed me the lines on his arm. "We're paying the price for playing the blues."

I'd never seen heroin tracks before and it made me sick to my stomach. *So that's why his eyes looked so dead,* I thought and wondered how long it would take for his addiction to overtake his talent. I couldn't wait to get out of the car. Carlos and Conway didn't pressure us to spend the night. They clearly only had room in their lives for two loves, heroin and music.

That night, I picked up my guitar and wrote my first song.

Funky Fanny did her thing
On the streets of New Orleans.
Man, that chick could really sing.
Conway and Carlos liked her sound,
But they were living underground . . .

I was one song closer to my dream.

5
ALL ROADS LEAD TO CALIFORNIA

Oh Lordy, Lordy, got those Hunting Ground Blues.
Brand new territory, help me choose.
Looking for a real man, a real good man.

Montana was, well, mountainous, and watching a geyser erupt in Yellowstone Park was not the kind of eruption that Melanie and I were looking for. We got on a bus to LA and sat behind a man who coughed non-stop the whole way. We didn't smoke during the entire ride and swore we would quit for good, but conveniently forgot when we got off the bus in Los Angeles.

The Sunset Strip turned out to be a major disappointment. It *definitely* wasn't our scene. There was a phoniness about it. Just a bunch of hippie wannabes—chicks with striped, department store bell-bottoms, and perfect hair standing on street corners trying to attract the guys in expensive sports cars cruising up and down the Strip. I felt like I was on a movie set, but this wasn't the movie I wanted to be in.

San Francisco was where it was at. Melanie and I splurged on a rental car and headed up Highway 101. Staring out the passenger window, I was struck by how uniquely beautiful the West Coast was, with mountains on one side and the ocean on the other. It was fertile ground to spawn new ways of living and revolutionary ideas that skipped over the backward middle of the country on their way to the East Coast. I felt hopeful and excited.

"Let's stop here! I think the beaches are free," Melanie suggested as we drove toward a sign for Carmel. We parked the car, jumped out, rolled up our jeans, flung off our sandals, and splashed our feet in the cool refreshing waters of the Pacific. It was official! *Now* we were in California!

A few hours later we zig-zagged up Lombard Street to the one famous place Melanie knew about in San Francisco: City Lights Bookstore. She filled me in about how it was started by Beat Generation poets like Allen Ginsberg and Lawrence Ferlinghetti in the 1950s and how the government had tried to ban their books because they wrote about sex and homosexuality and used obscenities. I didn't understand what the big deal was. All our friends said *fuck, fucked-up* and *fucking far out.*

I spotted a community bulletin board as we walked into the store. There were rooms for rent in San Francisco, but a summer rental in Berkeley caught my eye. "Berkeley's just over the Bay Bridge - we could go to San Francisco anytime we wanted. Besides, we might meet cool people from the university," I said to Melanie as I unpinned the index card. We walked outside to find the nearest payphone. What I didn't tell Melanie was that San Francisco seemed big and intimidating and a little scary to me.

We were in luck! The room was still available, so we drove our rental car over the Bay Bridge, and knocked on the door of a grand-looking Tudor house just a few blocks north of the Berkeley campus. I straightened out my army jacket, smoothed my hair, and stood there waiting like a hopeful mess. A hunky guy with wet, curly brown hair opened the door, holding a towel precariously around his waist.

"Hi, I'm Daniel. Come on in. Sorry, I just got out of the shower!" He flashed us a smile that seemed more directed at Melanie, who coyly smiled back. I sensed an immediate attraction between them. We walked into a huge living room with two worn couches and a big stone fireplace.

"That's Mark," Daniel said. A guy with a scruffy blond beard and bloodshot blue eyes sprawled on one of the sofas was unclogging his hash pipe with a pipe cleaner. He didn't bother to get up, just nodded and stared in our direction. Was I being paranoid and insecure, or did he stare a little longer at Melanie?

Uh oh. Both guys are digging Melanie. She was such a knockout that I hardly got a second look, although I knew I was attractive in a different, hip, spacey kind of way. My thick dark hair flowed down past my shoulders in soft, frizzy waves, and I often wore off the shoulder peasant blouses that showed off my slim arms.

"It's just the two of you?" I asked Daniel.

"Rob's in class. Wanna check out the room?" he pointed upstairs to a large loft area that overlooked the entire living room.

It was a decent-sized room at the end of the hall. A trundle bed draped with an Indian print bedspread gave off a faint scent of incense.

"We'll take it!" Melanie and I said in unison.

We learned later that Daniel was a pre-med student from Sacramento and Mark was a political science major from a wealthy Boston family. Whenever they weren't studying or screwing, they mainly laid around, watched old movies, and got stoned.

The third guy was the least cool of the bunch. Rob was short and wiry with reddish-blond hair, cut short. A philosophy major from Brooklyn with very strong opinions about nutrition, he ate a whole tomato with his dinner every night, convinced it was the key to good health.

The days took on a laid-back rhythm. The sun was always shining, the temperature never dipped below seventy-five degrees, and hunky guys with tight jeans and flowing hair were paraded everywhere. It was as if Peter Pan's Lost Boys had all flocked to Berkeley, just waiting to be found. I was in hippie heaven!

One of my favorite spots was the steps of the Student Center on the Berkeley campus by the fountain in Sproul Plaza. It was a great place to sit and check out the musicians holding impromptu jam sessions, playing guitars, wooden flutes, and conga drums. Some days the Hare Krishnas with their shaved heads and orange robes danced around the fountain, shaking their tambourines. I sometimes quietly chanted along with the chorus, *Hare Krishna, Hare Krishna, Hare, Hare Krishna.*

One day I spotted an interesting-looking guy sitting a few steps in front of me. I could only see the back of his pony-tailed head and the red handkerchief tied around his neck, but I was instantly drawn to him. His aura had a kind of magnetism to it. He must have felt my eyes on him because he turned around and looked right back. I could feel myself blush. Something in his clear blue eyes radiated inner peace. Both of us turned away, but for me he was a living, breathing symbol of what I was searching for—a path to spiritual enlightenment and peace.

I'd been reading *The Autobiography of a Yogi* and Castaneda's Don Juan series ever since I'd got to California. I still needed outside validation to know I was on the right path, and yet realized that it was ultimately up to me to discover my true karma. Melanie was following a different path. She'd let the chemistry she felt for both Daniel and Mark take over, and never knew if one had told the other. According to her, sex was to be celebrated and different partners kept things spicy.

It all caught up with her one afternoon when she ran into our bedroom in a panic.

"What's the matter?" I asked, looking up from my book.

"I can't go downstairs! You've gotta do something. Daniel and Mark are hanging out and so is that guy I met at the bookstore. You remember, right? I think his name was John. And some other dude I slept with, too! What should I do?"

I lay down *Be Here Now* on the paisley bedspread and tried to stifle a laugh. This was something that could only happen to Melanie! Ironically, being here now was the last place *I* wanted to be, but I had to help my friend.

"Just go down there and make something up," Melanie begged in a desperate voice. "Tell them I'm sick. Yeah, that's it! Tell them I have a stomach bug and I can't stop throwing up," she urged.

"Okay. I wish *I* had your problems!"

All eyes were on me as I walked into the living room and told Melanie's fan club that she was sick and couldn't come down. They looked bummed out but were cool about it. She hadn't committed to any of them, it was just casual sex. No big deal, just part of living in Berkeley.

Hitchhiking was the only way to get around. Hippies lined up on University Avenue waiting to get rides into San Francisco or beyond. I wasn't afraid to hitchhike on my own, but I did have one hairy experience on a ride back from San Francisco when a middle-aged Chinese man picked me up. I immediately got bad vibes, but it was too late to get out since we were already at the entrance to the Bay Bridge.

He had his car radio on and the newscaster was talking about a Manson sighting that didn't pan out the day before. A few weeks earlier Charles Manson and his followers had murdered Sharon Tate in LA. It was all over the news, every gory and gruesome detail.

"Manson, I knew him," bad vibes guy said.

Who would brag about that? I wondered. *This guy is seriously messed up.*

"Uh-huh," is all I said, looking straight ahead and all the while praying, *God please protect me! Please let me make it back alive!*

Then out of left field, he said, "I might be short, but I can kick butt if I have to. Feel my muscle. Go ahead, feel it!" He suddenly bent his elbow and made a fist, his other hand on the steering wheel. I closed my eyes and felt the biceps of his tattooed arm. I was hoping it was the *only* hard body part he wanted me to touch. I could already see the headlines: "Manson follower throws Jersey girl over Bay Bridge for refusing to squeeze his biceps."

As soon as we crossed the bridge, I jumped out of the car at the first stoplight. Shaken and scared, I stayed in Berkeley for the next few days and chilled out. I spent my mornings listening to musicians jamming at Sproul Plaza and my afternoons at Cody's Bookstore on Telegraph, perusing the latest books and the latest hunks in the New Age section. I was tempted to buy a book on casting spells but chickened out. Black magic was way too heavy and I didn't want to kiss any frogs and turn them into Prince Charming. With my luck, I'd screw it up and end up turning Prince

Charming into a frog! Besides, I needed to know I could attract a guy using my *own* powers.

Except for the Fillmore West and Golden Gate Park, San Francisco wasn't the happening place I thought it would be. Haight Ashbury's cool factor had faded, and its Flower Children had been picked over like a wilted bouquet. Many of the original hippies had moved north to start communes in Marin and Mendocino counties. Others followed the Yellow Brick Road all the way to Eugene, Oregon—The Emerald City. The only ones left were druggies who lived in the brightly painted Victorian houses on the Haight. Word on the street was the speed freaks lived in the purple house, the heroin addicts in the blue, and the coke heads in the grey house with the pink trim. I'd arrived a year too late.

"Daniel told me about a nude beach in Marin. Wanna go?" Melanie asked me a few days later while I was still laying low. I could see she was making an effort to perk me up, but I wasn't ready to come out of my funk.

"I don't know if I can take my clothes off in front of a bunch of strangers. I don't feel very sexy. Maybe because I've never had sex!"

Melanie must have sensed that I was feeling down about not meeting anyone.

"Oh, come on Carol! It'll be fun. Besides, you don't have to take *all* your clothes off. Anyway, once you get there, you might change your mind."

"Well, okay. I need a change of scenery."

We hitched rides with a Berkeley professor named Bentley and an out-of-work musician who claimed he knew the Grateful Dead. They acted like perfect gentlemen and I was able to put my scary bridge experience a little farther in the rearview mirror.

"What's the big deal about this place?" I asked Melanie as we walked on the sand at Muir Beach.

"I wonder why everyone's walking over the rocks down there? Let's check it out." Melanie headed off, looking determined. There was nothing left for me to do but follow.

When we got to the other side of the rocks, *Whoa! What a sight!* I didn't know where to look or not look. Nude sunbathers were nonchalantly hanging out everywhere, and acting like nothing was hanging out! For them, it was just a typical day at the beach—throwing frisbees, swimming, jogging, and sunbathing.

"Let's start with our tops," Melanie suggested. *I guess I could do that. I'm proud of my breasts.* We took off our t-shirts and bathing suit tops and put them on our towels. I tried acting cool as we walked on the beach. A muscular guy with a deep tan stopped to talk to Melanie, and I quickly walked back to my towel to sunbathe and body gaze. I was uncomfortable and so uptight that I quickly hooked the back of my bathing suit top and put on my grey GWU t-shirt. *No point in getting sunburned,* I told myself, but the truth was I felt too exposed both physically and emotionally. Maybe the next time we came here I'd do it, but that depended on other things changing. My virginity was still up for grabs.

A half an hour later, Melanie came back. "There's something about that guy, Carol. He's mysterious and I get strong vibes from him. Maybe it's those dark eyes. He wants to show me his treehouse in Sausalito. He has a friend with a motorcycle who could give you a ride back to Berkeley. Are you cool with it?"

I could tell she was *really* into him. She was talking fast and practically gushing as she clued me in.

"Sounds okay," I said half-heartedly.

I didn't know which was more dangerous. Me with no helmet on the back of a strange guy's motorcycle speeding down a mountainous coast with no guard rails, or Melanie spending the night with a mysterious stranger, god knows where whose name I didn't even know. I wasn't worried about her, she could handle herself. As for me, I was getting used to living on the edge. The ride was exhilarating! I hung on to my anonymous biker and closed my eyes for half of the trip. When I did have the courage to open them, I looked down at the Pacific waves crashing on the rocks. We were riding so close to the edge and were so high up, one wrong turn would send us plummeting to our death!

You've come a long way! I thought, and I felt empowered by every mile I'd traveled. I was no longer that sheltered teacher's pet, a goody-goody living in boring suburbia. I'd finally broken free. Unfortunately, there was zero attraction between me and "motorcycle guy," so I thanked him for the ride, jumped off the bike, and put my sandaled feet on solid ground.

The next day, a glowing Melanie described her romantic adventure.

"His name was Stacey and he *did* have a treehouse." She dreamily relived her magical night as we drank our coffee during one of our many round table discussions.

"It was the best! We did it on a bearskin rug! The vibes were so intense I swear I saw lightning above the trees! It was cosmic!"

"Unbelievable! I'd settle for a few sparks. But summer's almost over!" I whined, feeling frustrated with my fate. "I've *got* to go back to school a changed woman."

With only a week and a half left of my California trip, I was determined to find the right guy to change me from a "flower child" to a "de-flowered child."

Two days after Melanie told me about her amazing treehouse experience we were walking down Telegraph Avenue when a cute guy came our way. I felt an instant attraction. Our eyes met and we smiled at each other.

"He's mine," I whispered to Melanie and she winked and walked away.

"Hey," he said. "What's happening?

"Not much," I smiled up at him. "I'm gonna check out the music at the plaza."

"Cool. Want some company?"

We fell into step and started to talk. His name was Richard and he was from Buffalo. He was exploring the scene on the West Coast before he started graduate school in the fall. He was handsome, medium height and weight, with short black hair, round wire John Lennon glasses, and a nicely trimmed beard. Except for his short hair, he was my type.

Rich—that's what he liked to be called—asked me all about myself and seemed genuinely interested. Three blocks later he'd invited me to go to dinner.

"I could really be into you, Carol," he said as he planted a kiss on my cheek. "See you tonight, then."

Maybe he's the one! I thought as I rushed home to get ready.

During dinner, I broke the news as we ate our Wonton soup. We were at the Yahtzee River on Channing Street, a popular Chinese restaurant within walking distance from my place.

"I have something to tell you, Rich," I stopped to take a gulp of tea. "I want to be with you, but I've never *done it*," I whispered.

"You mean you're a *virgin*? Really?"

I nodded and stared down at my soup. I felt like crawling under the table and hiding behind the tea-stained tablecloth. When I finally looked up, Rich stared deeply into my eyes and said, "Carol, I think I could fall in love with you. I want to make your first time special."

I ate some of my chow mein and we made some small talk, but it was pretty obvious that neither of us could wait for the main course. Things were falling into place. After dinner, we got into Rich's rental car and drove around until we spotted a cheap motel on the outskirts of Berkeley. As soon as we walked in the door I went straight to the bathroom to inspect for bugs. I walked out to find Rich lying on the bed butt naked!

"Come here, Carol," he stood up, took my hand, and led me to the bed.

"Take your clothes off," it was more of a sigh than a command. I quickly undressed down to my underwear. We got under the covers and he rolled up on top of me and slid the only lace panties I owned down my legs as he gently kissed the inside of my thighs. Some awkward moments, a hesitant thrust, a little bleeding, and the deed was done. I still had no idea what an orgasm felt like. It was totally underwhelming. Afterward, we smoked our cigarettes and rolled over on our separate sides of the bed.

The next morning while Rich was still snoring, I wrapped a blanket around me and tip-toed over to the sliding glass door. As the sun came up, I spotted a middle-aged woman hanging crisp white sheets in a neighboring backyard. I was overwhelmed by a strong spiritual connection to her. This simple act was a powerful reminder of the bond we shared as women. She was an archetypal symbol of womanhood, and now I too was initiated.

Driving back to my place, Rich panicked and told me he was engaged to a woman back in Buffalo. "Last night was wonderful, but I don't want to give you the wrong impression about our future, Carol."

I felt hurt but knew all the same that he'd given me something way more important. I'd finally done it! How could I feel used? I'd crossed the line. We'd used each other, just for different reasons. A vague emptiness overcame me as I kissed Richard goodbye. *What would having sex with someone I was in love with be like?* When I got back to my room, I took out my guitar and let my feelings out in a new song.

I'm A Woman
Hello my friend, I'd like to make a confession.
I think you've got the wrong impression of me.
I'm not the girl who I pretend to be.
I've not yet given up my childhood fantasy
Of what I think my true love should be.
But I'm a woman and I need loving,
And I need someone to ease the pain
Of being a woman and needing loving,
And the man I'm lovin's got to feel the same . . .

6
THE FALL

Then I decided to be on my own,
And face my fears about being alone.
But my Daddy's words echoed in my head,
And I wanted to be loved like my Daddy said.

I knew California was not forever. Before we left on our cross-country trip, Melanie and I had found a furnished apartment near Dupont Circle. The neighborhood was a little dicey with students, hippies, and druggies, but it was within walking distance of GWU. Our place was on the second floor of a three-story building with two apartments on each landing. The best thing about it was our neighbors across the hall, Bonnie and Marsha. Our apartments looked exactly alike: a big living room painted a sickening hospital green, Goodwill furniture, a small kitchen, and three single beds in one bedroom. I was impressed by how Bonnie and Marsha used the extra bed as a place to pile their dirty clothes on.

Our new neighbors were also juniors at GWU and Melanie had been in English 101 with Bonnie, freshman year. Bonnie was a French major who had spent a semester in France. She loved to travel and was bubbly and animated, especially when she talked about the countries she planned to visit after she graduated. She was very pretty, with wavy, long blonde hair, blue eyes, and a mouth that turned up at the corners, even when she wasn't smiling. Bonnie was convinced that eating the French way was how to keep thin. She ate exotic foods like pate and camembert, but in very small amounts. She laughed easily and always had men circling around her.

Marsha was the calmest of the bunch, a real Earth-mother. She wore long dresses and hand-crocheted shawls and very little make-up. Chestnut-colored hair cut in a page boy framed her dark brown eyes and lightly freckled face. Marsha was wise beyond her years but loved to laugh and was always ready to get high. Evenings I often found her in the kitchen enjoying a joint and baking up a storm. Her banana bread was delicious, but it was her hash brownies we really looked forward to.

Marsha's mystery brownies weren't the only way we got stoned. At the start of the semester, Melanie had become friends with Big John. He owned an underground record store in Georgetown, but bootleg records weren't all he was selling. He was always in a mellow mood, mostly because of all the drugs he did. Big John started hanging out at our apartment, hoping Melanie would turn on to him, but that was not about to happen. He looked like a big teddy bear, tall and stocky with a full head of curly brown hair sticking out from his signature brown suede cowboy hat.

One night the three of us were passing a joint around when Big John came up with a business proposition. If we agreed to keep a grocery-sized shopping bag of LSD in our refrigerator, he would pay our rent. It seemed like a good deal. We would have some extra money since our parents would still be paying our rent every month. Big John convinced us that no one would suspect two innocent GWU girls of possessing drugs, and said we could take free samples. Melanie and I went for it.

It was Friday night and Melanie and Marsha had sampled some of the powder in Big John's bag. Bonnie was on a "study date" and the three of us were sitting around the kitchen table staring at an egg candle melting yellow wax. I was the only one who hadn't tried the LSD.

"Look at the way the egg cracks open the warmer it gets. It's like life. Never knowing what's on the inside," I mused.

"Yeah, that's deep," Melanie said. Are you sure you're not high?"

"No, it's a contact high. I'm picking up on your and Marsha's vibes."

By the following Friday night, my curiosity about tripping took over and I dipped my finger into the magic bag and waited for my free sample to kick in. I felt safe with Melanie and Marsha who were staying straight just in case I had a bad trip. They were sitting on either side of me on the couch when suddenly I felt a rush of energy. I jumped up and ran to the closet to put on my skunk fur coat with big shoulder pads, an unclaimed item I'd inherited from my grandfather's dry-cleaning store.

"I have to get out of here!" I ran down the stairs with Melanie and Marsha trailing behind me. Standing on the corner under the streetlight, I was filled with love for everyone in the universe and wanted to share this new revelation with them. It felt amazing! I started waving wildly, calling out to people walking by. "Hey, you wanna get high?" Luckily, no one took me up on the offer.

"Carol! Stop saying that. Come on, let's go back upstairs," Melanie coaxed.

"Shhh! You wanna get us into trouble?" Marsha was freaking out.

By then I was staring up at the stars. "I've gotta get to the country. Take me to the country. If I don't get to the country, I'm gonna die!"

"Okay, okay," Melanie calmed me down. "We'll get Big John to drive us to Rock Creek Park, but first you have to chill."

It was pitch black when we got there. I ran out of the car and immediately took off my boots and socks. The feel of the cool earth beneath my bare feet grounded me and instantly offered me relief. The gentle, reassuring sound of the water hitting the rocks in the nearby creek whispered to me, "You're safe. You're safe." The sound was like a natural mantra, breathing calm and oneness into my being, making me feel part of a force much bigger than myself. I was egoless—devoid of any separation between me and the outside world. Marsha and Melanie huddled around me, instinctively protecting me as Big John rubbed my neck. I still felt scared but agreed to go with the flow and ride back with them to the apartment.

It was when we got back that my hallucinations really took hold. I was on a trip I couldn't control. Bizarre images of mysterious creatures danced in the shadows of the walls and even my friends' faces became distorted and ugly. Everyone looked like the Wicked Witch of the West. Melanie and Marsha lovingly guided me through the kaleidoscope of emotions with music and reassuring words. I gradually transitioned from a bad trip to a good trip. Prismatic images of lights and colors shone like halos around my friends' bodies, and vibrations vividly danced in front of me. Toward dawn, Melanie put on *Abbey Road*. The lyrics spoke to me as if I were hearing them for the first time. The Beatles were bringing me a message from a higher plain to heal my soul with love.

Standing at the kitchen window, I watched the sunrise in the pale limitless October sky. Daybreak had never looked so beautiful. Across the street, a middle-aged woman in office attire stepped out of an apartment building and made the sign of the cross. A simple morning ritual to summon protection for the day. Another powerful message from the universe that spirituality and a higher power were everywhere.

It took me a few days to completely come down. Big John had neglected to tell us that the acid was laced with speed. The way I viewed life was changed forever. I vowed this would be my first and last trip. I'd heard of people who took trips and jumped out of windows or went insane and never came back. I was already having a hard enough time holding on to reality. Why tempt fate?

As the weeks flew by, I forced myself to go to more classes and smoke less pot. I was a sociology major, but the only class I liked was Marriage and the Family. The professor made a point of telling us that the United States was the only country that combined romance and marriage. European countries traditionally regarded marriage as a practical partnership and romance was found outside of marriage.

My father had proclaimed that one day I would fall in love and experience true bliss. But what he *really* meant was that I should wait for Mr. Right before I did something wrong. He was a hopeless romantic and proud of the fact that he was a virgin when he got married. But I wasn't buying it. I thought it had to do with those scary VD movies they showed him in the Army.

I was still questioning whether my Knight in Shining Armor would ever appear and writing songs about it.

When I was just a little girl, my Daddy said to me.
"A man's gonna come and love you some,
That's your Daddy's prophecy."
But it keeps on a-worryin' me
Oh Lord, It keeps on a-worryin' me.

Meanwhile, I was getting more and more disillusioned with school. How could statistics help me in any way? I wrote a note to myself during one of my classes:

Sit in the classroom and listen to the teacher, even though you're bored
to death. Copy down notes and read the bullshit, memorize it, and
take a test. Get your little word grade, which tells you where you stand
compared to the other goons who have done the exact same thing. Do
this process about forty times and whoopee—a piece of paper signify-
ing that you are in the educated elite.

I couldn't tell my parents how I was feeling about school. They were still recovering from the one time they'd visited me. I'd tried to clean up the apartment and hide the ashtrays and other paraphernalia, but they'd only stayed an hour and then took me out to dinner. I found out later that after they dropped me off, they sat in the car and cried. Maybe they got a whiff of what was going on in my hippie pad, but to me, it was just a typical apartment of a struggling college student.

I was home for Thanksgiving vacation when I got a frantic call from Melanie.

"Carol, Big John got busted! They arrested him and put him in jail! God—What are we gonna do?"

"I hear you. It's time to clean the refrigerator."

When we got back to Washington, the first thing we did was flush all the evidence down the toilet. Lucky for us, we were never contacted by the police. We never found out what happened to Big John either, and were too afraid to ask.

7
SEASON OF THE WITCH

I'm a girl-woman, I need a boy-man.
I'm gonna give him all that I can,
'Cause I've got a feelin' that I've got to share . . .

It was a gloomy Saturday afternoon in late November and Melanie and I were taking a study break. "Something about this time of year feels strange," Melanie said as we drank our chamomile tea and listened to a Donovan record.

"I know what you mean, there's some bad vibes brewing."

"Yeah, it's like Donovan's "Season of The Witch.""

I'd gotten past Big John's bust scare and was getting more into my music. One of Bonnie's boyfriends was an amazingly talented guitar player who was giving me lessons. Bonnie didn't seem that into him, but I was blown away from the minute he walked in the door. Michael reminded me of a cherub with street smarts. He had dark curly hair, large brown eyes, an olive complexion, and a soft, sexy voice. Added to his coolness was a small, gold stud that he wore in his left ear. He revealed to me that he was brought up by Jewish middle-class parents, but had quit high school and been on his own in New York City since he was sixteen.

Michael cupped his hand over mine and I felt a spark. "Here, let me show you how to bar that chord, Carol."

It was my second lesson and we were working on a traditional blues song, "The Sun's Gonna Shine in My Backdoor Someday." He had a soulful way of bringing out the music. I sensed he was feeling something for me too, but I didn't want to make the first move.

"Are you still seeing Bonnie?" I asked innocently.

"I don't think she's my type," Michael said. He pulled my face toward him and kissed me softly.

The next day Bonnie and I were having café au lait in her apartment while discussing our upcoming plans. The four of us were renting a townhouse starting in January, and Melanie and I were moving in with Bonnie and Marsha for the month of December. That was a big reason why I didn't want my feelings for Michael to get in the way of our plans. We all got along so well - even our astrological signs were complementary. I was an air sign, Gemini; Melanie was water, Cancer; Marsha was earth; Capricorn and Bonnie was a fire sign; Leo. Taken together we comprised all four elements—we were in our own little world!

"How are your guitar lessons going with Michael?" Bonnie asked out of the blue.

This was a conversation I wasn't looking forward to having. "He's a really good teacher, but he's a bit of a flirt. Are you still seeing him?"

I took a sip of my coffee and studied Bonnie's face. She was hard to read, with her mouth turned up in its ever-present half-smile.

"I'm not sure about him. I'm seeing a few other guys. He *is* a flirt and I don't get his whole music thing. Hmm, maybe *you* should be with him."

I tried to hide my excitement, "Are you sure? I don't want any bad vibes between us."

"Yeah, my life's been getting too complicated. If you want him, he's yours," she declared.

I was ecstatic, but I couldn't let Bonnie know. She'd find out soon enough.

My guitar lessons turned into make-out sessions, but I did manage to write a new song about Michael.

Hoping he'll find me, wherever I am,
I'm playing it cool, that's part of my plan.
Might take a day or a month or a year,
My love will happen, I know that he's here.

I was willing to let things heat up between Michael and me for a while longer. I knew it was just a matter of time until we "did it" and I experienced not just sex, but making love for the first time. Melanie and I were busy moving across the hall, trying to stuff all our clothes into Bonnie and Marsha's apartment. Marsha drew the shortest straw to see who got the couch in the living room. She seemed fine with it, knowing it was only temporary. Soon we would have an entire townhouse to ourselves.

"You wanna fly to New York with me for the day? My treat! I need to see some friends there," Michael asked during one of our lessons.

"That sounds like fun. I love New York!" A few weeks had passed and I'd finally finished moving across the hall. I would have gone *anywhere* with Michael.

"Great! But I need to tell you that I'll be doing a little drug deal. Are you cool with it?"

"Yeah, sure," I said, but felt disappointed. I wanted to be so much more than the chick he traveled with to avert suspicion. As for the drug thing, I kinda knew he couldn't be making money just from his music. I wasn't *that* naïve.

On Saturday Michael and I got on a plane to New York, met his "friends" and then walked around the city. It was a clear, cold December day and the stores on Fifth Avenue were decked out like a winter wonderland. We stopped in front of Lord & Taylor's window where two-tone hanging crystals glistened in front of a red velvet background and dancing dolls moved to the music of the Nutcracker. It was a magical world come to life and when Michael drew me to him and kissed me, I felt like I was living my *own* enchanted fairy tale.

"I think I could be falling in love with you," he whispered in my ear.

"Me, too, but there's one thing bothering me. Should I feel funny that I'm a little taller than you?"

"Is that all you're worried about?" Michael gently laughed. "My last girlfriend was a model and she was a head taller than me."

I should have said, "No, I'm worried that you're a dealer and we both could end up in jail, and you have no education and wear an earring," but none of that phased me. Instead, I answered, "You're right, I'm just being silly." Michael kissed me again, "Forget it, babe, you're perfect," he said. By the time we landed in Washington that evening we were a couple.

"Spend the night with me Carol," Michael said on the taxi ride home. He lived in an apartment in Arlington on the first floor of an old, two-family house that he shared with Doug, his friend from New York.

Michael referred to Doug as an "alligator"—someone who hung around musicians, but didn't play an instrument, a musician wannabe. I'd never heard that expression, but then again, Michael was teaching me a lot that I didn't know.

"I'm not sure if I should stay, Michael. Let me see how I feel. It's getting late and I've got to get some things at the apartment." He looked disappointed, but I didn't know if I was ready to sleep with him yet.

"Come on, Carol! You can take a cab. Arlington is just over the bridge. I wanna be with you tonight."

When I got back to the apartment, I still wasn't sure. It was already 8:30. Marsha, the only one home was busy baking Hannukah cookies. Her high-school friend Peter and his brother were coming over to sample them later. Melanie was playing catch-up at the library, sacrificing her Saturday night to study, and Bonnie had started filling in as a waitress at The Attic.

"You're glowing!" Marsha said as she looked up from her cookie batter.

"I'm in *love* and it happened in New York! He wants me to take a cab back to his apartment. I don't know if I should, it's already going on nine o'clock."

"What on earth are you waiting for? Go for it! Call Michael and tell him you're coming!"

Marsha had a way of giving advice without sounding pushy, so I took what she said seriously. I put a change of clothes and a toothbrush in my canvas army knapsack, called a very happy Michael, and caught a cab to his apartment. He opened the door and threw his arms around me. I knew right then and there that I'd made the right decision, but didn't yet know that it would be one of the luckiest decisions of my life.

"This is a big place!" I said as he showed me around. The dining room was set up as a music room. There were amps and mic stands and of course, Michael's guitars.

"Be careful not to trip on the wires," he warned, drawing me closer.

He picked up a red electric guitar from a stand, put it around his neck, and handed me a mic.

"Here, let's jam. Doug's out for the evening,"

"I'm not used to singing in a mic."

"Just hold it a little closer to your mouth," he said in his sexy, low voice. I knew what he was thinking about. I was a willing student, ready to learn everything he wanted to teach me.

"You better get used to it. You're a really good singer, Carol."

He plugged in his guitar and started playing "Summertime." The minute I held the mic in my hand and heard my amplified voice rise up singing, I knew this was for me! The reverb and bass gave my voice more presence and made for a bluesy sound. I spread my wings and let my voice take to the sky. Michael felt it too. When he played his solo, the vibes between us were so heavy I had to lean on the mic stand. As the last chord faded, he put down his guitar, took my hand, and led me to his bedroom. I felt like I was floating!

"This is my bed. I built it myself. Come up."

It was a solid wood loft about five feet off the ground. I had to climb a wooden ladder with six steps to get up there. Once I got used to our bed in the sky, I started to relax and get comfortable.

Michael was a very gentle, but passionate lover. Making love in his loft sent me to new heights, pun intended. The connection was cosmic, as if we were plugged into a spiritual force. There was nothing mechanical about it. I couldn't tell where my body ended and Michael's began. We were melting into one another and I didn't want the night to end.

The next morning, I was sitting at the kitchen table waiting for Michael to make us coffee when I felt inspired to write a poem. I grabbed a napkin and wrote:

Two fantasies in New York met, trembling to freedom's syncopated rhythm.
Airport, planes, taxis, trains. A universal harmony remains—
You, intensely bright, penetrating my protective shell,
Making love under vanilla fudge skies . . .

I'd just taken the first sip of my coffee when the phone rang. Michael picked up, then handed it to me.

"Carol, it's Marsha."

"Marsha, are you okay? You sound upset. How did you get this number?"

"Bonnie had it. Listen, we're at the police station. We're okay, but something really bad happened! *Really, really bad.* Last night three black guys knocked on the door and said they were looking for Big John. I got really bad vibes and closed the door but forgot to put the chain back on. They knocked again and my friend Peter said he'd get rid of them. He opened the door and they forced their way in. It was a nightmare! They raped us, Carol. *Raped* us!" Marsha broke down, sobbing.

"Oh my god, my god!"

My hand was shaking so badly, I could barely hold the phone. I'll be there," I said. "I'm coming to the station."

"No, my father is on his way to take us back to our house in Westchester. I'll fill you in when we get there."

I put down the phone, burst into tears and Michael threw his arms around me. In between sobs, I told him what happened. "They got raped! Guys broke in! If I hadn't come here last night, I would've been raped too! Marsha told me to come here last night. Both of you are my angels. This *can't* be happening."

In just a few seconds, I'd gone from heaven to hell. It was beyond a wake-up call. A few hours later, Marsha called back. She'd managed to steady her voice and her nerves and tell me more of what had happened.

"So, Melanie was back from the library, when these guys burst in. They tied Peter and his brother up to the kitchen chairs and locked me and Melanie in the bedroom. We could hear them ransacking the place, dumping every drawer on the floor. Then they came into the bedroom. Melanie and I were too petrified to move. Two of the guys were on top of me and Melanie and they held knives to our throats and started forcing themselves on us. They took turns raping us. We didn't struggle. They were so wired up on drugs we were afraid they were going to kill us. Then, Bonnie came home and before she could run out, one of them grabbed her. She twisted free and ran towards the bathroom, but he just grabbed her again, pulled her into the bedroom, and raped her, too. The last thing one of them mumbled as he split was "Love is just a four-letter word."

I was beside myself again. "Oh no! Oh God, I can't believe it!" I kept saying over and over again.

"They trashed *everything*. Every drawer, every closet. Everything we own is on the floor!"

"Do you think they were looking for money?"

"Money, drugs - who knows?"

Michael put his arm around me as I chain-smoked and told him the gory details. Now I was getting angry. "Why didn't Peter put the chain on? Why did he have to answer the door?" I kept repeating between inhales.

"No one wanted this to happen, Carol."

"I know, but if only . . ."

I was on an emotional roller coaster—devastated when I thought about what happened, and elated when Michael held me. There was no middle ground. How could I feel such extreme emotions? How could I not?

I shuddered just to think about what I'd escaped! I was practically a virgin. Even Michael, who I loved, had to be very careful with me. How could I have survived a gang rape? I couldn't even imagine it. Surely, I would have been damaged for life. How would my best friends be affected?

Later that day, Marsha called again, this time with better news. Her father had told our new landlord what happened, and he agreed to let us move into the townhouse right away.

"That's great news." I tried sounding upbeat.

"There's only one thing, Carol. Can you pack up the apartment for us? None of us think we can face going back."

"Of course," I said. I was terrified to set foot in there, but that was the least I could do.

"Just feel better. I'll take care of it. You shouldn't ever have to see it again. Michael will help me."

There was one more phone call I was dreading.

"Daddy, I have some bad news," I said in a shaky voice.

"Are you all right?"

"I'm okay." I took a long drag on my cigarette.

"When I was at my new boyfriend's yesterday, some guys broke into the apartment. I'm not gonna lie, it was really bad. They raped Melanie, Bonnie, and Marsha."

After a moment of silence, my father asked, "Are you okay?"

"I'm okay, I'm at Michael's house."

"Michael? Who's that?"

"I told you, Daddy, my boyfriend."

"Where *are* you? I'm coming to get you!"

"No, I'm fine! And Marsha's father took everyone to their house in Westchester. He talked to our new landlord and said we could move into the townhouse right away."

I could hear my father sighing and sounding a little out of breath. "Last night your grandmother came to me in a dream. You know you're named after her." After a moment he said softly, "I asked her if she could watch over you and she said, 'Can't you do something for her on earth?'"

"Oh my god! She did watch over me!"

"Carol, I want you to move back to the dorm immediately."

"I can't. I have to be with my friends. We need each other. We'll be safe, the townhouse is all arranged. I promise! We have to be together!"

I hung up the phone, grateful that my father relented, and did not insist I move back to the dorm. Maybe he just went with it because he was so relieved that I was okay. Or maybe he didn't want to upset me anymore, but something told me this was not the last I'd hear about it. I'd played it calm and brave and convinced my father that I'd be all right. Now I only had to convince myself.

8
PICKING UP THE PIECES

You keep your hurts in a private place,
What you've been through is hard to face,
But together we'll find a sacred space
And start life over again.

The next morning Michael and Doug helped me find some cartons. As we rode in Doug's car to the apartment, I snuggled up to Michael in the back seat. *What if they came back?* I was petrified. It took every ounce of courage I had to open the apartment door. I didn't know what I'd find. It was worse than I'd imagined. Everything the four of us owned was on the floor. It looked like a tornado had swept through and there wasn't even a clear place to walk. I sat on the couch and cried.

Michael and Doug tried to comfort me but made it clear that they couldn't help me pack. This came as a total surprise. Michael told me he had guitar lessons to give and Doug made up some excuse about where he had to be. I felt a growing sense of panic setting in.

"You'll be okay, Carol. Don't open the door to anyone. They won't come back. They know the police are looking for them." Michael tried to reassure me.

"I'm scared, I truly am!"

"Listen baby, you promised your friends that you would do this. I'll call you in a few hours and we'll go back to my place," Michael said sweetly and gave me a goodbye kiss.

I didn't have a choice. Michael *had* saved my life, but he wasn't going to help me pack. I kissed him back and told myself that this was a hellish job, but nothing compared to what had happened to my roommates.

I started in the kitchen. The uneaten Hannukah cookies were still on the counter. Why couldn't a miracle have happened *that* night? As I packed up the kitchen, I tried to focus on our new place. Most of the pots and pans belonged to Marsha. I carefully inspected each one to make sure we didn't bring any "unwanted guests" to our new house. We'd complained about the roaches to our sleazy landlord a week after we moved in. His words of wisdom were: "Girls, roaches are like men. If you don't feed them, they won't come." It took me a few hours to finish up the kitchen. Michael called to say he was on his way. I made doubly sure it was him before I opened the door. If only *Marsha's friend* hadn't opened the door that night!

"This is the hardest thing I've ever done," I told Michael later as he held me in bed. I felt guilty about complaining since he was understanding to a point. But still, he didn't offer to help.

Every day I went back to the apartment and forced myself to pack more things. Going to class was out of the question. Marsha's dad called the Dean of Students and explained the situation. Not only did he get us excused from classes, but arranged for us to get our grades without taking final exams. The major stipulation was that we keep the incident quiet. The publicity would be bad for GWU, the Dean explained. We could care less about GWU's reputation. We were just relieved that we didn't have to go to our classes.

Not until Friday did I find the courage to walk into the bedroom. Michael went with me. So many evil vibes hung in the room that it was impossible to turn my brain off as I imagined the horrific scene. I felt violated just thinking about it. A chill went through my body. Michael picked up on what I was feeling and held me closer. What had my roommates done to deserve *this*? Every drawer was emptied and every piece of clothing we owned was strewn on the floor. Michael sat on one of the beds, as I quickly threw clothes in boxes and suitcases. We would sort it out when we got to the new house.

A week later Marsha's father drove everyone back to DC. I got Michael, Doug, and two of their musician friends to help move boxes to our new place. As soon as my roommates walked through the door before they had a chance to take their coats off, we threw our arms around each other in a big group hug. My eyes welled up with tears, part sadness, and part joy. We were finally together! There was strength in numbers and nothing was going to separate us now. They all looked a little paler and thinner but were still the same beautiful women I'd always known. They inspired me to write a song about our sisterhood:

Four lovely women brave as Joan of Arc,
Living in a world of fear, trying to make their mark.
Stronger together, they stand their ground,
There for each other until their courage is found.

January 1970 brought a new year, a new decade, a new semester, a new house, and, with time, a new beginning. Marsha and Melanie shared the bigger upstairs front bedroom and Bonnie and I had the smaller one. We were messier than they were and not big on hanging our clothes up from the night before. Bonnie even kept her skis on the floor in between our beds. The first one to go to bed guided the other one. The whole room was like an obstacle course!

We tried to create a sense of normalcy but an oppressive cloud still cast its shadow over all our lives. From the black burlap curtains in the downstairs windows to my roommates repeated visits from the sex squad detectives, we were constantly reminded of the rape. Sometimes late at night, I peeked around the burlap curtain and was relieved to spot a police car slowing down in front of our house. Marsha's father had requested to the detectives, that the DC police nightly patrol our house.

My parents, still very worried about me living off-campus, made no effort to hide their concerns.

"Hi, Dad. What are you doing?" I asked on one of my Sunday night check-in calls, trying to sound casual.

"I'm doing some artwork," he told me.

"Great, what are you working on?"

"I'm designing tombstones for hippie children."

"That's not *funny*, Dad! We feel safe here. Don't worry."

"Someone has to."

"I'll talk to you next Sunday. Say hello to Mommy."

I quickly got off the phone and tried putting the conversation out of my mind. There was no way I was moving back to the dorm.

"What's gonna happen to those guys when they catch them?" Melanie wondered after yet another trip to the police station, to identify the suspects in a line-up.

"Don't tell me you're worried about them!" I said to her.

"I don't know. Do you think we invited this into our lives on some level? Were we flaunting our sexuality and drug connections?"

I couldn't believe what I was hearing. There was no question in any-one else's mind that they deserved to go to jail. "Think of it this way. Do you want them to hurt other innocent women? They have to be caught."

Every time life was starting to feel normal, another crisis caught us off guard. One night, Melanie was rushed to the hospital, doubled over in pain. It turned out she had a serious pelvic infection brought on by gon-orrhea. She'd tested positive the night of the rape, but no one had even bothered to contact her! Bonnie and Marsha were luckier. New tests showed they had never been infected.

I was still seeing Michael, and growing more and more in love with him. I was sure he felt the same about me, so when we started spending less time together, I never questioned it. I felt so secure in our love, I didn't see the end coming. Maybe I wanted to be fooled.

"Carol, I've got to talk to you," His voice sounded different, weaker. Something was off.

"What's up?" I tried sounding casual.

"I don't think we should see each other anymore. I don't want to hurt you, but I'm falling for someone else."

I hung up the phone, feeling like I was falling, too—falling off the face of the earth. I was still crying an hour later when Bonnie found me and made me go upstairs to bed.

For the next three weeks, I had a ritual. I'd come home from class, lie on the couch, and listen to Laura Nyro records. Her songs were filled with deep emotions and her strong voice wailed out in a woman's pain. From the regret of a lover's breakup in *I Never Meant to Hurt You,* to a man's inability to commit in *He's A Runner,* her music comforted and supported me. By the third week, I'd turned my grief into anger and stopped blaming myself for the break-up. Just like in one of Laura's songs, I realized that Michael was somewhat of a "Flim-Flam Man," and I mentally knocked him off his pedestal.

One day Bonnie made a new attempt to console me. "Look, this totally sucks," she said, "But it will make you a better songwriter." Something in me resonated with her words, and I stopped feeling sorry for myself and wrote a new song.

> *I wanted to be fooled, I wanted you to lie,*
> *Just to hear you say, you love me one more time.*
> *I knew you didn't mean it, I knew you weren't mine.*
> *I can't be mad at you babe, I wanted to be fooled . . .*

In time, the heaviness of the winter lifted. On a beautiful sunny late morning in March, Marsha and I climbed out her bedroom window and sat on the townhouse roof. It was so much fun sitting out there I spontaneously burst into Elton John's "Your Song." Passing below, a group of black school girls dressed in plaid uniforms looked up.

"Hey! You can *sing!"* one of the girls yelled up to me. I knew my voice was strong. It not only carried easily into the street. It carried me through my heartache, my fears, and my dreams of stardom.

Singing on the roof inspired me to answer an ad in Washington's underground newspaper. It seemed like it was written just for me: *"Grace Slick sound-alike wanted for DC rock band."* I decided to go for it!

I sang Grace Slick's "Somebody to Love" and got in the band. I was stoked!

The guys in the band were real characters and really good musicians. Tommy, the guitar player, was a sweet, mellow guy with long straggly black hair. He wore a plaid flannel shirt and faded jeans. My friends and I called guys like him "crunchy chewy" types. They were all about eating granola and getting back to nature. At the first rehearsal, I asked him if he was a Virgo. He nodded, looking surprised. I knew by the way he insisted that every note of every song had to be exactly like the record.

His best friend, John, was the bass player. They knew each other from high school in Virginia and their playing was tight. John had wavy, light brown hair that was parted in the center and fanned out to his shoulders. When he played the bass, he closed his eyes and moved his body back and forth as if he were in a trance. He was either stoned, really into the music, or both. It didn't matter, his playing was hot!

Jeff, the drummer, was the only married one. He had some government job during the day, so his dark brown hair was shorter than the other guys. "Music's the only thing that keeps me sane, Carol. Nine to five is not my thing." He took a toke off a jay. "But I like, have responsibilities, ya know?" I admired him for that.

During one of our rehearsals, John pointed to an old electric Wurlitzer keyboard in the far corner of the basement and asked me if I played. I explained to him that I mostly played classical piano and didn't know much about rock chords and improvising, but he wouldn't take no for an answer. He insisted I accompany myself on a blues song by Tracy Nelson of Mother Earth, "Down So Low," and I really got into it. It was a difficult song with two key changes and I spent hours learning the chords. If the guys thought it was worth taking the legs off the fifty-pound Wurlitzer and dragging it along to gigs just so I could play *one* song, I was going to do my damnedest to perform it well!

Our first gig was outdoors at the Washington Monument, as part of a Peace Concert featuring local bands. There was no formal stage or audience space. We set up on a grassy incline bordering the monument, as people walked around aimlessly, looking unsure as to why they were there. Organizers were giving out anti-war pamphlets and passing around petitions. A rock band a few feet from us was winding up their last song, Country Joe and the Fish's great ironic Vietnam protest, "Feel Like I'm Fixin to Die Rag".

We began our set with "Wooden Ships," which fit in with the anti-war theme. When we got to the chorus, our three-part harmonies sounded pitch-perfect! Our practicing had paid off! I started to relax into the music. We did two more Airplane songs and then I felt my nerves kicking in as I adjusted my mic stand and took a seat behind the keyboard. I played the intro of "Down So Low," then let loose and belted out the first verse, all about loss and heartache. All the hurt and pain from my break-up with Michael and the hell from my roommates' rape came pouring out of me. I stared down at my hands all through the song, playing the chords I'd memorized, not daring to look out at the audience. When I finished, the crowd burst into wild applause just as thunder began rumbling in the background. *Was it a sign from the universe that I was on the right track?* The oncoming storm cut our set short, but I left on a performance high I wanted to feel again.

I liked working with the band, and my new feeling of confidence increased my desire to write and sing my own songs. Blues was definitely my thing. I wanted to dig deep and express what I felt in my soul about being a woman. My passion spilled over into my music appreciation class, where I wrote a term paper about three groundbreaking women blues singers: Bessie Smith, Billie Holiday, and Big Mama Thorton. They didn't just sing the blues, they lived it. I would never know what it would be like to be a black woman trying to make it in a segregated society, but that didn't stop me from feeling their music. We were women trying not to get fucked over in a man's world.

April rolled around, but Melanie, Bonnie, and Marsha were still far from ready to open up to springtime romance, but unselfishly encouraged me to move on from Michael and "get back out there." Going deep into my music was helping me come out of my funk, and one day I realized I was eyeing the hunks on campus. They couldn't all be heartbreakers, could they?

9
THREE'S A CROWD

Just give me some real affection.
I won't waste time making my selection.
I guess I'll love anybody who'll let me.

"I'm almost there, slow down!" I screamed, but by the way the bed was shaking, I knew it was too late. I was so close but not close enough. Jerry lay on top of me like a dead man with a smile on his face.

"Did you come?" he whispered.

"Almost. I just needed a little more time."

"You really turned me on, Carol. I couldn't wait."

"That's okay, maybe next time." I tried sounding hopeful.

"Just relax, it's your turn now."

Jerry was one of two guys I was seeing. No one I knew used the word "dating" - it was *so* 1950's.

Jerry was high energy and a great guitar player. Whenever he got excited about something, he'd lean his head to the side and his dirty blond hair would cover one eye. I couldn't stop myself from touching his wayward locks and sweeping them behind his ear. He told me that sometimes when he played guitar, he got so into it, he came. *If he can do that while playing the guitar what could he do to me?* I still hadn't climaxed at the same time with any of my partners. Maybe he'd be the one to set me free.

We'd met in music appreciation class. I felt very comfortable with him. We shared a similar Jewish middle-class background. He was from Long Island, and I was from New Jersey, but it was really all the same.

Joshua came from a more affluent family. Melanie had been with him a few times Freshman year but found him too intense, so she introduced him to me. His energy was more subtle than Jerry's, but his piercing blue-green eyes could look right through me. I never knew what to expect when I was with him. He was funny and cute and liked to live on the edge.

He was doing the hippie thing with his long, dark hair, and moustache but driving around the city in a shiny red MG convertible. Joshua confessed that his family's house was so big it had an elevator and made me promise not to tell anyone. He also told me that his family would frequently vacation with the Governor of Maryland's family when he was growing up.

But there was a downside. His socialite mother and workaholic father didn't spend much time with him. He was the proverbial poor little rich boy, a refugee from his own family just like the guy in Joni Mitchell's "Rainy House Night." One thing was for sure, Joshua wasn't going to become a corporate lawyer and join his father's law firm, even though his father totally expected him to. The thought of Joshua with short hair, clean-shaven, and wearing a three-piece suit, made me laugh. He was a hustler and had his own "business" on the side, but nothing his parents would approve of.

My confidence level was at an all-time high and I was having fun! The only problem was that Jerry and Joshua both lived right across from each other on "O" Street, not too far from my old apartment at Dupont Circle. *I'm having orgasms on "O" Street!* I thought as I ran up the stairs to Joshua's. I wasn't "going steady"—another outdated expression—with him or Jerry either, so I casually said hello when I bumped into Jerry on the street the next morning as I was leaving Joshua's apartment.

"It's getting a little too much seeing both guys," I told my roommates at one of our roundtable discussions.

"That's one problem I wouldn't mind having," Melanie said, pouring herself another cup of coffee.

"There's gotta be one you like more than the other. If it's meant to be, you'll know it," chimed in Bonnie, the most romantic of the group.

Marsha nodded and offered me a slice of her homemade banana bread.

With its red and white checkered curtains and walls full of fun forties memorabilia, our kitchen was the most cheerful room in the house. Marsha's mother had given us a table cloth brightly printed with red cherries on a white background, and some real china cups and saucers with pink roses on them. They were a lot nicer than the plastic dishes my mother gave me.

"Yeah, I don't know. Jerry seems to be really into me, but I'm more into Joshua. I'm not that sure about him. I just hope he's not a player."

"He's got that reputation," Melanie warned.

"I know, but everyone's doing it with everyone. Maybe we'll fall in love, but I don't want another heartbreaker."

Just then the phone rang. It was Joshua.

"Carol, I'm in jail."

"Is this one of your jokes?" I asked, trying not to laugh.

"No, for real. I'm in jail and I need you to bail me out. You're my one phone call. I had a few unpaid parking tickets, about $400 worth. Bring your checkbook and I'll pay you back when I get home."

"Okay, I'll call a cab, give me the address."

I got in the cab feeling angry. How could Joshua have been so careless? I wasn't too worried, since I knew he had a safety net - his parents. I did too, and for me, it was a blessing and a curse. I felt lucky that my parents were there if I needed rescuing, but it interfered with my drive to succeed. Still, it was comforting to know I would never be out on the street.

My anger melted when I walked into the station and saw Joshua's scared little face. He looked cute and vulnerable, like a mischievous puppy who knows he's done something wrong but wants you to love him anyway.

On the cab ride back, Joshua sat very close and held my hand. "You're my one phone call, Carol. I think I love you. You get me and you laugh at my jokes. I don't want to be with anybody else."

"Me either," I whispered in his ear.

Bonnie was right about knowing. Joshua was the one, and I would have to stop seeing Jerry.

I called up Jerry and told him I was getting serious with someone. He was cool with it but sounded a little hurt. I didn't tell him who it was. That's why I was freaked out when I walked into the Student Center a few weeks later to find Joshua and Jerry sitting together. I tried running out the door, but it was too late. Joshua had spotted me.

"Carol, have a seat. Do you know Jerry?" I smiled and nodded.

"We were in a music class together last semester," Jerry said coolly.

"Jerry put up a sign looking for riders to go to Florida with him over Spring Break. I'm thinking of going. You know how I'm not into seeing my parents right now. You wanna come?" Joshua asked me.

"Why don't you come with us?" Jerry chimed in, with his familiar, soft-spoken voice.

"Thanks for the invite, but I'm going home to Jersey," I mumbled. "Good to see you, but I've gotta get going now." I couldn't come up with an excuse. I just had to get out of there.

"Hey, I'll walk you out. Jerry, I'll let you know about the trip," Joshua called back over his shoulder as he ran to catch up with me.

"Wow, that was uncomfortable! I had a little thing with him, nothing serious. You're my main man," I assured him once he caught up. He must have been feeling jealous since he gave me a passionate kiss.

The idea of Jerry and Joshua driving to Florida together and comparing notes put me in a panic. What else would they talk about on their long drive? The only thing they had in common was me. I prayed that it wouldn't work out, but I couldn't let Joshua know how shaken up I was. My prayers were answered later that week when Joshua told me he had decided to go to Long Island instead, to house sit for some friends while they were on vacation.

I sat on the train to New Jersey wishing I had gone to Long Island with Joshua instead of to my parents. What was a week apart going to feel like? We had started to bond and I was missing him already.

"Rode in the smoking car again, Carol?" my father asked as he gave me a big hug at the New Brunswick train station. I couldn't bring myself to tell my parents I was a smoker. They were in denial about a lot of things. Smoking was the least of it.

The next day, I woke up in my old bedroom with excruciating cramps and the heaviest period I'd ever had. I started to panic. Could I be having a miscarriage? I'd never gotten pregnant. For one reason or another, I'd never been able to take the pill but was good at remembering to use my diaphragm, even if it sometimes did get in the way of spontaneous moments. Many of my friends had to get abortions, legal or otherwise. One friend in high school had to travel with her parents all the way to the Caribbean to get one. Thank god, things had changed in this country and women could now make decisions about their bodies without risking their lives.

My parents' denial about my smoking paled in comparison to their level of denial about my virginity. They were completely clueless about my sexual escapades and I wanted to keep it that way. But when my mother asked me what was wrong, I told her about my heavy period.

"Why are you so concerned, Carol? Are you having sex? Do you think it might be a miscarriage?"

I was too scared to lie. "Yes, I admitted. I'm sleeping with Joshua."

Before I could say anything more, she went down to the basement to tell my father. It didn't matter that I could be bleeding to death! All that mattered was that their little girl wasn't a virgin. I didn't want to know my father's reaction. I couldn't spend another night in that house of shame. I ran upstairs to call Joshua before he left for Long Island.

"Carol, is that you? Are you all right? I can hardly hear you."

I was crying so hard I could barely get the words out. "I can't stay here. I just told my parents I'm not a virgin. I'm bleeding so bad I think I'm having a miscarriage. Can you pick me up on your way to Long Island? I'm scared, I'm really scared."

"Calm down, baby. Just give me the directions and I'll be there."

I pulled it together enough to give Joshua the directions, and closed the door to my room, and started packing. I lay down on the single bed where I'd spent so many nights dreaming of Prince Charming. I could never be the woman my parents wanted me to be. If they didn't accept me, then I would have to figure it out on my own. The truth had flowed out of me and I had crossed the Red Sea. There was no turning back. I was free.

As it turned out, I didn't have a miscarriage. The five days I spent with Joshua at his friends' house on "the Island," as the JAP-y girls from GWU referred to it, were relatively uneventful. But one night, Joshua's hustler personality took over and he came up with a crazy idea.

"Let's get married, Carol," he casually said, as we were walking on the beach. For one sweet minute, I felt my heart stop. Could this really be happening? Had my horrible nightmare turned into my dream come true? Before I had time to answer, he said, "We can get married, take all the money and gifts from the wedding, and split them. I told you, my family's rich! We could really make out!"

I didn't know what to say. My emotions were shifting like the sand below my feet, and it took all my energy just to keep my balance.

"What do you think?" Joshua asked as he put his arm around me. I nodded in agreement, never thinking he would go through with it. But that night he called his mother to tell her the good news. I listened in on the bedroom phone,

"Hi, Mom. I have some news. I'm getting married."

His mother sounded tentative. "Who is this girl, and how long have you known her?"

"Her name is Carol. Carol Marks. She's a student in one of my classes. I've known her for about six weeks."

"Oh Joshua, you're so mixed up!" she cried and abruptly hung up. He never brought the subject up again. His future had bigger and more dangerous hustles on the horizon.

On our ride back to Washington, I wondered when I would talk to my parents again. I knew I wasn't ready. I needed time to heal and make sense of what had happened. I told myself it could've been worse. What if I'd been pregnant and lost a baby? Another catastrophe averted!

Maybe I did have a guardian angel protecting me. When Big John got busted in November, no one discovered that Melanie and I were keeping thousands of dollars' worth of drugs for him in our refrigerator. Then in December, I had narrowly escaped being raped. I had fallen in love with Michael on the very day of the break-in. I shuddered to think what would have happened if I hadn't gone to Michael's that night. Another close call! If only my roommates could have been so lucky! I sent a silent prayer of thanks to Chia Sora, the grandmother I was named after but never knew. My father's mother who was murdered in the Holocaust. Maybe *she* was the one watching over me.

Back in DC, I kissed Joshua goodbye and thanked him for rescuing me. Melanie, Bonnie, and Marsha felt more like family to me than my real family did. I could hardly wait to see them as I opened the door to the townhouse. "I'm back!" I called out. I'd never been a touchy-feely kind of girl, but there at the door, as they all came to greet me, I said "I need a group hug." *It felt good to be home!*

Two weeks went by before I found the courage to call my parents. Only my mother would talk to me. My father was still mad. She told me that they wanted to visit me the following weekend. So it was on Saturday that I found myself sitting in the "hot seat"—in this case, a park bench by the Lincoln Memorial. My mother sat between me and my father. No one said anything, which was very out of character for my father since he was never at a loss for words.

My mother, always the peacemaker, prodded him to say *something*. When he finally did, I could barely hold back my tears.

"I will never condone what you did, Carol, but for the sake of keeping the family together, I'd like to put this behind us. I'm still your father and I will always love you and be there for you. Can we agree to go forward?"

I swallowed my pride, took off my scarlet letter, and shakily said "Okay."

10
REVOLUTION

How much will you give for an all-and-out war?
Two million people, mainly the poor.
Rich politicians, that's who it's for.
The lambs get slaughtered while the lions roar.

After our meeting on the park bench, my father wrote:

All is well that ends well. You are approaching the truth from your path, while I have looked it over from my life's angles. I recall a Chinese poem by Lu Chi: 'Running and standing still at once is the whole truth.'

School was okay and I was actually going to classes. The band got a few more gigs including playing at The Cellar, which was one of the biggest clubs in Washington. One night, while I was singing "Summertime," I felt such a strong connection to the audience that the high was better than grass or even sex. The crowd's vibes were merging with mine and I was singing from a place I'd never been before. It felt like one big vocal orgasm.

I was flying, but I didn't dare tell Joshua. He wasn't a musician and couldn't understand. I was more worried about his feelings than mine, and I didn't want to say anything to threaten his fragile male ego.

Things between us had cooled down. We were still seeing each other, but he was taking a lot of business trips to Philadelphia. He told me he was working on a deal to sell jewelry from Mexico and not to worry, but I knew there was something wrong. We were having sex less and less. He started making up excuses; too tired, too stoned, too stressed. His lack of desire made me feel unattractive and it was messing with my self-esteem. To feel better about myself, I borrowed a bicycle from one of the guys who lived next door and started riding around the neighborhood without a bra on. The sight of my boobs bouncing over potholes and cobblestone streets did bring me some much-needed male attention.

One night I got up the nerve to ask Joshua if I could go with him on his next trip to Philadelphia. "Wait till the semester's over. We'll work it out baby," he told me.

I tried putting my suspicions out of my mind, but as I studied for my exams the thought of Joshua with another woman kept popping into my head. I had trouble focusing and the text looked blurry, just like the lines between what Joshua was telling me and the truth. I wanted to believe that he truly cared and that he was going to Philly just for business, but I was starting to have my doubts.

When Joshua came back, he gave me a beautiful silver and turquoise bracelet. The turquoise center stone was huge and there were two smaller stones on either side. "I want you to have this, Carol. It's a sample of the jewelry I'll be selling."

As I lay next to him that night I felt hurt by his lack of sexual interest. It was as if someone turned off the juice. I felt the smooth stone of my bracelet against my wrist and rationalized that he wouldn't have given it to me if he didn't love me, but a tiny voice inside my head said this was a guilt thing. Was I being fooled again?

"There's a rally tomorrow. SDS's gonna take over one of the class-room buildings. Do you wanna go?" Melanie asked me the next morning after Joshua left.

"Cool, maybe I'll get my mind off Joshua. Something's wrong, but I don't know what."

"I thought he was really into you."

"Yeah, so did I, until he started going to Philly on the weekends. Something about a business deal and Mexican jewelry." As I reached for a coffee cup, the sleeve of my bathrobe slid up my arm. "Look, Joshua gave me this last night," I said waving my wrist at Melanie.

"Far out! That stone is the biggest turquoise rock I've ever seen! Things are probably okay. Don't worry. Look at the big picture and go to the rally with me."

I knew there were people in the world with much bigger problems than mine. In my sophomore year, I'd volunteered to be part of a literacy program. It was a real eye-opener for me. On the ride to the projects, where the third-grade girl I tutored lived, I saw nothing but slums for miles and miles. One continuous ghetto - the real capitol of our nation.

Then there was the war. Viet Nam was heating up and demonstra-tors all over the country were getting arrested. Guys my age were getting drafted, burning draft cards, or fleeing to Canada. Joshua had gotten out of the draft by taking uppers, staying awake for seventy-two hours, and ranting incoherently when he faced the draft board. They deemed him too unstable to kill people. He was one of the lucky ones. They were getting hip to the fact that lots of draftees were faking it.

One musician I knew got granted a conscientious objector status, but that was rare. He was a cute horn player who sat in with the band occa-sionally. His name was James, but everyone called him Jesus. It was easy to see why. He had an aura of peace around him. With his long, light brown hair, beard, and blue eyes, he looked just like the pictures of Jesus I'd seen in books. He always wore white Indian cotton shirts and sandals, even in the middle of winter.

I could never imagine Jesus holding a gun. One night when we were jamming in the basement, a big spider started crawling towards me. I screamed, but Jesus just calmly picked it up and took it outside. Later that night we started writing a protest song together:

The loser's the winner, people deceived

Wrapped in propaganda, lies are believed

It's all a distraction to cover their greed

And make us think that they know what we need.

We never got to finish our song. Jesus disappeared. I heard he moved to California to play in Guru Maharaji's band.

By the time Melanie and I got to the SDS rally the next day, a large group of students were already congregated on the steps in front of Maury Hall. Right on the front door was a sign that read, "*Liberate the restrooms!*"

"You can use any bathroom you want!" a guy in an army jacket shouted. "We're taking over. Sexual equality includes gender-free bathrooms!"

Melanie and I hung around for a while at the edge of the stairs. The crowd was growing and spreading to the street. I recognized the guy screaming in the megaphone. His face was turning the same color as his red hair.

"He's a hunk," Melanie shouted in my ear.

"I know, that's Peter Miles. He was in my European Lit class last semester. I thought he was a snob, but I guess I was wrong."

"Abolish ROTC! Draft beer, not students! Peace Now!" the crowd started to chant. Someone from SDS handed me a pamphlet with a picture of Uncle Sam pointing his finger on the cover. It said in big letters "FIGHT IMPERIALISM." Melanie and I pushed through the crowd to hear Peter.

"GWU is involved in the war machine. It is isolating itself from the rest of DC!" Peter was yelling. "Racial minorities continue to be exploited in the richest country in the world. Racism is not simply a question of individual consciousness but of institutions! Washington is seventy-five percent Black, and there are almost no Black students at GWU. Read the pamphlet! Our college president belongs to a country club that excludes minorities."

"We're taking over the classrooms!" Peter's voice boomed through the megaphone. Melanie was so into it that she was ready to follow the protestors into the building. I turned to see a line of DC police standing across the street with helmets on their heads and clubs in their piggy hands, just waiting to use them. I remembered the blood spilled on the sidewalk in front of the White House. Red, black and blue were the real colors of the freedom fighters. Violence didn't bring peace. I thought about my peaceful, conscientious objector songwriting partner. What would Jesus do if he was here? I knew the answer. It was time to split.

"Let's get out of here, Mel. Things are gonna heat up. I've had enough!" I grabbed her hand and we weaved our way through the surging crowd.

I stayed away from campus the next day. The rioting had gotten out of control. Demonstrators took over some classroom buildings and then the cops tear gassed the entire block. The GWU campus was a war zone.

It made the front page of the *Washington Post*, along with the College President announcing that he was canceling all final exams for Spring Semester! I couldn't believe my luck! Whatever grade you had up to that point, you got. Now I had two semesters in a row without taking finals—fall semester because of the rape and now this! I was doing well in all of my classes, but thinking about quitting school. What would I do with a sociology degree? I tried changing my major to music education, but I would have to take too many classes and stay an extra semester. All I wanted to do was write music and sing.

I was still in denial about Joshua when he called. He had just got back from another Philly weekend. Hoping against hope that he'd missed me, I picked up the phone.

"Carol, you know you're very special to me, but there's a reason we haven't been getting it on. There's someone else I have to be with."

"Let me guess, does she live in Philly?" I could feel my knees getting weak.

"It just happened. She was my business partner's roommate. I wasn't looking for anyone. I'll always care about you, but the chemistry was too strong to fight."

I couldn't believe what I was hearing. My knight in shining armor, my rescuer, my pretend husband, was cheating on me. How could this be happening again?

That was it! I was never coming back to Washington. I was quitting school and moving as far away as I could get from this awful city. I had to go back to California. A student revolution was going on in the country and I was going through my own personal revolution. No one could change my mind. I'd had enough. I'd find a way to break it to my parents, once I stopped crying.

When they picked me up the next day, there was no hiding my tears. I cried nonstop for an entire week. Everyone blamed Joshua except me. I blamed myself. First Michael and now Joshua? *Why couldn't I keep a man? Wasn't I attractive or sexy enough?*

My parents felt bad to see how inconsolable I was over losing Joshua. But when I announced on the ride home that I wanted to quit school and move to California you'd have thought I'd dropped the atomic bomb. This was the final blow that blasted all their dreams for me to smithereens. I swore I'd go back to school in a year, but my father wasn't buying it. "You'll *never* go back to school, Carol. This is the biggest mistake of your life."

Looking back now, I suppose they were torn between rescuing me from my misery and wanting me "to do the right thing." *Should they let the baby cry herself to sleep for hours or pick her up?* Ultimately, it was just too late to change the family dynamics. They paid for a plane ticket to California and stopped the crying.

11
BEZERKLEY

When I want a man, you know that is a chore.
I can't use my money, I can't go to the store.
I just sit and pray to the stars up above,
'Cause like the Beatles told me,
Money can't buy me love.

I had a plan when I got to California, but meeting Randy Loveman wasn't part of it. Yes, that was his real name! Like a sign from the universe that I'd made the right move, this tall, good-looking angel of a man asked me if I needed a ride as I walked out of the San Francisco Airport and breathed in the California air. He was about six feet tall, with dark curly hair, mischievous deep brown eyes, and a slightly sunburned face. I guessed he was a few years older than me.

"I'm going to Berkeley."

"I can take you as far as San Francisco."

"Far out!" Something about his smile and upbeat energy made me trust him.

"What are you doing in Berkeley?" he asked.

I blurted out my whole life story – every miserable thing that had happened that year: the breakups, quitting school, wanting to make it in the music business, and most importantly my California dreams.

"I'm never going back to the East Coast!" I said.

"I get it. California's where it's at. Sounds like you need a change!" Randy said sweetly as we neared San Francisco.

I could feel the chemistry between us. He must have felt it too because a few minutes later, he offered to drive me all the way to Berkeley.

We pulled up in front of a boxy, modern apartment building a half a block from Telegraph Avenue. Mark Greenberg, a guy in Marsha's philosophy class, was subletting an apartment there for the summer and he said I could crash for a while until I got my own place. He was going back to GWU in September to finish his senior year and apply to law school.

Randy insisted on coming upstairs to check out the place and meet Mark. The apartment was a one-bedroom with a galley kitchen and a big living room with beige wall-to-wall carpeting. Mark seemed warm, laid-back, and easy to talk to, but definitely not my type - too big-boned and all-American looking. In other words, the perfect roommate. I sensed he wasn't attracted to me, either.

Randy put down my bags and asked, "Write down your address, Carol, okay? I'd like to see you again."

"Sure, I don't know how long I'll be here, but I'd like to see you, too."

"You will! Do you like cats?"

"Yes!" I called to him as he ran down the stairs.

I wasn't the only student from GWU who'd heard about Mark's sublet. It seemed that word got out to everyone at school. I'd left Washington, but Washington hadn't left me. Our apartment became *the* crash pad for GWU. The living room and bedroom floors were covered with wall-to-wall sleeping bags. Mark and I were the only ones who slept on beds since we were the only ones paying the rent. There was a constant stream of hippies, frat boys, and even a pet raccoon for a few days. At night it was a zoo, but during the day the troops rolled up their sleeping bags and put them against the walls as they explored the Bay Area.

I looked forward to the early afternoons when I could grab a nap or wait for Randy's visits. A few days after dropping me off he'd showed up with two housewarming gifts: an adorable, six-toed calico kitten, and a bag of white powder. I kept the kitten and named her Orinda, after a town we'd passed on our drive from the airport.

True to his name, Randy Loveman was a *great* lover. Of course, our lovemaking was intensified by the lines of white powder we inhaled right before it. I could get used to this, I thought one lazy afternoon as we lay together coming off our highs. I knew we'd never be a couple. Randy casually mentioned he was living with his girlfriend in Sausalito, but that they had an open relationship. I was cool with it. I wasn't ready for anything heavy.

Still, Randy was more than just a pleasurable experience. He made me feel sexy and desired and was good for my bruised ego. Joshua and Michael's break-ups had left me with a deep wound that reached inside my very soul. Randy was sweet and fun, but I still needed to prove to myself that I was attractive to more than one guy. After all, I was in Bezerkley! A crazy good place to meet hippie guys who were looking for chicks to hook up with.

I spent most of my days just walking around town. I especially liked checking out Cody's bookstore on Telegraph. The cool guys hung out in the New Age section, and I spent a lot of time skimming through books on past lives, yogis, and astrology, and otherwise sampling the inventory. Faces, first names, body parts—I sampled many I met at Cody's, and anywhere else my loneliness led me to wander. Yet while all this male attention made me feel more attractive and desirable, it still was not enough to fill my emotional emptiness.

One afternoon I was daydreaming at Cody's, making a mental list of books I'd buy as soon as I got a job and had some money when some lyrics popped into my head:

When I get the urge to buy a brand-new pair of shoes,
I count up all my money, I know that I can't lose.
And when I get the urge to get my hair done up real nice
I go to my beautician and I pay him his price.
But when I want a man, you know that is a chore.
I can't use my money, I can't go to the store.

Meanwhile, the chore of making some money was staring me in the face whenever I opened my eyes from my daydreams. A few times a week, I made a feeble attempt to land an office job. I slicked my dark, thick, frizzed-out hair back in a ponytail and put on my grown-up uniform, one of my mother's hand-me-down tweed blazers, and a black A-line midi skirt. Then I hitchhiked to the business district in downtown San Francisco. The interviews always came down the same. Some suit behind a desk looked over my application and said, "You haven't lived here long enough. How do we know you're not a transient?"

It was a Catch-22: I couldn't get a job if I didn't already live here. But how could I stay if I didn't have a job? I guess part of me didn't give a shit. I didn't want to be working in the straight world. No skirt or pantyhose could cover up who I was, another spaced-out East Coast chick checking out the California scene.

What I really wanted to do was my music, but that wasn't easy to break into either. A week after I got to Berkeley, I'd auditioned for a band in San Francisco in an old rundown boarding house. Waiting in the dingy hallway with a few other hopefuls, I'd felt confident as I listened to the soulful sounds of an organ coming from behind the closed door down the hall. I knew I could sing and was determined to make some money to stay in California.

Finally, the door opened. A Janis Joplin wannabe sauntered out and said, "I nailed it. Your turn."

"We'll see about that," I said as I headed to the door. A tall black guy with a big afro stood up from behind the organ and motioned me in.

He was wearing a colorfully patterned Dashiki, and looked a little older, somewhere in his thirties. He gave me a warm smile and asked me what song I was singing.

"'Summertime' in C minor,"

"Cool," he said, and handed me the microphone. He started to play and I belted out the song, trying to sing above the organ. After the first verse and chorus, he stopped.

"You have possibilities, but you haven't reached your potential. I don't think you're ready for my project. You have a good voice but you need more training. Keep on it."

"Thanks for the advice," I said and shook his hand. I hated to admit it, but I knew he was right. Maybe I'd been a little too confident. I'd always been able to slide by on the power of my voice but I'd have to be more disciplined if I wanted to make it. But first, I'd have to go back to looking for a job in the boring straight world.

Just when my fragile ego was starting to mend, I got a letter from Melanie about Joshua that triggered all my old insecurities.

Joshua plans to go to Philadelphia with ego-boost security chick. What can I say, Carol? I have to tell you this shit, but who knows? Maybe he really loves you and isn't ready yet. Can I give you my interpretation? It isn't pretty, but you have turned Joshua into a man-god and it seems he's still a little boy. Your relationship was too equal. You both helped each other and shared with each other. It seems that Joshua feels that's too heavy. He needs a girl's (mother's) undying approval and awe—especially with his sexual ability. When will he learn that there is no ability in sex? It is only the joy in giving. I think he knows his fuck-ups and is treating them. Carol, you've grown into a woman, but he's still a boy-man.

Melanie's letter sent me into a tailspin. I ripped it up, ran out the door to the bookstore, and went home with the first guy who smiled at me. This was the second guy I'd slept with this week. His name was Steve something. After sex, he'd asked me why I was crying. I shook my head and turned away. I knew why. I felt hollow and lonely and disconnected. Instead of intimacy, I felt distance.

The next morning, I opened my eyes and looked at the naked body lying next to me. For a minute I didn't know where I was. *How did I get here?* I quickly pulled on my t-shirt, scooped up my jeans from the floor, and wriggled into them. I grabbed my Indian print bag and tiptoed into the bathroom.

I looked in the bathroom mirror and dragged a brush through my tangled-up hair. I didn't have to look at my watch to know what time it was—time to get real. With no job, no band, no place to live after the summer, no love, there would be no future for me here. For the next couple of days my head was full of "I-told-you so's," but I finally swallowed my pride. I made the phone call I knew my parents were expecting and asked them to book me a one-way ticket back to Jersey. I made a quick stop at the free clinic to make sure I didn't have VD or any other scary diseases and started packing my bags.

I couldn't leave Orinda without a home, so I stuck her in a canvas knapsack, gave her a quarter of a Dramamine, and hoped no one would notice how the sack was wiggling around. I got off the plane with one very unhappy kitten. My father was even more unhappy about having a pet, so I hatched a plan with Nina, who was staying at her mother's house to save money until she could afford her own place. Her mom loved cats, so I took Orinda over to show her to Nina. She was so adorable with her little spotted face and kittenish ways that Nina's mom fell in love and agreed to adopt her right away. I could even play with her as much as I wanted since Nina's mom lived just a few blocks from my parents.

My parents bent over backward to make me feel comfortable. They knew it would take some time for me to figure out my next move. They put a bed and dresser in the spare room downstairs so I could have some privacy and unhappily agreed to let me smoke.

I wrote Randy a letter to give him my new phone number and address, but I never thought I'd hear from him. One lonely Saturday night about a week later, I was slouched on my parents' couch smoking cigarettes and eating pretzels, watching the Miss America contest, and feeling like a total loser, when the phone rang. My parents were out, so I picked it up.

"Carol, how are you?"

At first, I didn't recognize the voice on the other end.

"It's Randy."

I couldn't believe my ears! A reminder of the life I'd left behind.

"I found you a place! It's in Marin, an apartment on the lower level of a lighthouse! Isn't that cool? It'd be perfect for you!"

"Randy, didn't you read my letter? I'm in Jersey. I'd love to live there, but I'm stuck here for now."

"Bummer! Okay, Miss New Jersey. Let me know when you're ready to come back to sunny CA."

"I will," I promised. "Oh, and I brought Orinda with me," I added. But he'd already hung up the phone.

12
HONEY, LET THE GOOD TIMES ROLL

In the morning when I look into your eyes,
Country sun is dawning, reflecting city skies.
Singin', "Honey, let the good times roll,
Honey, let the good times roll,
Merrily rolling inside my soul!"

For nine long months, I lived with my parents and worked as a sub-stitute teacher and part-time salesgirl at Sears. It all paid off in July when I was finally able to move out and Nina and I began sharing Marvin's apart-ment on West 72nd. The first thing we did was put curtains up in the front bay window. *No more parading around nude, like I did with Marvin!*

The bedroom was a narrow rectangle with a double and a single bed. It also had a tv and was the only room with an air conditioner. To escape the summer heat, I spent my nights watching *I Love Lucy* reruns. I was in a dry spell and feeling bummed out that I hadn't met anyone in New York.

"I won't need the double," I told Nina. "Nothing's happening for me in the romance department." How could I predict that two weeks later, my ex- roommate's older brother would move to the city and blow my mind? Marsha's brother Robbie was subletting an apartment downtown for the summer to work as an assistant still photographer for a movie being shot in New York. Marsha suggested I give him a call.

We met for dinner at a health food restaurant in the Village. "You're hardly eating, Carol. Don't you like your stir fry?"

"It's okay. I have this neurotic thing about eating out, especially when I'm nervous."

"It's cool with me. I love to cook. You can come over to my place. I'll just put the food on the table and you can eat it whenever you want."

"Thanks for not making me feel weird about it. I'm seeing a shrink. He thinks he can help me."

From that night on we were inseparable. Robbie had been on his way to a commune in Virginia when he got the offer for the movie job. His father had connections and Robbie figured he could earn some money, then drop out later and live on the commune. He had the soul of a country boy even though he grew up in Westchester, not far from the city, and went to college in Chicago. He'd hitchhiked cross-country a few times and loved camping and sleeping under the stars. My idea of camping was staying at a Motel 6.

Robbie was a strict vegetarian. He was so dedicated he managed to lug a twenty-pound bag of brown rice on the subway from the wholesale health food store downtown to his apartment. He was a good influence on me, but some days I would sneak out to a diner and have a big juicy hamburger with lots of ketchup. Therapy was helping me to be less neurotic about my eating habits.

Robbie and I were opposites in many ways, but we were both from the same tribe. We both had dark hair, light skin, and greenish-brown eyes. He wore his thick, wavy, shoulder-length hair in a ponytail to keep cool, and he looked cool, too. Sometimes when we made love, I looked up at him and saw myself. It was eerie and seductive. *Could I be in love with myself?*

We even joked about it. He called me Howdy Doody and I called him Rooty Kazootie. But his favorite pet name for me was Yoko. Maybe it was because John Lennon and Yoko lived across the street, or maybe because it was fun to say. Who knows? It was part of the world we shared, and that's all that mattered.

Some nights I took the downtown bus to 38th Street and walked two blocks west to 10th Avenue. It was an iffy neighborhood, and I felt scared, but nothing could stop me from spending the night with Robbie. His sublet was on the tenth floor of a low-income high-rise and the bedroom had a full wall of windows. After midnight the city quieted down and we were in our own little world. Making love to him and staring at the bright stars and the inky blue sky was what I lived for. It was the only time I felt like I belonged in this city of infinite possibilities. No one cared what you did. You could be anyone you wanted to be or slip into anonymity.

We were in bed at Robbie's one night when he brought out his camera and asked if he could take some nude photos. At first, I felt shy and uptight. He suggested we smoke a joint to relax. I started to get into it, but it wasn't the pot that did it. It was his desire for me. I could feel it coming through the lens. When I looked up at him it was as if the camera and his eyes were one. I'd never felt so sexy and adored. When he stopped, we were both so turned on we made love over and over again until we collapsed in each other's arms and fell asleep just as dawn blushed the horizon.

"New York has the best and worst of everything. It's a matter of where your head's at, Carol." I was in Bruce's office trying to make sense of my new relationship.

"Problem is, I don't know where my head is at, but I do know where my heart is. I'm falling in love with that guy I told you about last week."

"What makes you think that?"

"I feel so peaceful when I'm with him. He gets me. He doesn't care if I can't eat out in restaurants. The only problem is sometimes I can't have an orgasm. I feel myself holding back."

"Are you afraid of being hurt again?"

"I don't know. It feels more like I'm so into the closeness that I don't need the orgasm, or maybe I have performance anxiety."

"You mean, you can't let go?"

"Maybe."

"You told me that when your roommates got raped, you felt angry that one of their friends said he could handle things. Then he opened the door without the chain on. "Do you think that could be part of why you have difficulty trusting men?"

"Hmm. . . ." I took a long drag on my last cigarette in the pack. I hadn't planned on telling Bruce about the rape so soon, but in our last session, I'd felt a strong need to talk about it. "So you're saying it's a control issue?"

"Could be. What's more vulnerable than having an orgasm?"

"I *am* afraid of losing myself and just living for him."

"Why is that?"

"I don't want to give up on *my* dreams."

"Isn't that why you came to New York? What are you doing about your music?"

"I rented a piano. I might play at an open audition at an uptown club next week."

I took another drag on my cigarette, remembering the day the piano got delivered. They'd put it on a crane and hoisted it through the living room window. Only in New York! I immediately sat down and started playing "Home Again," and it was true. Accompanying myself on my very own piano, I felt like I was home—home to my music. I looked out the bay window framed by tie-dyed curtains, just like the ones on Carole King's *Tapestry*. It was dusk and the city had a hazy pink glow. I was where I belonged. I was finally living my dream.

It was as if Bruce could read my mind. "When you walked in here that first day, you had a light around you," he said. "If you worked at it, who knows what could happen?"

I took a minute to catch my breath. I felt flattered and a little embarrassed that Bruce thought so highly of me.

"That's mind-blowing. I want to be famous but I want to be able to enjoy it."

"You know what they say—'Once you make it in the Big Apple, everything else is applesauce.'"

When I got home I found a note from Robbie that made me smile.

Yoko,

Going to Din-Din with my father and then on to film preview. Will be back here afterwards. Probably around 10:30. I'll see you later.

Love & butterfly kisses,

Robbie

P.S. Karate man called. Says restaurant below him wants to try you out as a waitress if interested.

Robbie was sweet, but Karate man, whoever he was, would have to wait. Besides I didn't want to be a waitress. I sat down at the piano and started playing around with some melodies as I thought about Robbie. It was time to trade in my blues and let the good times roll.

The summer rolled along. I got a job in a health food store not too far from Bruce's office and Robbie worked on his movie. Nina was out so much that I couldn't keep up with her comings and goings. She'd met a shoe salesman down the street and was spending a lot of time at his West Village apartment, enjoying the summer as she waited to get into grad school

Robbie was spending most of his nights at our place. Some nights he'd play his flute and I would play the piano. I even started to write a new song:

Let me tell you a story about two people I knew.
He whistled fire while his lady sang the blues.
He promised to love her and they were doin' just fine,
Days filled with music, healthy livin', and wine.

Life was a perfect duet.

Until it became a trio. Robbie had casually mentioned that his ex-girlfriend Susan had called a few times just to say hi. He assured me that there was nothing between them, just old friends catching up. I wanted to believe him, but this little voice in my head made me feel uneasy. One night I confronted him.

"I think Susan wants to get back with you. It's the third time she's phoned in two weeks. Why else would she be calling?" I asked him while eating my miso soup.

"No, she knows I love *you*, Yoko."

I let it go, but I knew he was wrong. Men could be so clueless. Only another woman could pick up on what was *really* happening. Still, I persuaded myself to take him at his word and somehow managed to put Susan out of my mind.

And then Robbie told me about his plans for the fall. "I love you, Yoko, but I hate the city. I feel so torn. I only planned to stay until the movie ended. I never expected to meet you."

"I know you're a country boy, but what about us? Maybe you could work on another movie?"

"They offered me one, but I turned it down. This is such a hard decision but I have to go to Virginia."

The heaviness of his words felt like the world was crashing down on me—our world, the one we'd built together. It was like I was sitting in a movie theater unable to leave, glued to my seat as the credits rolled and *The End* flashed boldly on the screen.

A week later Robbie was gone and my life was left in shambles, like the popcorn-strewn aisles of an empty theater.

13
CROSSING THE GREAT WATER

There's a lonely woman in New York City who wants to know,
Does her man still love her? Just a simple yes or no.
If the answer is yes, she'll sing a happy song,
But if the answer is no, she'll be gone, gone, gone.

After Robbie left, I prayed for a letter, a sign, anything to make me feel he was still mine. Saying goodbye was hard for both of us. I didn't want him to go, and he told me he loved me, but he had to get out of the city. The country was calling to him as strongly as the city had called to me. It was tragic. We told each other it was just for a while, but how long was that?

I wanted a letter so badly that I dreamt there was one waiting for me. But the next afternoon my mailbox was empty.

I was still working in the health food store during the day and writing blues songs at night. Looking through some old lyrics, I came upon a note my father had written to me before I moved to the city. He knew I was into the *I Ching* and had gone out of his way to buy me some coins that were blessed by a Chinese wise man. At least that's what the shop owner told him. He was trying to get inside my head by any means possible, even using quotes from the *I Ching* to get his point across. He wrote:

It furthers one to cross the Great Water.

Whatever your decision may be, and wherever the winds may carry you,

My heart will always be with you.

That was it! My mind was made up. I had to cross the Great Water! I had to find Robbie in Virginia!

The next day I told Bruce about the mailbox dream and coming across the note from my father. "What do you think? Should I go to Virginia? Were the dream and the note a sign?" I asked.

"Let's start with the note. You have a lot of anger towards your father, but he's trying to show you how much he loves you. You're never going to change him and you can't change your childhood. You can only change how it affects you now. Your parents were doing the best they could at the time. The only place to get in touch with your anger is here."

I knew why he brought that up. I'd visited my parents two weeks earlier, right after an intense session with Bruce. All the anger that I'd suppressed throughout my childhood was starting to come to the surface. When they said they wanted to talk to me, I sat down on a plastic-covered dining room chair, my anger mounting, knowing what was coming next: *What were my plans for the future? When was I going to go back to school so I could get a real job?* They made me feel like a fucking loser.

"Everything in this house is plastic!" I exploded. "Plastic dishes, plastic cups, plastic furniture covers! Plastic and beige and boring! I'll *never* live like this!" I screamed even louder. "*No way* am I living in a cookie-cutter house with 2.5 children and neatly pruned shrubs. I will never be who you want me to be!" I simply couldn't stop screaming. All the times my parents had made me feel like I wasn't smart enough, pretty enough, well behaved enough, came bubbling to the surface and I just let it rip.

My anger turned to sadness on the long bus ride back to the city. I felt bad for upsetting my parents. Back at the apartment, I turned to my trusty journal:

There's a raging fire of anger inside me. Real anger, the forbidden, shiny red fruit of every socialized, civilized person. The secret wish of every child who swallows down 'I hate you, mommy. I hate you, daddy.' Then goes to bed and turns off the TV, or sings in front of the dinner guests. . . . The list is endless.

The message was clear. I was feeling so down about Robbie, and my rage had been buried so deep inside for such a long time, that I'd lost control and let it out on my parents when they'd started asking me about the future.

"Carol?" Bruce's voice was soft but strong enough to bring me back to the present.

"I get it," I said, feeling guilty. "What I did was wrong. I should have never yelled at my parents that weekend. I realize I upset them and I know they're worried about me. My anger surprised even me."

"You need to get your anger out here, where it's safe to express it. That's when you'll start to feel better. It takes energy to suppress feelings and that's what causes phobias and neurosis."

"Yeah, but what about going to see Robbie? That's happening now. Should I go?"

"I can't decide for you. You tend to be impulsive. Sometimes it works for you and other times against you. Can you handle either outcome, good or bad?"

"I don't know, but it's torture not knowing where I stand. I need to find out."

"There's your answer. See you in a week."

On the train ride to Washington, I was nervous and scared. I had no idea how Robbie would react to my surprise arrival. I looked out the window at the Chesapeake Bay. *It furthers one to cross the Great Water.* This is my destiny, I told myself. I'm meant to be with Robbie. And yet, I didn't know how I was going to find him once I got to DC! I knew the town in Virginia was called Flint Hill, but I had no idea where the commune was. I was crazed, on a mission to get my man back, and nothing was going to get in my way. Not even not knowing where the hell I was going was gonna stop me!

It was as if a force was guiding me back to Robbie. When I got to Union Station in DC, I found out the bus station was in the same building. I easily found the bus that was leaving for Flint Hill. Everything was falling into place. The farther we got from DC, the more beautiful the scenery became, with lush rolling hills and large stately farmhouses. I could understand why Robbie liked living here, away from the crowds and cars and graffiti. After about an hour's ride, I moved up to the front seat and told the bus driver my predicament. By this time, there were only two other people left on the bus, and they were getting ready to get off.

Miraculously, the bus driver offered to drive me around until we found the commune. I don't know if it was because he felt sorry for me or because I was the last one on the bus. He said he had an idea of where it might be. Within ten minutes we stopped in front of an old, white, colonial-style farmhouse. He drove the bus up the unpaved dirt driveway and waited for me to give him the thumbs up. I knocked on the door, and a minute later Robbie's handsome face appeared in the side window. I turned and waved goodbye to the bus driver with a big smile.

Once he got over his initial shock, Robbie was happy to see me. He held me tight in his suntanned arms right there standing at the doorsill. I was elated! I'd followed my instincts and they'd paid off big time!

There was just one minor detail I hadn't planned on, and her name was Susan.

"Hi," I heard from behind me. I turned my head as Robbie dropped his arms and abruptly drew a step back. She was a big-boned, waspy-looking woman with straight, mousey brown hair and blue eyes. Her most obvious feature was her over-flowing, D-cup breasts, which even her heavy denim overalls failed to successfully disguise. In the spirit of commune-ism she reached out her hand to welcome me, then quickly disappeared.

"I *did* write to you, Carol." We were lying in Robbie's bed after a desperate move on my part to reconnect physically. The sex was as good as I remembered, but we needed to communicate in a different way now.

"You *did*? I never got it. Wow, I guess my dream was real after all."

"Of course. I missed you, Yoko. And I didn't know Susan was going to come. She showed up on her own a few days after I got here. We're not a couple, you know, but who knows what the future will bring? I like it here and so does she. Could you picture yourself living with me out here?"

"I don't know. Let me think about it."

I might not have known the answer, but my body did. That night I came down with a doozy of a bladder infection, probably from the intense love-making with Robbie that afternoon. Adding insult to injury, there was no indoor plumbing, and I spent the entire miserable, rainy night running to the outhouse every hour. It was one of the worst nights of my life.

Bruce was right. Sometimes my impulses paid off and sometimes they didn't. At least I knew where I stood now and it wasn't with Robbie. It was just a matter of time before he and Susan hooked up and became a couple again. I couldn't wait to recross the Great Water, get back to New York, and get Robbie out of my life.

14
KEY CHANGE

You captured my spirit in your magic picture box,
Catalogued and epilogued and looked at now and then.
Damn it, I want my spirit back.
Take me out of your photograph.
I positively won't remain your negative!

I knew it wasn't going to be that easy to "uncross" Robbie out of my life. When I got back to the apartment, everywhere I looked reminded me of him: the bean sprouts and avocado plants on the windowsill, the Pero cereal drink we shared in the morning, the pint of chocolate Haagen Daz in the freezer that tasted so decadent after we made love in the middle of the night.

I gulped down two glasses of cranberry juice for my bladder infection and started rummaging through my underwear drawer where I'd stashed some photos Robbie had taken of us. We looked so happy and innocent it was clear that we were in love. In a fit of rage, I grabbed a scissors and cut up the pictures into little pieces, and threw them in the air. They fell on the bed in a pattern of black and white images that made no sense, just like what had happened to us. I took one last look and tossed them in the trash. There was one set of pictures I didn't have the heart to throw away—the collage of the nude photos he'd taken of me and fit into a heart for our one-month anniversary. It must have taken him hours to do. I couldn't toss it, so I stuck it back in the drawer under my panties.

A few days later, I received a letter from Melanie and Marsha from Boulder, Colorado. Marsha had moved there with her boyfriend right after graduation and Melanie had gone to visit, met a musician, and decided to stay. I hadn't told them about breaking up with Marsha's brother, Robbie.

Oh! How far out, you are in love!!! Melanie began. No Libber raps. Yes, souls fly if we let them. My Mark and your Robbie are both Aries! Come see the mountains and feel the sun and trip on life and sing all day and wear shorts and smiles! Carol, you are so much, and always know it, and feel it, and understand it. I love you and miss you and am happy you are happy.

What is there to say? Marsha wrote in a postscript. *I can feel your energy! And we know you can feel ours!*

The letter made me so sad I wondered if I should leave New York and move out to Colorado.

We were strong women who would always be connected through the unimaginable things we'd survived together. I was so proud of my friends for getting through the rape and coming out on the sunny side of a dark, dark cloud. That they were able to feel love and joy again was nothing short of a miracle. We'd lost touch with Bonnie, but Melanie thought she was probably somewhere in the middle of Africa, riding an elephant and living her dream with her college boyfriend.

I *was* tempted to move to Colorado, but I knew if I wanted to make it in the music business I had to stay in New York, no matter how lonely and miserable I felt. I again poured out my feelings in my journal, my new and only bedtime companion.

She sleeps with six pillows to cushion her, stays on her side of the bed. The emptiness embraces her like a living, breathing thing.

The life that they once shared is buried in the sunlight that is suddenly the past,
And tomorrow is confused by how the patterns changed so fast.
Friends tell her that she's acting brave, but the night-time knows her better,
And the morning's her reward for getting through.
Nothing was everyday, every day they spent together,
No night will ever be like the nights that they once knew.

I hoped to turn my ramblings into songs someday, but for now, I just needed an outlet for the raw emotion and pain.

Every day I dragged myself to work. The rows of vitamins, protein powders, and royal jelly creams, the whole alternative health vibe, reminded me of Robbie, and I went out of my way to eat a Big Mac for lunch in protest. That was the least of my bad habits. I was up to a pack and a half of cigarettes a day. I'm sure I looked like the unhealthiest health food store clerk in the city. I was only hurting myself, but I didn't care.

"It's no coincidence that you're wearing all black," Bruce commented. It was my first session with him since my Virginia trip and he could tell from looking at me how things had gone.

"No, it isn't. I'm in mourning," I said as I lit a cigarette.

"In your last session, you said you were prepared to deal with the outcome whatever it would be."

"I guess I wasn't expecting Robbie's ex to be there. I knew she'd been calling him when we were together, but he told me it was over."

"He wasn't the right one for you."

"Why do you say that?"

"From what you told me, he had commitment issues. He dropped out of college with only one semester to go, and he turned down an opportunity to continue his career in film-making."

"I guess, but what does that have to do with being in a relationship?"

"It's all tied in. You need someone who knows where he's going. Who's not afraid to plan more than a season at a time."

"But we *loved* each other!"

"Did I ever tell you the story about the widow who just started dating?"

I shook my head no.

"She came home from a date and started talking to her late husband's picture on the nightstand. 'Abe, you're the only man for me,' she said. Then she went on another date and another date, and every time, as soon as she got home, she looked at her husband's picture and said, 'No one measures up to you, Abe.' After about the fifth date, she came home, walked over to the nightstand, and placed her late husband's picture face down on the table."

"Is *that* supposed to make me feel better?"

"You may not feel that way now, but there *will* be another man that you'll fall in love with."

"Maybe, but what do I do until then?"

"What do you think?"

"Frame a picture of Robbie and talk to it?" We both started laughing. Only Bruce could change my mood like that.

"I think you know there are other areas of your life you can concentrate on now."

"Yeah, like my music."

"And your work here."

That night some music ads in the *Village Voice* caught my eye. Two musicians in Brooklyn who claimed to have a manager were looking for a female singer. It sounded interesting, but it was in Bay Ridge, and getting there was a hassle. I still couldn't take the subway by myself, and even when I'd tried riding the train with Robbie, I was a total wreck.

Nevertheless, I decided to go for it. It took me two buses and a whole hour to get to the try-out. I walked the three blocks to the audition nervously clearing my throat, wondering if I would fit in.

I rang the doorbell, trying not to get my hopes up. *This is just an experiment to explore my options,* I told myself. A cute twenty-something guy with a Beatles haircut opened the door and introduced himself as Peter, the keyboard player. He led me downstairs to the basement where his partner Frank was playing a few runs on the bass.

Peter asked if I sang any Beatle songs. When I shook my head no, Frank asked, "What would *you* like to sing, Carol?"

"What about 'House of the Rising Sun'? I sing it in B flat."

"All right, let's hear it," Frank said and handed me the mic. They were solid players, and I belted my heart out. I held my last note, still sounding strong, then turned around to see what they thought. They were looking at each other with big grins, and Frank was nodding yes. "Wow! You really can sing!" Peter exclaimed, flashing me a smile. "You wanna hear some of *our* songs?"

"Sure," I said casually, flooded with relief. My heart stopped racing, I tossed my head back, sat down on the beat-up sofa near the guitar amps, and stretched out my legs.

Peter and Frank are good musicians, I thought, listening. *Their songs have strong hooks and are probably commercial enough to get on the radio.* I was trying to convince myself I could be part of their music even though "commercial" was far from my style.

"What do you think Carol? Are you feeling it?"

"Yeah! You guys sound great!"

Peter handed me a stack of lyrics with a big smile, "You're in! Welcome to City Beats!"

It was official. I made the band! I hadn't really lied, I just didn't tell the whole truth. And maybe this *was* the change I was looking for. A music project to get my mind off Robbie and change my blues to a major key.

Going back to Manhattan I was tempted to hitchhike, but knew it was too dangerous. It was one thing to hitch a ride in California where everyone did it, and another to do it in New York. Even in California, I'd had some close calls. I waited twenty minutes for the bus and vowed to work harder in therapy to get over my subway phobia.

"What's the worst thing that could happen if you're on the subway?" Bruce asked at our next session.

"What if I can't breathe, or the train stops and I never get out?"

"Let's break it down. It's true, sometimes the air in the subway feels heavy, but there is air, and if you take a deep breath and close your eyes, that feeling will pass. Everyone else is breathing. And sometimes the subway indeed stops for a few minutes, but it always starts again."

"I guess, but the way I feel isn't logical."

"There will come a point when your desire to get somewhere outweighs your need to be scared."

"I get what you're saying. Last week, I went to the Whitney and saw this short film that was like that. A girl about my age was sitting in a chair, staring blankly into the camera. She looked like a character in a Warhol film. You know—straight dark hair with severe bangs and dark eyes with hollows underneath. But it wasn't how she looked, it was what she was saying that got to me. First, she listed all the things she needed: food, a place to live, love, friends, freedom, etc. The list went on and on for about ten minutes. Then she listed all the things she wanted: a big apartment, money, fame, nice clothes, etc. It made me think about the difference between wants and needs."

"What do *you* want, Carol?"

"I want to be understood. I want someone to accept me. I want love and I want my music to be on the radio. There, I said it. I want love and fame. I want it all!"

"What do you need?"

"I need to be free from my hang-ups!"

"How about free from your parents?"

"What do you mean? I don't live with them."

"You don't have to—they're still living in your head."

"Yeah! It's like there's this imaginary cord that's pulling me to them. Like an umbilical cord." I inhaled deeply and let this thought sink in. "Yeah," I said, exhaling. "I need to cut the cord."

"Recognizing it's there is an important step. You have a lot to think about. Whatever you do, don't hitchhike in Brooklyn. See you in a few days."

"Okay, I promise."

I kept my promise and continued to take buses to Brooklyn. Everyone was in their own little world and no one cared what I was doing. I worked on memorizing lyrics and singing the songs in my head during the long rides. Rehearsals were going well and Peter and Frank seemed like nice, normal guys—for musicians, that is. The songs were upbeat, catchy, and commercial. *Let's face it,* I told myself. *They're fluff, light-weight, bubble-gum rock, but that's what's selling. I can use The City Beats to break into the business and do my heavy women's blue thing down the road.*

We taped some practice sessions for Peter to play for his manager. Right away, he requested a private meeting with me at a midtown bar near the theater district. I was psyched and nervous as I walked into the dimly lit, upscale room with its heavy wooden furniture and Tiffany-style lamps. As my eyes adjusted to the smoky darkness, I spotted a man in a corner booth waving me over to his table. Mark Leonard, whose real name must have been Mario Leonardo, appeared to be in his early forties and was a few inches shorter than me. His dark, dyed hair fell just below his ears in a Beatle cut, not exactly flattering for someone his age. From his designer jeans to his half-buttoned paisley shirt to his hairy chest and gold chains, everything about him screamed *I'm trying too hard to be young and hip.*

He laid on the compliments as I sipped my ginger ale and smoked a cigarette, trying to keep an open mind.

"You're *very* talented, Carol," he began. "I'm working on getting The City Beats a record deal—they're good, even if I'm not crazy about the name. But *you*, Carol, *you've* got something *really* special. I could make *you* a star. You think you could handle it?"

I'd told Bruce I wanted it all. Could it *really* be happening?

Mark slid his hand over my wrist, making the expected move. I took a drag on my cigarette and tried to look cool and aloof.

"I don't know. I guess. Doesn't every singer want to be famous?"

"Your wish is my command, Carol. Are you free Saturday night?"

I'd promised myself a million times I'd never sleep my way to the top. But still, I wanted so badly to believe he could make me a star that I gave Mark my number and left on a high from the pedestal he'd put me on. At the same time, I was also dreading what he'd probably expect in return. I was so full of nervous energy that I walked the whole thirty blocks back to my apartment, chastising myself all the way for giving him my number and agreeing to see him.

Along the way, I suddenly remembered the summer I'd worked at a hip little record store in New Brunswick owned by Guy DeLuca, who'd started an independent jazz label. He was in his fifties and very worldly. One slow afternoon, we got talking about women making it in the music business.

"Would you ever have sex with someone to get a record deal?" he asked.

"I would *never* sleep my way to the top!" I answered indignantly.

"Too bad, kid, that's how most women do it. There's too much competition out there."

At the time, I was too naïve to think he was coming on to me. I simply didn't want to hear it. Now here I was, telling myself I could handle a date with a sleazy manager and not sell my soul.

I spent the rest of the week hoping I hadn't made a deal with the devil. As I gathered the courage to knock on my new agent's door in a modern high rise on East 87th, I hoped that Guy DeLuca had been wrong.

"Come in, Carol," Mark said, looking even more duded-up than when I'd first met him. He was wearing an op-art polyester shirt, open halfway down his hairy chest, bell-bottoms, and snakeskin cowboy boots. All I could think was, *Yuck!*

"Let me show you what success looks like, Carol."

I walked into a sterile, boxy apartment with white walls, low ceilings, and a fake fireplace. But what caught my eyes was the real deal—a row of gold records hanging over the mantel. Mark motioned me towards the balcony and I started to feel even more nervous.

The view from the 29th floor was dizzying. "This is what the view from the top looks like, Carol," Mark did his best to give me a meaningful look. Leaning in a little closer, he whispered in my ear, "It's all waiting for you if you make the right moves."

Clearly, he is making all the wrong moves," I thought, as he took my hand and led me to the couch, following a classic, sleazy old scenario. When he sidled up close and started playing with my hair, I knew I had to get out before it was too late.

"I don't think I can do this," I stood up and announced. "I like working with the band and I'm sure you're a good manager, but I'm not looking for anything else."

Mark stood too and put both hands on my shoulders. "Carol, if you walk out that door, you'll be making the biggest mistake of your life," he said, staring up at me.

I grabbed my coat and ran. Maybe he was right, but I swore to prove him wrong. The next day I quit the band. Getting to Brooklyn was a hassle and the music we were playing wasn't my thing. I might have lost an opportunity, but I know for sure I kept my self-respect.

15
DRIFTING

I don't want to be nobody's woman, don't want to call no one my man.
I don't want to fit in with your rhythm, don't want to be part of your plan.
If you see my eyes a-smiling, if you brush up against my hair,
If you hear my heart a-sighing, it still don't mean I care.

Nina had moved out in September. She was going to Columbia grad school and had found a room in a pre-war, three-bedroom West End apartment with two other grad students. She was getting her Masters in Political Science and then planned to get a job as a community organizer. I hadn't seen her in almost a month and was looking forward to meeting for lunch on Columbus Day at a Jewish deli near her new place.

"I never see you!" I said, hugging her.

"Are you able to manage the rent by yourself?" Nina asked as we walked toward a booth at the rear of the restaurant.

"Yeah, I'm still working at the health food store and my parents are paying for therapy. But I have mixed feelings about living by myself. I feel more independent, and if I want to get up in the middle of the night to write a song, I can, but it's lonely."

"I know. How's therapy going?"

"I can actually have lunch with you! Let's order, I'm starving." We ordered two cups of matzah ball soup and a corn beef sandwich to split. Nina nodded her chin towards a table nearby.

"Look at those two old yentas talking and laughing. That's gonna be us someday."

"*Oy!* They do kinda look like us—you could be the one with the dyed red hair and I'd be the one with the wild salt and pepper mop!"

Just then, the waitress went over to their table. "What'll it be, ladies?" she asked. The redhead pointed toward us and smiled. "What are they having?"

Nina and I burst out laughing. By the time we stopped, her face was bright red and I was gasping for air. I'd never laughed with anyone like I laughed with Nina. I'd often go home with her after class in high school. Nina's mom was an ardent traveler who spent little time on housework. Her house was the direct opposite of mine: brochures and magazines piled on the living room coffee table, souvenirs from exotic places scattered about, brightly woven Mexican blankets slung over the couch, and hand-woven baskets overflowing with newspapers. Best of all, I felt free and accepted as soon as I walked in the door.

Not surprisingly, our mothers were as different as their houses. Mine was finicky and organized and made sure that every object had its place. Hard-working but very rigid, she banned all clutter from the house, which she'd beautifully decorated with French Provincial furniture that my father bought wholesale in New York. My father, who toyed with becoming a part-time artist, had even painted a mural of an 18th-century French country-side on one of the living room walls, but our house still had a sterile vibe. Nina appreciated the uncluttered feeling and told me she felt calmer there.

Nina's mother was divorced and raising Nina and her younger sister on her own. She worked all day and didn't have time to sweat the small stuff. She was an avid reader, worldly, and a lover of the arts. Ahead of her time, she was into things like health food, yoga, and Adele Davis before anyone else I knew had even heard of them. Her philosophy was "live and let live," and the vibe in her house was "do your own thing." Dinner at

Nina's always featured a wide variety of exotic foods with interesting textures and tastes: avocados, hummus, pomegranates, falafels. Of course, my definition of exotic was something that you didn't have to put ketchup or mayonnaise on.

"What's happening in the man department?" Nina asked, looking up from her steaming soup.

"I met a guy at the park the other day. He lives down the block and is some kind of artist. I could use a friend, but I don't know if that's all he wants."

"Are you attracted?"

"I don't know if I'm ready to be with anyone new. I don't trust myself and I don't want to get hurt again."

"That's a *no*! But I get what you mean. I met this Latin musician in a club a few weeks ago. He sings and plays the congas."

"You mean like Ricky Ricardo? Let's hear the spicy stuff, Senorita!"

"That's *your* favorite show, not mine." Nina bit into a big sour pickle. *This is gonna be juicy!* I thought.

"Anyway, he was short, dark, and handsome, and really good with his hands. The first time we did it, it was behind the bar after the club closed. It was hot!"

"Far out! Did you see him again?"

"Once. I went back to the club and we had a repeat performance. Then I realized it meant nothing. I want more than a diversion."

"At least it's a step up from that shoe salesman you met at Tip Top Shoes last month."

"You mean the one whose girlfriend climbed up the fire escape and tried to break into his apartment to kill me?"

I shook my head yes, and we both started laughing. *I'm so lucky I have Nina to laugh with about our man trips,* I thought as I bit into my overstuffed corn beef sandwich.

"Maybe I *will* sleep with that artist down the street. I've got to get over Robbie, but I don't think I'll ever fall in love again."

"Yeah, right. That's what you said before you met Robbie. Is Marvin ever coming back from California?"

"He called last week. He's in love with a woman there and is taking a temporary legal job in L.A. or something. I can stay in the apartment for at least another year!"

"Cool! He was a really lucky connection."

"I know. I was on the corner of 72nd and Going Nowhere. He turned me on to Bruce, too."

"You *do* seem better," Nina smiled, eyeing the slim remnants of my sandwich.

"I have my good days. This is one of them."

Later that day, I gave my neighborhood artist a call. "Hi Tom, it's Carol. We met in the park the other day. Wanna hang out?"

"Sure. Meet me at the entrance of the park in twenty minutes. I'll bring my charcoals. I'd like to draw you." I felt flattered that he sounded so enthusiastic. *Did he want a friend or a lover? Or maybe just a model?* It was a beginning, but the details were still a little sketchy.

The sketches Tom did of me blew me away, and we were soon hanging out together. Cute, with a cherub-like face and frizzy, shoulder-length light brown hair, he was a sensitive, artistic type who tried to hide behind a macho exterior, but his army jacket and hiking boots didn't fool me. The best part was that he lived just one block down the street, between Columbus and Amsterdam.

Tom made his living as a commercial artist, but he had unusual talent and a very gifted eye. The sketches he'd made definitely looked like me, but they had an ethereal quality. I fantasized about asking him do my album cover if I ever got a record deal. What I *wasn't* fantasizing about was sleeping with him. I liked him as a friend but didn't feel any chemistry.

Tom was a year younger than me but somehow seemed immature. I assumed he didn't feel the chemistry either, since he never came on to me, but he was a Scorpio and hard to read. Besides, from what I'd heard, Scorpios and Geminis weren't a good match.

One Saturday night while we were eating Chinese take-out at my place, he confessed that he'd only slept with two women. One was a one-night stand at a St. Patrick's Day party in college when he'd drunk too many green beers. The other was his ex-girlfriend Lauren. She was a nude model in one of his drawing classes at Pratt, and he was the lucky artist who got to bring out her other dimensions.

After six months, he couldn't stand the idea of everyone else seeing what he felt belonged to him, and he insisted that she quit her modeling gig. Typical possessive Scorpio, I thought to myself. I didn't dare say anything to Tom, though. He felt bad enough. Predictably, Lauren had told him to hit the road. No man was going to tell her when and where to take off her clothes. I secretly admired her for that!

I liked spending time at Tom's. It was a large studio facing the street, which had a good amount of light coming in through the two windows. He'd managed to use every inch of space, building a loft bed and setting up his wooden drawing table beneath it. Instead of a couch, he had a brown, imitation suede bean-bag chair and colorful pillows strewn on the floor. The bed reminded me of Michael's loft back in Arlington. That seemed like a lifetime ago.

It was a rainy Friday night and I was at Tom's, smoking weed and listening to Miles Davis's *Kind of Blue*. Tom was showing off the new stereo components he'd just put together and wanted to turn me on to jazz, which I knew very little about.

"It's relaxing and intense at the same time," I mumbled through half-closed lips, taking another toke.

"Yeah, it's his best album. Can you believe it came out in 1959?"

"That old? *Wow*—it's still out there!"

I struggled out of the bean bag chair and walked over to the window. Half-tranced, I stood there for a while, listening to the rain. It sounded like a dozen drummers were jamming up on the roof. "It's really coming down. I feel wasted, but I should go."

"Why don't you crash here? Then you don't have to get soaked."

It seemed like an innocent invitation, and I was too stoned and tired to disagree.

"Cool. I can barely move and it's really coming down hard. Where should I sleep?"

"With me. It's a double bed, there's room."

"Can I borrow some toothpaste?" I'd been through the toothpaste-on-my-finger routine more than once. What I *should* have asked was, *Can I borrow some common sense?*

When I came out of the bathroom, Tom was already in bed. I took off my bell bottoms and climbed the steps to the loft in my t-shirt and panties. I'd just gotten under the covers when I felt Tom's hands on my breast and crotch. My whole body instinctively stiffened. For a moment I lay there frozen, like a bug who knows it's going to get caught but still is weighing its options.

"What are you doing?" I asked, pushing away his hands.

"What's wrong?"

"Why are you touching me? I thought we were just friends."

"But you *want* me to. Why else would you take your clothes off? You *know* you want me to fuck you, Carol."

Before I could answer, Tom was on top of me and I was too out of it to fight him.

"Okay, just do it!" I said as I felt him slide off my panties. I closed my eyes and prayed he'd come quickly. He did, I didn't. I fell into a dead sleep, woke up at dawn, threw my clothes on, and went home. Not until I got undressed to take a long shower did I realize I'd left my panties buried under the covers at Tom's.

I felt utterly disgusted with myself for giving in. *What was I thinking when I got into bed in nothing but my t-shirt and underwear?* As the day wore on, I felt sad, empty, and lonely. More importantly, I'd lost my only friend in the neighborhood.

I was embarrassed to tell Bruce what had happened, but when I sat down at my Monday night session, he could tell something was wrong.

"How was your weekend, Carol? You look upset."

"I am. Wait, how can you tell?"

"You're wearing all black and thick makeup. It's a dead giveaway."

I couldn't help but smile. I knew it was his job to be observant, but I was impressed that he noticed I'd piled on the eyeliner and mascara.

"You're right, I screwed up. Friday night I was at Tom's. It was raining, and we were smoking pot, and he asked me to stay. I was wasted and didn't want to get soaked, so I agreed."

I paused to put out my cigarette and quickly lit another one. This was even harder than I thought it would be. I couldn't look Bruce in the eye.

"We've been just friends, so when he said I could sleep with him, I didn't think much of it. But I stupidly climbed into bed with just my underwear on. He thought I was coming on to him and started touching me."

"What did you do?"

"I should have run home, but I let him have sex with me."

"Why?"

"I don't know. I was stoned and tired, and part of me felt sorry for him."

"So, you sacrificed your own needs to please him and did something you clearly didn't want to do."

"Yeah, it doesn't make any sense."

"What would you have done differently?"

"I wouldn't have let myself get so stoned, and definitely wouldn't have stayed over or assumed he wasn't interested in me."

"You're an attractive woman, Carol. Many men will be attracted to you."

I felt myself blushing as Bruce's electrifying words sunk in. *Are you one of them? Are you attracted to me?* I so wanted to ask him, but I didn't dare.

"Thanks. I guess I have to be more aware or something," I finally managed to say.

"Yes, and ask yourself, why am I not worth putting my needs first? Any thoughts?"

"I don't know. Not feeling good enough?"

"That's part of it, but don't be too hard on yourself. Many young women have problems with low self-esteem."

"How can I get over that?"

"Keep at it—you will. It's a process."

I felt lighter as I walked out of Bruce's office. He didn't make me feel ashamed or bad for what I'd done, but he didn't agree with it either. But what made me the happiest was that he said he thought I was attractive!

16
WEEKENDS

Women together have got to be strong,
And follow our freedom and sing our own song.
Be brave and discover the place we belong,
For our art, our life—
Chained and tamed woman's blues.

After Nina moved uptown and got busy with school, I started hanging out with my Jersey friend Stevie on weekends. She was quickly becoming one of my most interesting friends. Stevie found her new digs on a bulletin board at the Rutgers Student Center posted by an artsy couple, Joe and Sandy, that everyone called Mutt and Jeff. Joe was six-foot-four, with a little slouch, long straggly blond hair, light blue eyes, and a ruddy complexion. He was a true gentle giant. Sandy was petite, barely five-foot-tall, with long, dark straight hair and bangs that accentuated her large brown eyes. Their backgrounds were as opposite as their looks. Joe felt right at home living with a bunch of women, since he came from a working-class family and grew up with three sisters. He even let Sandy paint his fingernails weird colors sometimes as a joke. He liked wearing corduroy overalls and plaid shirts and went barefoot no matter the season.

Of course, I said yes when he asked me to be an extra in the original hippie horror flick he was working on for his Senior project as a film major. It sounded like such fun! He wanted me to be a hippie zombie, with white face makeup, blackened eyes, a bandana around my head, and my hair all teased out. My part was to lure a group of curious teenagers to the hills behind a haunted house, where other zombies were waiting to ambush them. But as it turned out, the film never happened.

Sandy grew up on the Upper East Side and her father was a big-deal executive in an advertising agency. She had a thick New York accent and was studying to be a fashion designer. She came up with the brilliant idea to transform a pair of jeans into a maxi skirt by cutting the inseam of the pants and inserting a contrasting color in the center. I proudly wore one of her first creations, made from a pair of purple jeans that Robbie had left behind. I felt hip and sexy whenever I wore it and sometimes a little sad.

A lot of creative people hung out at the house and I never knew who was going to drop in. It was in South River, less than a mile from the New York bus stop and a few miles from Rutgers. The house was an old, run-down two-story colonial on a corner lot surrounded by overgrown bushes and trees. Sandy and Joe occupied the two upstairs bedrooms, using one room as a studio. Stevie had the large corner bedroom downstairs. It was big enough for the double bed with the light blue wicker headboard that she bought at a garage sale. By the window, her artist's easel proudly displayed her latest painting. Next to her room was a smaller bedroom where I stayed. A stone fireplace was on one wall in the living room and an old upright piano stood against the wall next to the spare bedroom. It was probably too expensive to move, so the previous tenants left it there. Some of the original ivory keys were chipped, and it needed tuning, but it was good enough for me to bang out some chords and accompany myself.

Stevie loved music, too. Although her main talent was in the visual arts, she was taking blues piano lessons from a middle-aged professor who gave private lessons at his house. She was really into it and practiced every day until his jealous wife called and told her not to bother coming back until she put some clothes on. It was what Stevie *wasn't* wearing under her skimpy halter tops that bothered her teacher's wife. Like me and most of my women friends, Stevie had "burned" her bra and liberated her breasts. She *did* have a thing for older men, though. She was having a hot and heavy affair with one of her other married professors but was thinking of breaking it off. She was growing tired of her backdoor man's 1:00 am phone calls, 2:00 am knocks on the door and 4:00 am door slams.

"It's all so cliché," she said one Saturday afternoon as we sat at the dining room table drinking tea from mismatched floral cups and saucers bought at one of her recent garage sale trips. "Young, naive coed has affair with older, married professor, waiting for him to leave his self- described miserable marriage," Stevie yawned, as she flicked an ash from her newly acquired long, black cigarette holder. She was trying to look sophisticated but she wasn't fooling anyone. Her suburban upbringing was just as sheltered as mine, no matter how many posters of Greta Garbo and Lauren Bacall hung in her room.

"Let's write a blues song about it. You've gotta let it all out!"

"Yeah!"

The next weekend, Stevie handed me a sheet of yellow-lined paper with lyrics on both sides in red ink. Her angry words nearly leaped off the page. We called it "The Angry Woman's Song."

Well, you can have your wife and that crazy life
Of not knowin' where you're going or what you're living for.
And all I gotta say is that mine's a different way . . .
You know I want to be free from all that pain and strife.
Close the door, Daddy, and go back home to your wife.

For sure, this song will give Stevie the guts to break up with her bad-boy professor, I thought, but I was wrong. A week later, his wife caught them in a New Brunswick hotel room not far from campus.

"Do you think he wanted to get caught? You know, the whole guilt thing?" she called to ask the night it happened.

"Maybe. I'm learning in therapy that the unconscious is very power-ful and it can influence us in mysterious ways."

"Yeah. Why else would a smart man like him do such a dumb thing? How could he leave the hotel info on a pad by the phone?"

I didn't want to hurt her feelings, but I was thinking, *How could a tal-ented, beautiful, smart woman like you do such a dumb thing as sleep with your married English professor?*

"You know you're better off without him. He probably wouldn't have left his wife."

"Yeah, but the sex was amazing!"

"You know what they say: Is the fucking you're getting worth the *fucking* you're getting?"

When I saw Stevie at the South River house the following weekend, her newest creation was sitting on her easel. It was a large charcoal draw-ing of a woman in a long black dress with one arm up in the air making a fist. Wrapped around the wrist of her other hand was a broken chain falling from her waist. Her head was tossed back and her thick dark hair was flying freely. Her mouth was open as if she were shouting. She was the very embodiment of defiance, freedom, and strength. It was one of the most powerful pictures I'd ever seen. I stood there for a few minutes, caught up in its raw emotion. It spoke to me in a way that went straight to my soul.

I turned around and saw Stevie standing in the doorway, arms folded, with a rose-colored fringed shawl wrapped around her shoulders. She was waiting for my reaction.

"When did you do this?" I asked her.

"The night Paul and I got caught. I stayed up all night drawing and drinking tea."

"Nothing stronger than tea?"

"No. I didn't want to water down my feelings."

Just then Dani Melber walked into the room. She and her husband Rich had lived in the house before Stevie moved in, and she still liked hanging out here. She was the smartest woman I knew and my first friend who was actively involved in the women's movement. At the time this seemed ironic since she was also my only married friend. She spoke fluent French, played classical piano, and was working on her second Masters.

Dani was only five feet tall, but the big, dark bun piled loosely on top of her head made her look much taller. She was a force to be reckoned with. She had an opinion about everything and everyone, but nobody minded, because she was so smart and tried very hard not to hurt anyone's feelings.

"Oh my god! Oh my god! This is a masterpiece!" Dani cried, spotting Stevie's picture. "It's everything we've been fighting for! We *are* that woman!" She bobbed her head *yes* with such excitement that her bun almost toppled over.

Inspired, I ran to the piano and improvised some blues chords. Dani and Stevie were right behind me.

"I've got to find a melody that goes with your picture," I said to Stevie, trying out chord progressions.

"Yeah!" Dani yelled as she danced around the room à la Isadora Duncan. "So chained and tamed, chained and tamed, so chained and tamed!" she sang, then gave out another drawn-out *Yeahhh* that sounded even breathier and sexier.

"That's it, *Chained and Tamed Woman's Blues!*" I said.

"I can't believe you got all this just from my picture." Stevie flipped her shawl over her shoulder and turned towards the kitchen. She looked detached and cool, but I could tell she was pleased by the way her voice sounded a little higher.

"Anyone want a cup of tea?" she asked, glancing back at us.

The next weekend when I came back to the house, Stevie's picture was hanging over the piano. Dani and I got inspired to finish our song, and it almost wrote itself.

Chained and Tamed Woman's Blues
Straightjacket night, blanket so tight

Wrapped up in a woman who's waiting to fight.

Burstin' with something, knowing the time must be right

For her art, her life—

Chained and tamed woman's blues,

So chained and tamed, so chained and tamed,

So chained and tamed—Aah, aah, aah . . . yeah!

I guess you're wondering what I'm smiling for.

I used to be a prisoner, but not anymore.

I'm breaking, breaking, breaking through every door

For my art, my life—

Chained and tamed woman's blues.

It might break my heart to break my chains,

No one knows my pains, my pains.

I love you so, but I'll love you more

When I own my soul, and not before.

So chained and tamed, so chained and tamed,

so chained and tamed—Aah, aah, aah—Yeah!

It might break our hearts to break our chains,

But oh the gains, the gains, the gains,

We're breakin' through, we're wanting more

Than the life we've lived before.

17
DEMO

I live my life like a song, I'm a dreamer. So long!
I began my life with lullabies, now I'm saying my goodbyes.
My music is what I feel, it's the only thing that's real.

If I wanted to make it in the music business, I'd need to record a demo. My problem was coming up with the money. Then Joe made me an offer I couldn't refuse. He'd pay for my demo tape in exchange for being my manager/producer. I couldn't believe my luck!

When Stevie told me he had a "business" on the side, I knew exactly what she meant. Her housemate, Joe was a small-time drug dealer, mostly marijuana and occasionally cocaine—no big deal, pun intended. Musicians and drug dealers went together like disc jockeys and payola. Money was money, clean or dirty, and nobody cared where it came from as long as the music kept playing.

I agreed to record five original songs: four women's blues songs a la Laura Nyro, and a lighter one a la Carole King. Joe knew some musicians who were willing to do the recording in exchange for "free samples."

Everyone was excited for me and my father even sent me a couple of song ideas. He was reaching out, trying to connect in ways I could relate to. I rejected the first set of lyrics:

Spaced out like a bird in flight,
Spaced out like a runaway kite . . .
Space is my reality, a spiritual mentality . . .

I had to admit, though, that the second idea had possibilities.

I live my life like a song, I'm a dreamer, so long,
I heard lovers sweet, sweet songs
And I had to follow, right or wrong . . .

I put a catchy melody and rhythm to my father's lyrics. I thought "I Live My Life Like a Song" might have commercial potential, and I wanted to appeal to a wider audience, not just broken-hearted women. But I was going to include "Chained and Tamed Woman's Blues" and another original blues song. The upbeat song I chose was the one I wrote for Robbie, "Honey, Let the Good Times Roll." Maybe something positive would come out of our relationship after all.

I wrote down the lyrics and chords and sang and played all five songs into my Panasonic cassette recorder. The next weekend, Joe brought the musicians to the South River house. They looked like a motley crew, half awake and kinda quiet until Joe passed a joint around while we listened to my tape. Then they picked up their instruments and the fun began. I got good vibes from the keyboard player. He was a cool-looking black dude, with an earring in one ear and thick leather bracelets on each wrist. He was a music major at Rutgers and classically trained, but could he play the blues! "I dig your songs, Carol. I can really feel you."

The drummer and bass player played around with different rhythms. "Playing music is like flying a plane—takeoffs and landings," the drummer advised as he took a big toke on his joint. "Let's work on these intros and endings." I nodded, trying to suppress a smile. I'd only sung with a few bands so far and still felt like I had to prove myself. Sometimes musicians copped an attitude toward singers who didn't play an instrument in the band. But these guys were the real deal—they liked my songs and it was clear that they weren't just phoning it in. We went through the songs, spending a lot of time on beginnings and endings. We avoided long solos since the demo was meant to showcase my songs and my vocals.

I was flying high! My songs were coming to life and I couldn't wait until the actual recording. The rehearsal went so well Joe scheduled the recording session for the following week. One of his "business associates" had a studio in his parents' basement.

I felt happy and fulfilled on the bus ride back to New York. For the first time, this feeling had nothing to do with being in a relationship. My music was a reflection of my experiences and it was uniquely mine. It came from a part of my soul so deep that no one could take it away—not my parents or my old boyfriends or even Bruce.

As I got closer to the city, I thought about my last therapy session. I'd told him how I ran out on big-shot manager Mark Leonard, and that he'd said I was making the biggest mistake of my life.

"I quit the band," I matter of factly told Bruce.

"That was the smart thing to do," he answered.

"Really? I'm shocked. I thought you'd be on my case for not sticking with them and trying to work it out."

"Just the opposite, Carol. You took care of yourself by not compromising your self-respect. That took courage! You should feel proud of yourself."

"Thanks. I wasn't really into their music. I'm gonna concentrate on what *I* want to sing."

How ironic that the recording was coming together in New Jersey, just a few miles from the very place I was trying to escape from. But I had roots there and, most importantly, friends who knew my struggles and shared my dreams. The geography didn't matter—we were figuring it out together. What was important was that we supported each other's need to create and make sense of the chaotic world we refused to accept. I had no idea where the road ahead would lead, but at least I knew I was on the right path. The future would have to reveal itself one song at a time.

18
REUNIONS

Why were we so blinded by the love that speaks our name?
While sitting round the fire, living life so tame.
Now we're weaving bluesy blankets, wearing lost men's threads
Keeping all the women warm who'll never love again.

My music was fulfilling, but it couldn't keep me warm at night or make me feel sexy. Yes, I felt proud of myself after recording my demo. The feeling stayed with me, but I had to face the fact that I was still addicted to love! Besides, where else could I get material for my songs?

Just as Melanie had predicted, Joshua, my college heartbreaker, came back into my life. He left "ego boost chick" and got his own place in Philly. He tracked me down through Melanie and wormed his way back into my heart. His timing was perfect.

I'd been having some casual flirtations, but was only dipping my toe in the water. I didn't feel ready to take the plunge into the deep end, but the minute I heard Joshua's voice on the phone, I was back to swimming in dangerous waters. He used the magic word "love." That and a bunch of "I'm sorries" was all it took. He was a gifted salesman and he had something I was in short supply of.

It was easier for Joshua to drive to New Jersey than New York, so we began meeting at the South River house on weekends. It was a match made in heaven. Not me and Joshua, but Joshua and Joe. Two hippie dealers nickel-and-diming it until they could score the big one. The deal that would make them a ton of money and get them out of the business so they could pursue bigger and better things.

Melanie had left Colorado and was living at her parents' house on Long Island until she figured out her next move. After reading her last letter, I wasn't surprised she'd come home.

Dear Carol,

Oh! So many heavy things. Everything seems so nowhere. Where are we going? Doing? Wanting? . . . My head is in a weird place! I'm digging doing nothing but my parents are pissed. I have little desire to do anything. . . .

Lately, I've wanted to be cold and calculating—get myself a rich man. Promises are so empty. I dig Mark—but the minute he has a cent—he buys cocaine. I'm not complaining—but I'd think he'd like to pay his rent or eat something other than peanut butter!

Oh yes, I love the hippie life— naked, smoking dope, snorting coke, rapping, honesty, drinking beer, playing, balling—but I want me a rich hippie.

I don't know what to write really. I'm feeling good and bad, lost maybe, no goals, only love. And that gets you nowhere.

I found it disturbing that Melanie wanted to find a rich hippie to take care of her. She was an intelligent, educated woman who was more than capable of taking care of herself. Somewhere buried in her psyche was a need for security. I could relate. No matter how hard we embraced the hippie life, our middle-class suburban upbringing wouldn't allow us to commit fully to a life of sex, drugs, and peanut butter sandwiches.

I had no right to judge her. My only career path was working in the health food store and going for my music dream. If I were, to be honest with myself, I would have to admit that there was a part of me that still thought a man was going to swoop in and save me. I'd read all of the books of Betty Friedan, Gloria Steinem, and Germaine Greer, thanks to Dani's recommendations, but it was hard to escape my childhood conditioning. Melanie and I had to remind each other that we were strong women and had been through a lot. It was easier to acknowledge *her* strength than accept it in myself. In the meantime, maybe we could encourage each other to believe in ourselves.

While Melanie was figuring out her next move, she started meeting me at the house in South River. It was becoming my second home. Some weekends Joshua and I stayed there and the three of us hung out. Joshua and I were reconnecting, and our sex was even better than before the breakup. But there was still a voice inside my head that told me to be careful and not trust him completely. I tried ignoring that voice, but I worried about him living in Philly, where his ex-girlfriend was. Melanie, Joshua, and I had fun together, smoking, laughing, and talking about some of the characters we'd known at school. It was pretty clear that Melanie wasn't over Mark. She talked about him a lot and was feeling lonely. He called her collect from Colorado once a week and told her he wanted to come East to see her. So much for our "liberated women" plans!

Melanie asked if Mark could stay at the South River house for a few weeks. I said I'd find out but couldn't guarantee anything. Joe, Sandy, and Stevie were still the only ones paying the rent, and although they were very cool about us being there on the weekends, a long-term guest was a different story. Joshua, Melanie, and I did contribute food and weed whenever we came, but we weren't there during the week. When Stevie started spending weekends at her parents' house, I knew she was getting a little pissed off about all the extra people.

It turned out that Joe and Sandy were cool with Mark crashing at the house. Joe had a soft spot for musicians, and Sandy went along with whatever he decided. Stevie said she didn't care. She had turned off to the house scene and confided in me that by the summer she was planning to get her own place.

Mark tuned up his old Ford pickup, threw a sleeping bag in the back, and in three days he was in New Jersey. We were like one big, happy hippie family! We had some fun jam sessions with me banging out chords on the piano and Mark playing amazing guitar riffs. Joshua got so inspired he learned to play the harmonica and joined in.

Melanie and I were only there on weekends. She was working on getting her teaching certification, mostly to stop her parents from bugging her. Meanwhile, Joe, Joshua, and Mark were bonding, and the "match made in heaven" between the two dealers was now a ménage-a- trois. One November Sunday afternoon, I walked in on the three of them whispering in the living room and they suddenly stopped talking. That night when Joshua and I were in bed I asked him what *that* had been about.

"Just some business we might do together."

"I know what *that* means. You're doing some deal. Whose idea was it? Yours?"

"Be cool. I mentioned that I had a lead on a really big score of hash and Joe said he had a connection in Pennsylvania who might be able to take it off my hands. He knows someone in New York, too."

"Hmm. Is that college professor, Howard, you took me to see on Riverside last weekend part of it?"

"Forget it, babe. I've got this." Joshua said. He planted a big kiss on my breast, turned his back, and stopped talking, signaling the end of all discussion.

I lay awake putting the pieces together. When Joshua and I'd gone to visit Howard, I was flattered that he wanted me to meet one of his old "college" friends. I kissed him on the cheek on the drive uptown and he gently patted my thigh. I was beginning to let my guard down. Maybe I *could* trust him again, and leave behind the hurt he'd caused me. We were both a few years older and hopefully more mature than when he cheated on me with that Philly chick.

The day felt magical. We had good parking karma and found a spot just a few blocks from his friend's apartment. We were in the flow!

Howard Sachs looked like a typical college professor. He was short and balding, with tortoiseshell rimmed glasses and brown leather sandals. His apartment, however, did *not* look like a place that a college professor could afford. He led us past a tall potted fern in the entranceway and through the dining room, which had a black lacquered dining room set and a brass buddha sitting atop a pedestal in a lily pond.

Walking into the expansive living room, I felt like I was in rich hippie heaven. Not a cinderblock or plastic milk crate in sight! It looked like something out of a newer, hipper, version of *Architectural Digest*. A spiral staircase in the center of the living room led to a loft with floor-to-ceiling bookshelves and the largest hi-fi speakers I'd ever seen. The color scheme was black and white: white wrap-around couch, white baby grand piano, black, and white zebra print rug. Expensively framed prints hung on the wall. I recognized a few of them, but couldn't name the artists. *Why didn't I pay more attention to the art museums my father dragged me to on family vacations?* I felt unsophisticated and outclassed by the plush surroundings. My old insecurities about being from the other side of the tunnel rushed back to haunt me.

It was clear who'd done the decorating. Mona sashayed into the room. Dressed in a bright fuchsia Indian cotton tunic with silver tassels and a long, flowing white skirt, she looked and walked like an exotic runway model. Little bells hanging from the silver belt wrapped around her waist made a ringing sound as she moved. Her wavy black hair complemented her heart-shaped face with its dark almond eyes and full lips, exaggerated by bright rose-colored lipstick. Mona exuded confidence, class, and a faint scent of sandalwood and patchouli. How Howard Sachs had landed such a goddess defied all logic!

I carefully sat down on the pristine white couch and declined a glass of red wine, opting for a Perrier. *Where were my parents' plastic seat covers when I needed them?* Howard passed around a joint, and after a few minutes of small talk, he asked Joshua to go upstairs with him. He mentioned something about showing him his state-of-the-art stereo components.

"I like your belt," I said to Mona.

"Thanks. I got it in Morocco."

"Far out! Did you go there with Howard?"

"No, that was before I met him. My parents sent me to a Swiss boarding school, and as soon as I got out of there, I took my graduation money and hit the road."

"Were you by yourself?"

"Some of the time. I usually found people to hook up with. I hitched rides overland from Europe to India."

"You were brave! I only hitchhiked around California for a summer."

"I had some close calls, but I guess my angels were with me. I ended up in Goa. It felt like paradise! I stayed for a few months, but then I got restless and went to Morocco. That's where I met Howard, and he convinced me to come to New York with him."

"I can't stop looking at your piano."

"Do you play?"

"Yes, I accompany myself," I said, eyeing the elegant white piano.

"Really!" Mona said her interest perking. "What type of music are you into?"

"Lately, I've been writing some of my own songs," I said, taking a breath. "My favorites are Carole King and Laura Nyro."

"All right! Why don't you play me some?"

The piano sounded as rich as its surroundings. I took another deep breath to calm my nerves, closed my eyes, and started singing *I'm a Woman*. By the time I got to *Chained and Tamed Woman's Blues,* my voice was warmed up and I gave it all I got.

"Wow, Carol! You can belt out a song! I dig your woman's blues vibe. I would never have guessed you could sing like that! Your speaking voice is so much quieter."

"Thanks," I said softly, and quickly went back to sitting on the couch. I felt happy I'd spoken up about my music.

"You're really talented! You know, I know some people in the music business. They're starting up a record company in LA. Do you have a demo?"

"Yeah, I just finished one a couple of weeks ago."

"Want me to show it to them?"

"Would you? That would be great!" Mona and I had connected woman-to-woman, but it remained to be seen if she'd actually go out of her way for someone she'd just met, or if she even really had connections in the music business.

A few minutes later, Joshua and Howard came downstairs. Howard sat down, and looked at me a moment, "You're really good!" he said in a surprised voice, then turned to Joshua, "Why didn't you tell me Carol could sing like that? You two wanna have dinner together? We can go to our favorite Chinese place, my treat."

Thanks to therapy, I was able to go and enjoy myself. I also took advantage of more time with Mona, who turned out not to be a snob at all, even if she did look like a goddess. The very next day I mailed her my tape.

Now, as I lay in bed listening to the steady breathing of the man I loved, my dread of what was really coming down between Joshua and Howard crowded out my music dreams of just a week ago. I turned my back to Joshua and tried to fall asleep, but I felt angry and hurt. Maybe he was trying to protect me by not telling me Howard was part of a drug deal, but I felt duped. I shouldn't have let my guard down. Melanie and I had always called November "The Season of the Witch." I tried to stop thinking about all the bad things that'd happened in Novembers past, but they kept playing in my head like a bad trip.

I knew I wouldn't be able to talk Joshua out of the deal. The wheels had been set in motion. This was the big one, the dealers' dream score. I had bad vibes, but there was nothing I could do to change things. Had I imagined the intermittent clicks on the phone when I was talking to Stevie that week? Was it just routine maintenance that had a utility truck parked in front of the house when I got there the following Saturday? I tried sharing my suspicions, but no one wanted to hear them.

19
BUSTED

Judges and lawyers determine what's true,
Hands tied up with paper and glue.
Juries hear the shouting, "Let's sue!"
From a man who just tripped over his shoe.

Except for the utility trucks parked outside, it seemed like a typical Saturday at the South River house. Stevie was at her parents for the weekend and Sandy was upstairs sewing. Melanie and I were in the living room and I was at the piano, playing her a new song I was working on. But we knew the deal was going down that day. Mark had left for the city in Joshua's car and Joe and Joshua were in the basement. The Pennsylvania guy would pay them for the hash and Mark would meet the New York connection somewhere in midtown, exchange the drugs for money and hightail it back to Jersey. Joshua assured me that the three women—me, Melanie, and Sandy—wouldn't be affected by what was going on. That's how it was supposed to happen.

What really happened felt like an atomic bomb hit the house. Thirty state, local and federal agents broke in—a sheer implosion of sounds and screams. At first, I thought the walls were going to come crashing down on top of us. Most of the agents ran down to the basement but some burst into the living room where Melanie and I huddled on the couch, holding each other for dear life. Another ran up to the bedroom, grabbed Sandy's arm, and pulled her down the stairs.

"Stay right there!" a narc commanded Melanie and me, and I found myself looking down the barrel of a gun. My body went stone cold and I couldn't stop shaking.

"Ca–can I get my cigarettes from the kitchen?" I managed to stammer. He shrugged and motioned me to go with a little sideways jerk of his head. I walked shakily into the kitchen and peeked down the stairs. The basement swarmed with narcs and pointed guns. I could make out Joshua and Joe with their hands cuffed behind them. Two of the sweetest men I knew were now captives.

Melanie, Sandy and I sat smoking on the couch as the agents marched Joshua and Joe into the living room. They were handcuffed and I noticed Joe had purple nail polish on his pinkies. A narc was pushing him toward the door and calling him a homo. Both guys had their heads down, and Joshua made no eye contact with me. The agents "escorted" them out the door and into one of the police cars. Melanie had no idea what had happened to Mark, and no way to get in touch with her midnight cowboy to warn him not to come back. We were numb, in a total state of shock, and Sandy was sobbing out of control.

And then the narcs began to ransack the house. They opened every cabinet, every drawer in the kitchen, looked under the rugs in the living room, took every piece of clothing in the hall closet, and threw it on the floor. When they got to the bedroom where Joshua and I slept, one of them yelled and all the rest went running. Joshua had hidden his private stash of marijuana in the back of the closet, enough pot to last for twenty years, stuffed in a big green trash bag.

"Do any of you girls know about this?" The narc didn't speak, he shouted the question, his face red from excitement. We shook our heads and I felt a strange calmness come over me.

"I thought it was my boyfriend's laundry. He brought it sometimes when he stayed here on weekends." I'd kicked into survival mode.

"Did any of you girls know what was coming down today?"

Again, we all solemnly shook our heads no. "They didn't tell us anything," I spoke up. "Did you tell your wife what you were doing today?" I was playing the dumb broad and he was buying it.

"We'll see. We're taking all three of you to the station for questioning."

When we got to the station, a dikey-looking woman pointed to me and took me into another room. "Take off your clothes!" she ordered! "All of them!"

I didn't know my rights and I didn't have time to think about it. I did what I was told and stood there shivering, naked.

"Bend over," she barked. *Does she think I'm hiding drugs in my orifices? They had just confiscated about a thousand pounds, probably the biggest hash bust in American history, and she was worried about the little bit I could have stashed in my ass and vagina?*

I didn't come to my senses until after she threw my clothes at me and told me to get dressed. "We need a lawyer," I said as I walked out. "This is against the law. We have rights. You can't just strip search us!"

My words did some good because Melanie and Sandy were spared from the humiliation I'd been forced to go through. We weren't allowed to leave until we each signed papers stating we would take a future lie detector test, which in itself was a lie. We didn't care what the papers said. We just signed them and the cops drove us back to the house.

As we got out of the car, one of the cops looked at me hard.

"What's a nice girl like you doing in a place like this?" It was a line right out of a B movie.

At the time, I didn't answer him. Later, I thought I should have asked myself the same question, but I never did. This was my lifestyle and these were my friends. I never thought of it as dangerous. Drug dealers, musicians, lovers—they were my people, and this was my scene, and that's where I wanted to be.

We walked into the house like three zombies. We hadn't eaten all day and that was the least of it. Melanie made herself some instant coffee and I found some flat coke and a bag of stale potato chips. Sandy poured herself a glass of milk and we all shared a package of chocolate chip cookies, stuffing our mouths and trying to make sense of the cyclone that had just torn through our lives. And then it struck me.

"Oh my God!" I jumped up from the table and ran into my room. I opened the closet and dug my hand into the pocket of one of my vests that was hanging under a sweater. The wad of cash Joshua gave me to hide was still there.

"Look! They didn't find Joshua's cash!" I shouted, proudly holding up a fistful of money. "The narcs got so excited when they found the weed, they stopped searching!"

"Wow!" Sandy and Melanie said together.

"What's weird is, Joshua and I had a big fight about hiding it. I felt hurt at first when he didn't want me to know where he was going to put the money, but I guilted him into letting me find a good place."

"How much do you think is there?" Sandy asked, looking wide-eyed.

"I'm not sure. Could be thousands. Let's go to the living room and count it. Sandy, make sure all the doors are locked and the blinds are down." I plopped down on an overstuffed chair in the living room and counted out piles of hundreds.

"It's three thousand and fifty dollars! We can use this to get them out of jail!" I was trying to sound hopeful.

"Cool, but we don't even know where Mark is," Melanie reminded us.

Just then there was a knock at the front door. I grabbed the money, stuffed it under the chair cushion, and sat on it. Sandy opened the door to be met with two policemen. They flashed their badges and she let them in. Again, they started questioning us.

"This is very serious. If you don't tell us the truth about what you knew, you could end up in jail with your boyfriends."

I prayed they wouldn't ask us to stand up or go back to the station. How much more of this could we take?

No one said a word. Melanie, Sandy, and I just shook our heads and looked down at the floor. After some heavy silence and a few mumbled "I don't knows," the policemen looked like they were about to leave when one turned around. "By the way. We found your friend in New York. He's in jail, too."

Melanie's face turned white and I reached for her hand as the front door slammed. I retrieved the money and put it back in its hiding place.

When I woke up the next day, I wished it had all been a terrible nightmare. But when I looked around the disheveled room I knew it wasn't. There were so many unanswered questions! How did the narcs know about the deal? Who tipped them off? Where would Joshua and Joe end up? What jail in New York City was Mark in and how did he get arrested? And most of all, would Melanie, Sandy, and I be arrested, too? Just thinking about it made my head spin and I reached for a cigarette to calm down. I didn't want to go back to the city until I got some answers, so I called in sick to the health food store. My voice must've sounded hoarse from too much smoking and too little sleep because my manager was very understanding.

Melanie made a pot of coffee and we began straightening up the house. Sandy was still sleeping. Around 11:30 the phone rang. Melanie and I froze a moment and then I picked up. It was Joshua's lawyer, Ronald Gilbert, calling to tell me he'd been hired by Joshua's parents. He didn't want to talk on the phone since it could be tapped, and asked if I could come to his office in New Brunswick the next afternoon at 2:00. I asked if Melanie could come with me and he agreed. When Sandy finally woke up I told her about the phone call, and she said she was gonna try to go to some classes instead. I promised to find out as much as I could about Joe.

Monday afternoon, Ronald Gilbert led Melanie and me into his office in a converted house on Livingston Avenue. He was a middle-aged, slightly overweight man with a pleasant face, dressed in an expensive suit. As he filled us in, I kept staring at his tie, a paisley pattern of purples, pinks, and blues. It helped me to focus on the dreaded details.

"Joshua and Joe are being transferred to Middlesex County Jail, here in New Brunswick, until their trial and sentencing. Your friend in New York is in a downtown jail. I'll have my secretary tell you the exact location."

"How did this even happen?" I asked.

"The connection from Pennsylvania was working for the Feds. He'd been busted and cut a deal to be an informant."

"So I was right! The phone *was* tapped!" This was one time I wished I'd been wrong.

"How did Mark get caught?" Melanie asked.

"When he got out of the car in New York, they arrested him and impounded the car. His charges are more serious because he crossed state lines, which is a federal offense."

Melanie and I just looked at each other. Mark didn't have a wealthy Daddy to get him a high-priced lawyer. He was as good as gone.

"Joshua said you had some of his money, Carol. He'd like you to use it towards legal fees."

"Okay, but it will have to be in cash."

"That's okay. I'll let you know. You girls were very lucky. It's a miracle you weren't arrested on possession charges!"

Another close call, I thought as I unsteadily walked to Melanie's car. I'd narrowly escaped going to prison and having a police record. My grandmother, who I was named after, may have been watching over me, but it was time to stop pushing my luck. I'd help Joshua as much as I could, but I needed to get my priorities straight. I'd worked too hard on myself to risk losing my dreams for some guy living on the edge of his.

20
JAILHOUSE BLUES

Darlin', don't let them take your man,
'Cause when the judge says "One to three,"
They're gonna lock that door and take the key.
Darlin', you gotta speak up for your man.

Joshua slid a piece of paper through the small slot in the glass between us at the county jail. It was a blues song he'd written for me, scribbled on the back of some Jewish Federation stationery he'd received from a visiting volunteer. It was a shock to see him looking so lost and innocent in his blue prison work shirt and sweat pants. The whole scene brought back memories of the day I bailed him out of jail in DC for not paying his parking tickets. What a pivotal day that was—the day I realized I was his one phone call and we would be a couple.

Now the stakes were much higher. He was facing major drug charges, yet I still refused to believe he deserved to be in jail. To my mind, he was providing a service, selling something that was no more dangerous than a few beers. It was my generation's prohibition and no one was dying from a few tokes on a hash pipe.

His face lit up when he saw me.

"How are they treating you?" I asked. He looked thinner but other than that, okay.

"The food is horrible! The milk they gave us at lunch was past the expiration date."

"That's fucked up." I was trying to sound sympathetic, but in the back of my mind I was thinking, *You got arrested for the biggest hash bust in American history and you're worried about the date on your milk cartons?*

"You made the front page of the Sunday paper. They even compared it to *The French Connection*!" I tried joking, but no one was laughing. My parents weren't laughing when I'd gone with Melanie the day after the bust to give them a watered-down version of what had happened. They would've recognized Joshua's name and Stevie's address, so I had to confess in person. It was bad enough that I'd started seeing Joshua again and was spending weekends at the South River house. Not to mention it was only a few minutes from their place, and I didn't even visit them. Melanie and I tried to act reassuring and claimed we weren't in danger of getting arrested, but the paper made it sound so bad that our mission was doomed from the start.

1.5 MILLION WORTH OF HASHISH SEIZED

The Federal Bureau of Narcotics and Dangerous Drugs yesterday arrested four men in connection with the largest domestic seizure of hashish ever made in the United States.

Standing before a mountain of suitcases full of the brown-colored drug at a news conference yesterday, Regional Director Donald F. Malley announced that federal agents seized 1,500 pounds of the narcotic in Saturday raids in Manhattan and South River, New Jersey.

The raids took place after three months of surveillance in the New Jersey/New York metropolitan area.

The sting netted the four suspects and a huge cache of hashish, cut into one-pound "bricks" and wrapped in clear plastic. The drugs are valued at $1.5-million wholesale.

Hashish, like marijuana, comes from cannabis, but is produced from the resin of the plant and therefore much more potent. An agent holding up a single brick explained: "This single pound of concentrated illegal euphoria can produce 4,554 highs. Think of it—a purchaser could stay high for life!"

Questioned about the commitment of resources to stemming the influx of non-addictive drugs like hashish, Mr. Malley replied, "While heroin is our main concern, the illegal sale of a thousand pounds of any controlled substance calls for extensive investigation. The case is similar to The French Connection: The smugglers likely obtained the drugs in Morocco and hid them in the cavities of cars to be smuggled into the United States."

Bail of $100,000 set.

The following have been arraigned in Manhattan Federal Court on $100,000 bond each:

Howard Sachs, 25, of West End Avenue, a lecturer at Hunter College

Mark Thompson, 21, of Boulder Colorado, a musician

Arraigned on $100,000 bond each in Middlesex County were:

Joe Martin, 21, of 364 Main Street, So. River, a teaching assistant at Rutgers, the State University of New Jersey.

Joshua Goldman, 23, of 364 Main Street, So. River, occupation unspecified.

The purchase and seizure

The distinctive nutmeg odor of hashish permeated the room as Mr. Malley explained the sting. The operation was initiated when an undercover agent disguised to fit into the long-hair crowd arranged to buy 500 pounds of hashish at a bulk rate of $450 a pound rather than its current $1,000 a pound rate.

The undercover agent arranged to purchase the first 50 pounds at Mr.
Martin's house in So. River on Saturday. Driving from So. River,
Mr. Goldman picked up a suitcase at Mr. Sachs' West End Avenue
apartment, then returned with it to New Jersey, where he was arrested.
Agents made further arrests in New York and allegedly seized the rest of
the cache at Mr. Goldman's residence.

Asked if educators and other professionals were often involved in the
illegal dealing of drugs, Mr. Malley replied, "People in the educa-
tional field, so-called "intellectuals," are just as likely as anyone else
to be implicated—and maybe even more so."

I promised my parents I would break things off with Joshua. Given
everything that had just happened, I meant it. I wasn't being brave. The
universe stepped in and decided for me.

I visited Joshua just one more time to say goodbye before his parents
coughed up the $100,000 bail. What I did not tell my parents was that I'd
promised Melanie to visit Mark, who was jailed in downtown Manhattan.
As for Joe, we had no idea what happened to him. I asked Sandy, but all she
knew was that he came from a big family in North Jersey. Her parents had
threatened to pull her out of school if she tried to contact him. I prayed he
would be okay in prison, but feared that he was an easy mark with his laid-
back attitude and that purple nail polish Sandy had painted on his pinkies.

Melanie and I were shaking as we walked into the massive building
in downtown Manhattan where Mark was being held. The place had evil
vibes and the reputation of being one of the worst prisons in New York. The
name said it all: The Manhattan Detention Center, aka "The Tombs." Our
nerves only got worse as we waited for him in the dismal visitors' room.
When he finally dragged in, we barely recognized him. His long, musician's
hair had been shaved in a crewcut. Thin and pale, he picked up the phone
on the other side of the glass and looked at us, expressionless. Melanie told
him she was working on getting him a decent lawyer, and he described what
happened on the day of his arrest. When he got to New York and opened

the car door, an agent put a gun to his head and told him to freeze. If he'd moved even an inch, they would have shot him.

Melanie and I promised to visit again. This was our new reality. It could've been worse—it could've been us in jail. Joshua had told me that a detective came to his cell every day and asked him if "the girls" had anything at all to do with the deal. Lucky for us, he kept his mouth shut. But in reality, it was true—we actually didn't know that much.

A few weeks later, I got a letter from Melanie, who was still living with her parents on Long Island. She needed to vent.

Dear Carol,

Mark is finally being helped . . . the lawyer I wanted for him is the official lawyer. . . He also is very good. He might be released in my custody, which would mean I would be responsible if anything should happen— it sort of puts me up-tight . . . but anything is better than thinking about my gentle friend being locked up in a world where he doesn't belong . . . in a world where very few care about him. I've been trying to compose a letter to Goldman without sounding too bitter, but have been unable to simply ask him for Mark's belongings without flying into a rage. I've heard Goldman should be out by now, but I really have no desire to see him. It must be nice to have a rich daddy to bail you out of jail, but what about Mark and Joe? Who's going to help them? I just can't shake the turmoil that is inside of me—I carry it around every minute—so many mixed feelings about all the people involved. I know my attitude is very selfish and even hateful . . . but even my friends didn't turn out to be that separate from the world around me … and maybe that is what hurts me the most.

Mark's mother thought it would be better if he remained in jail and got it over with. What the fuck is wrong with people? This is no game. Can't she envision the reality of her son in a place like that? Ignorance and absurdity and horrible visions . . . nightmares . . . worlds of guilt and pain . . . Must I swim here the remainder of my life? God made Mark's road a little rougher, and because of that, God made him a little more beautiful. And it's not that I want him for a lover, but I want him to be able to love again. It would be wonderful if you two could play music together. . .

I will probably see Mark on Saturday to tell him the good news . . . I hope all is well with you. Love to Sandy and Joe . . . What has happened with Stevie? Will be in touch with you soon.

Much love,

Melanie

Why are we both in love with outlaws? I wondered as I put down the letter. *Is it a way for us to feel empowered? A "fuck you" directed at the uptight society we were raised in?* Politically and culturally, the country was deeply divided. You couldn't be a little bit pregnant. You had to choose a side. That's one explanation, I thought. But what if it has nothing to do with being idealistic and political? What if it's just that Melanie and I are attracted to "bad boys"? Weren't nice guys boring? Whatever the reason, I knew I had to kiss *my* bad boy goodbye. It was time to explore boring.

21
WAKE-UP CALL

The energy between us grows stronger all the time.
You are my strongest weakness, the tie I can't unbind.
I've tried so hard to give you up, replace you with a stable love.
And though I keep on trying, I find myself
Back in the arms of heartache . . . .

When I heard the phone ringing at 6:30 a.m., the first thing I thought was, maybe one of the guys was calling from prison or something else terrible had happened, but I was wrong.

"Carol, this is your father."

"Is everything okay? Is Mommy alright?"

"Yes, but I haven't been able to sleep since you and Melanie told us about the bust."

I took a big gulp. *Here it comes*, I thought, mentally trying to prepare myself for the lecture of a lifetime. "I've been doing a lot of thinking, and you cannot keep going down the road you're on," my father continued. "Am I going to spend the rest of my life saying *I told you so*? It's clear to me that you have not been exercising good judgement and I don't think that therapist is helping you. I will not continue to pay for you to see him. It's been over a year and you're still hanging out with the wrong crowd."

I opened my mouth to defend myself, but couldn't get a word in edge-wise. He just kept on lecturing. "I'm still your father and you should know I have your best interests at heart. I want you strongly to consider moving back home no later than next summer. Working in a health food store is not a career. Unless a miracle happens and you make it in the music business, I want you to keep the promise you made after you dropped out of school and go back to college next fall."

It had been a little over a year, and I was still seeing Bruce Pasternak twice a week. I'd called him to cancel my Monday appointment and fill him in on the drug bust. Now, back in the waiting room, I stared out the window at the dark, cold, cloudless sky, waiting for our Thursday appointment. I had some bad news to tell him and wasn't looking forward to our session.

"My friends got busted, but I got busted by my parents," I blurted out.

"What do you mean, Carol?"

"They're not gonna pay for therapy sessions anymore, and if I don't get something going with my music by next summer I have to move home and go back to school."

"What made them decide this?"

"The bust. At first, when Melanie and I told them what happened, they didn't say very much. My mother looked like she'd been crying and my father looked like he was trying not to lose it in front of Melanie. But yesterday morning I got a call from him at 6:30."

"What did he say?"

"He wants to stop paying for therapy. He doesn't think you're helping me make good life decisions. Like I said, he wants me to move home and go back to school in the fall unless, as he put it, a *miracle* happens and I make it in the music business."

As I sat waiting for Bruce to process what I'd just told him, I thought back to the day my father brought me to Rider to start my Freshman year.

It was a very conservative school. All the coeds were walking around in shirtwaist cotton dresses with perfect little front pleats and pastel floral patterns. I was in bell-bottoms and a tie-dyed tee shirt. I could tell my father wished I could be more like the shirtwaist girls. That's when he turned to me and said, "I've dreamed about this day since you were a child, Carol. The day you would be a college coed and become an adult. I never pictured you looking like *this*."

I told him I liked the way I looked. But that didn't make him or me feel any better. I had disappointed him. Little did I know this was only the beginning.

"What are you going to do?" Bruce asked, jolting me back to reality.

"I'm gonna concentrate on promoting my music until next summer, but this may be my last session with you. Without my father's help, I can't afford to come here," I said through my tears. "Are you crying out of sadness because you have to stop seeing me, or frustration brought on by your father not understanding?"

Was that a look of sadness on Bruce's face? An emotion hidden behind his cigar smokescreen? Would he possibly miss me as much as I knew I would miss him?

"I guess a little of both." I was crying harder. It felt like I was saying goodbye to my best friend.

"Your father doesn't understand that therapy takes a long time. There are patterns formed in childhood that are hidden and deeply embedded in your psyche. Not to mention trust issues and parental interactions which need to be analyzed. It's a slow and deliberate process. I think you *have* been making progress. Would you agree?"

"Yes, but I can't convince my parents."

"What if I reduced my rate to something you could afford yourself?"

"I don't know what to say. That would be amazing!"

"I think you're at a crucial place in the therapeutic process. I want to see you continue. All that I ask is that you don't tell anyone about our arrangement."

I couldn't believe my ears! Bruce Pasternak, one of the top analysts in New York, was cutting me a break. Now if I could only get a break in the music business….

"There is something I do agree with your father on. You might want to think about the people you are associating with and the men you are drawn to. From what you've told me about your experiences with the first drug bust and the rape you narrowly avoided, you've been very lucky. When you start to pull yourself out of the mud and get healthier, you may have to leave some friends behind. They will try to pull you back in there with them. Think about it. I'll see you Monday."

My mind was reeling as I walked out of Bruce's office and headed for the bus stop. Maybe he and my father were right. Maybe it was time to change the type of people I hung out with. I couldn't give up my girl-friends—they were way less neurotic than me, and I was the one who intro-duced Melanie to the hippie life, not the other way around. My other two college roommates seemed to be doing just fine. Marsha was happily living with her man in Boulder and working toward a degree in Education, and Bonnie was living out her travel dream somewhere in Africa. As for Nina, she was in grad school, and even though her man thing was pretty wild, she always gave me good advice. No, it wasn't my women friends, it was the men I chose to get involved with who were pulling me down.

The whole way home on the crosstown bus, my mind was plagued with questions. Why did I give in to temptation and go back with Joshua, after the way he'd hurt me? This time he'd found another way to break my heart and it was way more dangerous than cheating on me. I could have gone to jail. Was I willing to ruin my whole life for a man? A song title came to me: "Back in the Arms of Heartache." Yeah, that was it! That was the blues song I was going to write, not one about my man being in jail, like the song that Joshua gave me. My new song was going to empower women. More important, empower me.

By the time I got home, I had some of the lyrics in my head. I fever-ishly wrote them in the notebook I kept on top of the piano. It was one of the fastest songs I'd ever written.

Back in the Arms of Heartache

The energy between us grows stronger all the time.

You are my strongest weakness, the tie I can't unbind.

I've tried so hard to give you up, replace you with a stable love.

And though I keep on trying, I find myself

Back in the arms of heartache, making the same old mistake.

Lovin' in reverse ain't nothin' but a curse, and what makes matters worse—

When you tell me that you love me, I can see it in your eyes.

Then you turn around and leave me and I'm taken by surprise.

I've got to fight against my fate, bouncing between love and hate.

And though I keep on trying, I find myself

Back in the arms of heartache, making the same old mistake.

Lovin' in reverse ain't nothin' but a curse, and what makes matters worse—

Why does everyone I meet not measure up to you?

My life would be much easier if I found someone new.

I've got to stop the circle, stand firmly on the ground.

Release this old emotion, get off the merry-go-round.

I know it's just a numbers game 'til love takes hold of me again.

And though I keep on trying, I find myself back in the arms of heartache.

After I wrote it, I felt as if a weight had been lifted. Bruce believed in me. From now on it was all about my music and I wasn't gonna get side-tracked by boy-men, outlaws, dreamers, rebels, and schemers. Besides, I had enough song material for at least three albums!

22
GUILT TRIP

And time will come when you'll start believing
In your own strength, the way that people do.
You're so afraid 'cause the child is leaving,
But you fight your fear, 'cause you know 'round here
Grown-up children can't survive.

A few days after my wake-up call I got a letter from my father. He must have been upset when he wrote it and feeling a little guilty for coming down on me so hard. He was trying to reach out to me. Now it was my turn to feel guilty for upsetting him about the bust and my hippie lifestyle.

Dear Carol,

I am truly sorry. I assure you again and once more that my actions were initiated from the purity of a father's love and heart, and not from the darkness of some devilish, psychological scheme.

However, it remains quite evident that we are going through hells of pain, indecision, and insecurity. How much longer anyone of us will be able to endure this only God knows. The trust and faith lie with you; whether you'll be able to muster the strength to take some positive steps in order to persevere and emerge victorious, or give in to the same forces which have brought you to this turmoil of weakness.

The question remains of how a person who is endowed divinely and earthly with all the elements of success, seems to, almost as if in a deliberate way, avoid success? Why should the great fountain of youthful energy misdirect itself into the channels of unrealistic pursuits?

The great assets are still with you – they are far too many to enumerate. Yet, constant paradoxes of intentions seem to overwhelm them and at times even destroy them.

For example: You have a beautiful voice, which you cherish, you have healthy lungs, yet you have allowed yourself to become addicted to a poisonous inhalation that drains you of voice, breathing, life, power, and money.

Oh, for heaven's sake, Carol, I do love you, we all love you and cry out for you. We are all reaching out our hearts to help you. Don't turn your back on our truth, our beauty.

Phew! That letter was hard to read. On one hand, he was building me up by telling me that I had everything going for me to become successful, and on the other, he was taking away my confidence by telling me I was weak and making bad decisions. No wonder I needed a shrink! I brought the letter to my next session.

"You seem very upset by the letter you just read me, Carol."

I nodded and threw a big wad of tissues in the wastebasket. I'd been crying so hard my voice was shaking. I searched his handsome face to get a clue about what he was feeling. The warmth and kindness in his eyes betrayed his usual practiced, expressionless look.

"I feel really bad that I'm upsetting my parents."

"Your father is sending you mixed messages."

"Yeah, he builds me up and then he cuts me down. But it still hurts."

"You're an adult woman now, Carol. You're making it on your own and not asking your parents for help. Give yourself some credit."

"Then why do I feel like such a fucking loser?"

"You and your father have a complicated relationship. Something is going on unconsciously that's blocking you from succeeding. We talked about one aspect of it in your last session. You seem to pick people who put you in dangerous situations."

"Mostly the men." I wasn't going to let him put down my girlfriends. They were more together than I was.

"Have you ever heard the term "survivor's guilt?"

I nodded my head.

"For example, you told me about the rape in Washington, but we never explored how you felt about your roommates getting raped and not you."

I took a deep inhale on my cigarette and shuddered as I thought about how close I came to being gang-raped.

"I asked myself, 'Why me? Why was I spared?' a million times."

"That's an impossible question to answer. There's no logical explanation for it. What helped you get past it?"

"Well, I tried to help my roommates by packing up our apartment and listening to them talk about it. They were so strong and determined to get past it, that it helped *me*. And something weird my father told me about that night affected me. He told me the night of the rape, he prayed to his mother to watch over me. I was named after her—- my Hebrew name is Chiah Sora. She was killed in the Holocaust. He told me that same night, she came to him in a dream and asked, 'Can't you do something for her on earth?' Isn't that eerie?"

"Was your father in the Holocaust?"

"No. My father came to this country before the war, but his parents and five out of his six brothers and sisters were killed. My Uncle Leo was the only one who survived the camps."

"How must your father have felt when he found out that practically his whole family had been wiped out and suffered unimaginable horrors?"

"He never talked about it."

"Exactly. But that doesn't mean he didn't experience survivor's guilt. Many people directly affected by the Holocaust consider it a taboo subject to talk about with their children."

"How does that have anything to do with me?"

"We can discuss this at your next session. I'd like you to spend some time thinking about your family history relating to the Holocaust. See if there's anything you can remember."

"I'll try. See you Monday."

As I left Bruce's office, I felt a heaviness throughout my whole body. I walked past the upscale boutiques on Madison Ave. and past the perfect mannequin-like women walking their miniature French poodles and felt a sense of unreality. What had happened to my closest relatives was unimaginable. But, somewhere in my soul was a karmic wound buried so deep, that I didn't allow it to enter into my day-to-day consciousness.

Something inside of me resonated with what Bruce was saying about survivor's guilt. There were missing pieces of my family history that could be influencing my life now. I wanted to break the silence and unlock the secrets of the past, no matter how painful.

When I got home that night, I didn't feel like thinking about anything. I made my favorite comfort food, macaroni and cheese, watched some *I Love Lucy* reruns, and got into bed. I was getting used to living alone, but tonight I was feeling needier than usual. It would have been nice to have someone to cuddle up to.

The next morning I made a pot of coffee and got out a notebook so I could write down any memories about the war and the Holocaust. Uncle Leo and Aunt Roz lived outside of Boston, and we used to visit them every summer. I remembered a lot of laughter and good times. I enjoyed playing with my three girl cousins, and my Uncle Leo had a zest for life. He never spoke about what he had gone through in the Holocaust. The only reminder was the number tattooed on the inside of his forearm.

One night, when I was around twelve, I woke up to the hushed sound of voices in the living room at my aunt and uncle's house. I tiptoed toward the stairs and quietly sat down on the top step. My uncle was telling a story about being a boy in Poland before the war.

"We were all living in one room," my uncle said, speaking in hushed tones. "It was horrible. We had no food. Very late at night, I would take a bicycle I kept hidden in the bushes, and ride to the farmlands. If the Nazis had caught me, I would've been killed, but I had to feed the family. They were starving us to death. When I got to the peasants' houses, I traded trinkets, anything to get some food. I was lucky that I never got caught and that no one turned me in."

I crept back upstairs. It sounded so scary and so secretive! My uncle was very brave! I waited until we came home from Massachusetts to ask my mother what had happened to Uncle Leo. I sensed that my father wouldn't want to talk about it. I didn't want to get into trouble for eavesdropping but I needed to know the truth. I thought my mother might tell me since it wasn't *her* brother. I hoped that she'd understand why I was listening in on the stairs that night.

On a hot July evening, a week or two later, my mother and I were sitting in the driveway in front of our two-car garage, on our plastic outdoor lounge chairs. We were waiting for my father to come home. We had just finished dinner. My mother and I always ate before my father got home, except on Sundays, when we all ate together. I looked forward to our Sunday dinners. Sometimes we would get cold cuts from the Jewish deli and my father would quiz me on current events. He made a game out of it and it was fun.

Tonight our street was unusually quiet. There were no kids playing softball in the road or neighbors taking an evening walk in the twilight. The day had been a scorcher and the air was hot and heavy. It was just the two of us, me, and my mother. That's when I asked her what the grownups had been whispering about at Uncle Leo's.

"What did you hear?" my mother asked me. She looked surprised.

"Something about Poland and a bicycle and Uncle Leo getting food for the family."

"Yes, your uncle was very brave. The Nazis wanted to get rid of all the Jews in Poland. Uncle Leo survived because he was young and strong and the Nazis used him as a laborer. Even when he had a fever he had to keep on working or he would've been killed."

"When did Daddy come here?" I knew part of the answer but wanted to know more.

"His Aunt Mary and Grandma were already in Boston. They begged Daddy's family to leave Poland but his father didn't want to go. He had a good business and no one believed that the war was going to happen. So since Daddy wasn't getting along with his father, his mother asked Aunt Mary to send for him and bring him to America."

"What happened to the rest of the family?" I knew they had been killed in the war, but didn't know the details.

"I'll tell you, but promise me you won't talk to your father about it. He doesn't like remembering. It's too hard."

"I promise. I won't say anything." I felt closer to my mother at that moment than at any time I could remember. She was trusting me with a family secret, and I wasn't going to let her down.

"When Uncle Leo first came to this country, he didn't talk about the war. A few months later, your father and I went to visit him in Boston. It was summer and we were staying in a small motel outside of the city. Uncle Leo came to the motel and we were sitting around the pool when your father asked him what had happened to his family."

"Did he tell him?"

"Not right away. Uncle Leo said it would upset him too much, but your father begged him."

I took a deep breath and waited for my mother to continue. Her voice sounded a little shaky as if she was trying not to cry. I hoped *I* wouldn't start crying.

"Uncle Leo said that his father died of starvation in the Warsaw Ghetto before the family was taken away. He described the day the Nazis came for the family. His mother, your grandmother Chiah, stood in the street with the other children holding tightly to her skirt. The Nazis called for all the strong men to step aside. Your grandmother pushed Uncle Leo and told him to go. That was the last he saw of his family. They were killed in Treblinka, one of the worst concentration camps."

I closed my eyes and pictured that awful scene. It was hard to understand. Why did the Nazis hate my innocent family? Just because they were Jewish?

"How did Daddy take it?"

"He cried, and then he never talked about it."

I kept my promise and never asked my father about his family in Poland. Once he told me that I was named after his mother and that she was a beautiful and caring woman, but that's all he ever said.

The subject never came up again until a few years later. I was in high school, and my mother shared a letter that Uncle Leo had written to my parents about the day he was liberated from the concentration camp. I guess she thought I was old enough to handle it by then.

Many years have passed since the day of my liberation from Belsen-Bergen in 1945. I still can recall that joyous but painful moment. Yes, I was weak, a walking skeleton at that, but my mind was as clear as a child's.

I wept and thought of the years of great suffering. Years so long and yet now they seem to be nothing more but a dream.

My thoughts reached for my family whom I loved so much. They were so close to surviving and yet so far from living. I lay on the grass and looked at the English tanks passing by and could only utter, why, why so late?

Love always,

Leo

I tried to imagine how my father must have felt when he got the devastating news about his family, *my family*. It was almost impossible to conceive of it. How could the world allow this to happen? Because of Hitler, my relatives along with millions of Jews had suffered an unbearable and unfathomable fate. I would never get the chance to meet my grandparents and my aunts and uncles. I felt a pain in my heart and a hollowness inside that was different from any heartache I'd felt in the past. I wanted to believe in a higher power, but how could God allow something this horrific to happen? Was life that random? There simply was no answer.

Even though it was a windy December day, I bundled up and went to the park. The cold, brisk air shocked me back to the present. I thought about my uncle and what he had survived. He had overcome so much, yet instead of being bitter, he had embraced life.

I felt a new strength and determination to live a full life but on *my* terms. My dreams were not my parents' dreams. I couldn't wait to tell Bruce what I'd discovered.

23
COUCH DREAMS

Those nickels and dimes
Are of another time.
Life is believing in you.
It's pulling you through the bad times too.

At my Monday night session, I filled Bruce in on what I remembered about Uncle Leo and my father's family in Poland.

"This is very significant. As we talked about in your last session, your father has survivor's guilt."

"But what does that have to do with me?"

"He has transferred his feelings of unworthiness on to you."

I was becoming aware of where Bruce was going with this and I asked, "Are you saying that I have survivor's guilt, too?"

"You're an only child and given the loss your father experienced, it's understandable that he would want to over-protect you. By not talking openly about what happened in his past, he's repressed painful emotions and memories. They still have power over him, and make him feel unworthy. Somewhere in your childhood, you got the message that the only way to deserve happiness was to suffer."

"So I was like a sponge?"

"You could say that. You were a sensitive child."

"That's true, but my father always told me I could do anything I set my mind to."

"He didn't do it consciously."

Bruce paused and looked at me. He could tell I was deep in thought.

"You know, Carol, there've been studies on children of Holocaust survivors. Even though your father wasn't actually a survivor, he was deeply affected by the loss and suffering of his family."

"How could he *not* wonder why it didn't happen to him? Why *he* was alive?"

"You told me that he came to this country before the war?"

"Yes, his aunt sent for him. He was the oldest boy and he wasn't getting along with his father."

"He wasn't getting along with his father. Sound familiar?"

I needed a minute to let this sink in.

"Because he and his father didn't get along, his life was saved. And now *we* don't get along. That is deep. It's so ironic!"

"Yes, Carol, and you're rebelling against him."

"But how is that the same? My life isn't in danger."

"Survivors often need to have extreme control over their children and desire to inhibit their children's separation from them. Why *are* you rebelling?"

"I guess because I don't want to be who my parents want me to be."

"Exactly. You are saving *your* life by rebelling. Not literally, but symbolically. Your parents, especially your father, still have power over you. You are repeating a family pattern."

"But how can I change, if my father won't talk about the past?"

"By talking about your feelings *here*. Remember, you can't change your father but you *can* change the hold he has on you. The more we explore these feelings, the less power your anxiety and phobias will have over you. You haven't talked about your mother very much."

"My mother had her own way of making me feel guilty. When I would get sick as a child, she would say things to me like, *I didn't sleep all night. I was worried about you.*'"

"That was her way of showing that she cared about you."

"I know, but I felt smothered."

"What other thoughts do you have about her?"

I stopped for a minute and tried to think objectively about my mother.

"My mother always did what was expected of her. She always had a serious look on her face. She wasn't depressed, but there was a heaviness about her. Whenever she laughed or smiled, it felt like the sun breaking through the clouds."

Bruce gave me a quizzical look.

"My mother hated messes and made me feel guilty about accidentally spilling things. Everything had to be just so. She wasn't exactly big on body fluids either."

"That's hard for a child to live up to."

A sudden wave of sadness washed over me. I nodded. There had been so many lost opportunities to connect with my mother.

"My mother usually goes along with what my father says, but she tries to make peace between us. I feel guilty about upsetting her, too."

"For our next session, I'd like to explore your feelings of separation anxiety regarding your mother and father. I think it would be helpful, Carol, if you laid on the couch."

I was jolted out of my childhood regrets. I wasn't expecting to hear about the couch.

"How do you feel about that?"

"I was wondering when you'd ask me to move to the couch."

Of course, I left out what else I was wondering, like when my favorite daydream would come true. The one I flashed on any time there was a pause in the conversation, or things got too painful. The one where Bruce is lying on top of me on the couch, and I'm looking into his eyes and there's nothing left to say. When even words lose their power and we let our bodies do the talking. I felt an intense attraction between us, and at times I thought that Bruce felt it too. He was still smoking those big cigars, using smoke to put out the fire.

"How do you feel about that?" he asked me again.

"You mean lying on the couch?" Even if I told him what I was thinking, it wouldn't do any good. He would just tell me it was transference. There was no way I could share my fantasy with him, not yet.

"I don't know. I guess I'll have to find out."

As I walked out of the office, I thought about the sponge analogy. According to Bruce, I was absorbing my parents' unspoken fears and uncried tears. *Uncried Tears—that would make a good country song*, I thought. But this wasn't a song, this was my life, and it was something I had to face.

24
MOVING ON

Straightjacket nights, blanket so tight,
Wrapped up in a woman who's waiting to fight.
Burstin' with something, knowing the time must be right
For her art, her life—
Chained and tamed woman's blues.

I was getting used to waking up in the double bed by myself, but couldn't shake the feeling that something or someone was missing. Oh, for a nice, warm body next to me, I thought as I faced another freezing, frigid December day. Maybe I wouldn't feel as alone if I slept in the smaller bed, but it was piled high with clothes and I was too lazy to hang them up. It was a throwback to my Washington college days when my roommate Bonnie and I dumped our clothes in the middle of the floor. I'd lost touch with Bonnie but still heard from Marsha in Colorado. I was glad that breaking up with her brother Robbie hadn't affected our friendship. When I wrote to her, I left out the part about how badly he had broken my heart. I didn't want her to feel guilty about it.

Marsha knew that I'd gone back to Joshua, and she knew about the bust. What she didn't know was that I'd never really gotten over Robbie. He'd hurt me more than Joshua ever had, and that was saying something!

Even though Joshua had come back into my life, there was a part of me that never fully trusted him. He was exciting and sexy and familiar, but there was something dangerous about him. I was always waiting for the other shoe to drop, and it did.

Melanie and I talked a few times a week. She'd managed to get her boyfriend Mark a decent lawyer, and Mark was to be temporarily released into Melanie's custody. She planned to ask her parents to loan her the money for his plane ticket back to Boulder so he could stay with his mother until his sentencing. The lawyer thought he'd be sentenced to a year or two in federal prison. Today Melanie was going to see him at the Manhattan Detention Center to give him the good news. She and I were meeting for dinner in the Village later.

I walked into the kitchen, made my usual cup of instant oatmeal, ate it robotically, and then sat down on the couch in the living room. It was Saturday, and I didn't have to get to the health food store until eleven. I put on Carole King's *Tapestry* album, lit a cigarette, and drank a cup of instant coffee. No more Pero, the healthy substitute that Robbie and I used to drink together in the morning. Besides, it tasted like shit! Back to my decadent ways, I needed something stronger to start my day. *Some* of his healthier habits had rubbed off on me, though. I wasn't eating as many hamburgers and was taking more vitamins, bought with my employee discount at the health food store.

Katie, the store manager, had noticed the change. She was a whole-some-looking all-American girl, with thick strawberry blonde hair and per-fectly placed freckles sprinkled over the bridge of her nose. Katie and her husband had moved to the city from Nebraska so he could go to NYU med school. She looked innocent, but her baby blue eyes could turn into cold steel blue whenever a male customer started to come on to her, which was a daily occurrence.

"What? No running to McDonald's for lunch today?" she'd asked me earlier in the week.

"No, I'm not craving Big Macs like I used to."

"I knew you'd see the light if you worked here long enough. Here, have a protein bar. It's on me. Go ahead, take your lunch break."

I was hanging onto the job, trying not to let my crazy life distract me. Now, more than ever, I had to prove to my parents that I could be independent and take care of myself financially. They didn't even know that I was still seeing Bruce, let alone that he had discounted his fees for me.

I'd learned what most of the vitamins were for and recommended the store brand whenever possible. I was feeling less spacey and my ability to concentrate was improving. Katie said it was because I was taking B-complex, Bruce said it was due to my therapy, but I thought it was because there was no man in my life screwing with my head.

I was glad the job had worked out. It wasn't too stressful, my manager liked me, and more importantly, it paid the rent. It hadn't been my first choice. A week before I got the job, I'd had an interview with a music licensing company. I was psyched as I walked into the lobby of the ultra-modern office building on East 42nd St. I was wearing a white knit top, my favorite long skirt with purple, red, and blue patterns and my brown suede fringed sandals. My hair was pulled back in a ponytail, showing off my new silver hoop earrings with the purple beads in the center that I'd bought from a street vendor in Times Square. I knew I looked good! A thirty-something, cool-looking guy named Derek led me to a glass cubicle. There was a pad of lined paper, a pencil, and a set of earphones on the desk.

"We are a music licensing company. Your job will be to listen to music and identify the songs by title and artist. Your application says you're a musician, Carol, so that should give you an advantage."

I'm meant to have this job, I thought to myself. Then Derek said, "I'm going to give you a short music test to help you understand what the job will entail. Put on these headphones and simply write down the names and artists of the ten songs you hear."

It sounded like a no-brainer until the first song came on. Elevator music! All the songs sounded the same — no singing and a watered-down, homogenized musical arrangement. I got three out of ten. I handed Derek my nearly blank paper. He mumbled something about getting back to me, but we both knew I wouldn't get the job.

I got on the elevator and instantly recognized the song playing. It was the end of *Song Sung Blue,* by Neal Diamond. I knew the next song, too, *The Day the Music Died,* by Don McLean. Why couldn't I have done that well during the test? I guess I had to actually *be* in an elevator to recognize elevator music! I laughed out loud! I hated to admit it, but I was better off *not* getting the job. Listening to that boring stuff all day long might've killed my love for music. A week later I'd seen the "Help Wanted" sign in the "Sunshine Health Food Store" window and the rest was history.

That Saturday when I got to work, the store was almost empty, and it stayed that way all afternoon. Maybe the cold weather was keeping customers away.

"Hot date?" Katie asked me.

"I wish. Why'd you ask?"

"You keep looking at the clock."

"Just meeting a good friend."

"We're pretty slow today. You can leave an hour early if you want. I'll lock up."

"Thanks! I'll come in earlier on Monday."

Even though I wasn't meeting Melanie downtown until 7:00, I decided to head to the Village and walk around. The subway would be the fastest way to go, but I wasn't ready to take it yet. That was still one of my therapy goals. I walked over to Fifth Avenue instead and took the downtown bus, with a transfer to the West Side.

Nothing could dampen my spirits. It was Saturday night and the Village was hopping despite the cold weather. A long-haired hunk in an army jacket and suede boots with a guitar slung over his shoulder caught my eye. I smiled at him, but he was walking too fast to notice. Probably going to meet his lover. I went into a vintage clothing store to get out of the cold. I was drawn to a light blue, embroidered satin nightgown that looked like it could've been from the 1940s. It reminded me of the sophisticated gowns worn by movie stars like Lauren Bacall and Greta Garbo, strong, confident women who were comfortable with their sexuality. Their femininity was mixed with an aloofness that only added to their seductiveness. On impulse, I bought it. Was I signaling the universe to send me a new lover?

I walked down Bleeker Street and stopped to read the sign in front of the Bitter End. A singer named Melissa Manchester was performing that night. My friend and fellow singer, Shelley had mentioned her to me, and if she was playing at the Bitter End, she had to be good! Maybe Melanie and I could catch her show later.

When I got to the pizza place, Melanie was already there. Her perfect complexion looked a little paler than usual, reflecting the heavy stuff she was going through with Mark.

"How'd it go? How's Mark?" I asked her.

We both lit a Taryeton and inhaled. "Let's talk low," she said. "It's crowded in here."

I looked around the restaurant. There were mostly people our age or younger. Some were NYU students looking as if they didn't have a care in the world. That's how Melanie and I should have been feeling too, enjoying our twenties, full of promise. Instead, we were talking about prisons, sentencing, and drug busts.

"Mark looks terrible. He's lost a lot of weight and I'm afraid he's gonna have a breakdown. He cried when he saw me."

"When's he getting out?"

"In about two weeks. I hope he makes it. I heard Goldman is already out."

"Yeah, but I'm cutting him off. I promised my parents I wouldn't have anything to do with him."

"Good! You have to look out for yourself. No one else will."

Melanie was getting tougher. This experience had hardened her in a different way than the rape had. The rape had shown her the randomness and evil in the world, but the bust had made her disappointed in friends, people she thought she could trust. And in a way, that was harder to take.

"I can't stop thinking of that line in the Carly Simon song."

"Which one?" I was hoping to change the subject and our mood.

"I Haven't Got Time for the Pain"

"Yeah, that says it all. We've gotta get on with our lives. You wanna go hear some music?"

"Cool, let's go for it!"

25
INSPIRATION

Just listen to your special rhythm.
Your timing is right,
Get on with the fight.
There's lots to do.

Melanie and I lucked out and got the last two seats at the Bitter End. Our table was in the back of the room, but we could still see the stage. I couldn't remember the last time we'd had fun together. Being with her tonight reminded me of our cross-country trip when we were carefree and all excited about going to California. That was before all the bad things happened like the rape and the bust. Maybe, starting tonight, we could put those times behind us.

The lights dimmed and the announcer came on stage. "It is my pleasure to introduce Arista recording artist, Melissa Manchester!"

Melissa Manchester walked confidently onto the stage and sat down at the keyboard. She was wearing a long skirt and peasant blouse with a colorful flowered shawl wrapped around her shoulders. It was just going to be her and an electric bass player. From the minute she started singing, I was blown away. Her voice was powerful, her keyboard playing soulful, her songs uplifting.

"She's amazing!" I whispered to Melanie.

Melanie whispered, "You could be famous too if you worked at it."

I smiled back at her. Melanie always had been my biggest fan. But what if she was right? Could I actually be talented enough to make it in the big time?

I looked down at the makeshift leather bracelet I wore around my wrist. I noticed Melanie still had hers on, too. We had tied a piece of leather around each other's wrists during our California trip. It was our symbol of strength. We were part of an underground sisterhood that empowered and supported each other through the good times and the bad. I felt very lucky to have a friend like Melanie.

As the show went on, I felt more and more inspired. Melissa Manchester was everything I wanted to be: a strong female singer who accompanied herself on the piano and played her own songs. I knew I wasn't there yet, but seeing her performing in front of me was beyond inspiring. It was mind-blowing! I knew I had talent alright, but I knew I needed voice and possibly piano lessons. It was time to come up with a plan.

"Promise me we'll go out again soon!" I said to Melanie as I hugged her goodbye.

I picked up a copy of the *Village Voice* on the way home. Back at my apartment, an ad for voice lessons in the classifieds caught my eye: *Experienced voice teacher specializing in Broadway and popular music. Convenient mid-town location.*

The ad made me think about Shelley, who I'd met at a music show-case a few months ago. She was so driven and focused on making it in the music business that she worked as a waitress, sometimes doing double shifts, so she could afford her very expensive singing lessons. A week later, she invited me to her cramped walk-up apartment on West 4th in the Village to demonstrate some of her vocal warm-ups.

Shelley was my age and spoke with a pronounced English accent, but confided in me that she'd only spent a year in London. Everyone who met her assumed she was English, and she never bothered to correct them.

She looked very waspy, with her long, curly strawberry blonde hair and turned-up nose. No one would ever suspect that she was a middle-class Jewish girl from Passaic, New Jersey.

The only window in Shelley's apartment led out to the fire escape. She'd opened the window and positioned a floor fan in front of it, but all it did was move the oppressive air around. We were sweating like crazy, but that didn't stop her from attacking her voice exercises with gusto.

"Ugh, Ugh, Ugh!" she sang up the scale.

"Are you okay?" I lept up to slap her on the back.

Shelley started to laugh. "Yeah, that's one of my exercises. It helps to loosen up my tongue."

"I thought you were choking to death! That helps your voice?"

"That's what Joel Conlin says, and he's the best voice teacher in New York. He has a lot of famous students."

"Like who?"

"Bette Midler and a new singer he says is gonna make it big, Melissa Manchester."

"Far out! I think I'll sit on the fire escape until you're done practicing." Even though Shelley had a good voice, listening to her sing those exercises was like hearing someone throw-up!"

Twenty minutes later she waved me back inside.

"Do you want to see my sight-singing homework?"

Shelley was also taking music theory classes with Helen Katz, a teacher Joel Conlin recommended to all of his students. She was learning to sight-sing so she could audition for commercial jingles. I admired Shelly for being so ambitious. I'd thought about taking voice lessons, but wasn't impressed with Joel Conlin's method and knew I couldn't afford *him*. As for jingle singing, I had no desire to sing the Meow Mix song, no matter what it paid. Shelley told me that one of Helen Katz's sight-singing students had landed that commercial. I was impressed, but it wasn't for me. I just wanted to do my own thing.

All day Sunday I couldn't stop thinking about the ad. I had no idea what this voice teacher charged, but I knew I didn't have much extra money. Even the half-price deal Bruce offered me was stretching it, and I *definitely* couldn't afford the $85 Shelley was paying for lessons.

In the last few months, my singing voice had been getting lower and I was losing some of my high notes. I told myself it was allergies, but I knew it was from smoking. If I wanted to reach the next level as a singer, I'd have to give up cigarettes. But *God* was I dreading it. But wait, it could be a win-win —- if I stopped smoking, my voice would improve, and I could use the extra money to pay for voice lessons!

By Sunday, I was down to my last pack of Tareytons. I smoked the last one and flushed the butt down the toilet. I knew it wouldn't be easy, but I had to think of my bigger goals. Monday morning, I called the number in the ad and scheduled my first voice lesson for Friday afternoon, my day off. Maxine Adler put me at ease immediately. She sounded warm but professional. She gave me her address and requested I bring a blank tape and one or two pieces of music to work on. Best of all, she charged $45 for a one-hour lesson, half of what Shelley was paying. What a relief! With the money I was saving on cigarettes, and if I cut back on Chinese takeout, I could probably swing it. The protein bars in the health food store would come in handy as a cheap alternative to lunch.

On my way to work, I bought a big pack of Doublemint gum. That was the brand my grandfather, Zeida, chewed when he gave up smoking. It had worked for him, so I hoped it would work for me. Zeida was the one person in my family who understood me. He was a wise man who'd been studying to be a rabbi in Russia, but because of the pogroms, his father sent him to apprentice as a tailor in Brooklyn. When I was very young he taught me Yiddish songs and encouraged me to sing them for his customers at his dry-cleaning store. Whenever I told him I wanted to quit piano lessons he got very upset and made me promise to keep practicing.

Zeida loved telling me about a movie he couldn't remember the name of, where a young woman was playing the piano on a ship and a man on the ship fell in love with her and asked her to marry him. More than anyone else in the family Zeida encouraged me to do my music. I guess it was fitting that he would be my role model when it came to quitting smoking.

At the health food store, Katie noticed right away I wasn't smoking.

"No more cigarette breaks, Carol? First, you give up McDonalds and now cigarettes. Working here is starting to rub off on you!" She gave me a little hug and handed me another protein bar.

"I quit smoking," I proudly told Bruce later that day as I eyed the couch.

"What made you decide to quit now?" he asked with a not-so guarded smile.

"Voice lessons. I want to pay for voice lessons." It was the first time I ever talked to him without smoking. Cigarettes were like a punctuation mark at the end of every sentence. A smokescreen I hid behind to mask the sexual energy I felt between us. Today was also the first time I would be lying on the couch. I felt vulnerable and exposed. I wrapped my bulky black cardigan sweater tightly around me and stared at the water stain on the ceiling. A built-in Rorschach test? I closed my eyes and still wasn't sure what the purpose of lying on the couch could be. Bruce had mentioned something about free association and uncovering repressed emotions.

The one emotion that I did *not* want him to uncover was the way I felt about *him*. Why couldn't he have been fat, bald, and middle-aged instead of tall, dark, and handsome?

"In our last session, I said we'd work on separation anxiety."

"Yeah, I have separation anxiety—- from my Tareytons."

"I know it's hard, but try concentrating. Was there a time when your father scolded you for doing something wrong, Carol? Let me know the first image that pops into your head."

I took a minute to think back. "Okay. It was the first day of school, I think first or second grade, and I refused to go. My father insisted that I stand in front of our house and watch the other kids go to school."

"What happened after that?"

"I got embarrassed and changed my mind and went."

"Interesting. Your father was using reverse psychology on you."

"I guess." *How is this going to help me?* I thought to myself, but I decided to just go with Bruce's questions. I concentrated on the sound of his voice, which always calmed me down. The rest of the hour dragged. I didn't know if I liked this couch idea. I assumed he knew what he was doing and that lying on the couch would uncover thoughts and feelings that were buried in my inner psyche. Still, there were some feelings I could *never* share with him. My head might be "shrinking," but my heart was expanding.

It was torture, but I made it to Friday without smoking one cigarette! Cigarettes were a huge part of my persona, something I reached for so many times during the day: drinking coffee, finishing a meal, talking on the phone, songwriting, waking up in the morning, and especially after making love if I ever found someone to do that with again!

Every time I reached for a piece of gum I heard my Grandfather's voice saying, "You're a *shaina maidel*, my pretty girl. Don't be afraid of anything." One of the last things he asked me was, "Doll, will you talk about me when I'm gone?" I was sure *thinking* about him now and I knew he'd be in my thoughts forever.

Friday morning, I slept later than usual. I was so excited and nervous about taking my first voice lesson that I'd had trouble falling asleep. It didn't help that I was going through nicotine withdrawal but heard Zeida's encouraging voice in my head as I popped an extra B complex to calm my nerves, and made myself an English muffin and coffee.

I put on my hippest outfit, a blue denim mini-skirt, black tights, brown suede boots, and my favorite beige cable knit sweater. Before I walked out the door, I glanced in the mirror and liked what I saw. I put on the navy pea coat that I'd just bought in a secondhand store in the Village and strategically positioned my black corduroy Bob Dylan cap to show off my new mod haircut. The day I bought my pea coat, I walked into a hair salon and had my hair cut into a layered style with bangs. I did it on a whim and liked the way it looked. The young woman who cut it had safety pins in her ears and tattoos on her arms. She tried talking me into dying my hair purple, but I nixed that idea. A long, layered shag was radical enough!

I took the downtown bus to 56th Street and walked down Seventh Avenue repeating the address in my head, checking out the doorways as I went. I was reading the numbers on the buildings—881 Seventh Ave. *This can't be right*, I thought. *It's Carnegie Hall!* I pulled the address out of my pocket. *Wow, it is right. Her studio is actually in Carnegie Hall!*

I entered the iconic building, took a deep breath, and rang the buzzer for Studio 902. "It's Carol Marks," I announced. "I'm here for my lesson!" As I rode the elevator to the ninth floor, my heart was pounding and my expectations were soaring! *I'm coming up in the world!* I thought.

Maxine Adler opened the door and led me toward a black baby grand in a corner of the room. I took in the high ceilings, the skylights, and the large floor-to-ceiling windows. What wowed me was the wall of framed publicity photographs. They were all signed and some even had personal messages on them. I recognized many famous faces —- movie stars, recording artists, TV personalities.

"Johnny Carson!" I couldn't help commenting.

"Yes, nice man. His wife gave him two months of singing lessons as a Christmas gift. He said it was his dream to learn how to sing."

Speechless, I just smiled at her.

Maxine took a seat at the piano. Music books and sheet music were scattered in piles on top of the closed lid of the baby grand. In her mid-fifties, a bit matronly, but slightly eccentric, she was wearing a blue paisley printed blouse, a black wool skirt, silvery satin bedroom slippers, and black cat's eyeglasses with rhinestones on the corners. She motioned for me to sit on a tall, wooden bar stool next to her. I welcomed the chance to sit down and get off my shaking legs. I didn't know if it was nicotine withdrawal or if I was intimidated by her studio.

"Why do you want to take voice lessons, Carol dear?"

I cleared my throat and said in a bold voice that even surprised me, "I want to sing my own songs and make a record."

"I see. What music did you bring?"

I handed her my old stand-by, *Summertime*. She played the intro and I belted it out.

"Good! Do you think your voice is loud?" Maxine asked.

"Yes, I've always been able to belt out a song."

"True, but we need to work on placement and projection. I think you've been placing your voice in your throat. I'll give you some voice exercises to help with that. Think of your throat as an open vessel so that the sound doesn't get stuck there. You can improve your voice and protect it at the same time."

"Wow! I had no idea I was singing incorrectly!"

"Yes, but it can be corrected. Did you bring a tape to record your lesson? Good, let's get started."

26
ANYBODY WHO'LL LET ME

Anybody who'll let me have it all without feeling small,
Anybody who'll let me take the time to cross over the line.
Don't try and understand me,
Just let me show you how easy it'll be
When I give my love to anybody who'll let me.

"I slipped," I said softly to Bruce as I took my position on the couch.

"What, Carol?"

"I slipped up. I gave in."

"Don't feel bad. It's very common for people who give up smoking to have a cigarette in a weak moment."

"No, I'm not talking about *smoking*! I let a guy pick me up at a bar and I slept with him."

Staring at the water stain on the ceiling trying to decide if it looked like a phallic symbol or the map of Italy, all I could hear was the sound of Bruce puffing on his cigar. *Say something, say anything, make me feel like I'm not the slut I feel like.*

"What happened?" Bruce finally asked.

"Saturday night I came home from work, had dinner, and tried to work on some music, but I couldn't concentrate. I was feeling lonely. It's the Saturday night thing." I paused and heard more puffing, more silence. *Why did I say anything to Bruce about it?* "I put on my good jeans, piled on the makeup, and went for a walk. I heard music coming from a bar on Amsterdam and went in. I met this cute guy there and it just happened."

"Did it just *happen?*"

"Maybe not."

"You hoped to meet someone before you left."

"Yeah, you're right," I said sheepishly.

I'd walked into Jake's, a local club down the street from me, and found a seat at the bar. It was crowded and smoky and the band was playing a Stones song. I treated myself to a Kahlua and cream, closed my eyes, and listened to the music. The band was too loud and the lead singer was no Mick Jagger, but the songs were good. Someone tapped my shoulder and I swiveled around to see a tall guy with wild black Dylan hair and a thick mustache smiling at me. He looked part hippie, part mountain man with his red plaid flannel shirt, faded jeans, and hiking boots. He was my type, except a little taller than the men I was normally attracted to. Before I had time to think, he gently grabbed my arm and led me through the crowd to the dance floor.

The closer he danced to me, the more I felt like I was being drawn into his energy field. We were dancing to the Doors' "Come On Baby Light My Fire," and the music was getting more and more intense. It seemed like the song was never gonna end. I tried averting my eyes from mountain man but all I could see was his dark eyes staring at me, following my every move. When the song was finally over, he put his arm around me and I melted. All the frenetic energy was gone, and I was spent. "Let's get out of here and go someplace where we can talk," he whispered in my ear.

I was in an *I don't give a shit* mood. I nodded yes and grabbed my coat from the barstool. We walked out into the sobering cold January air arm and arm. Halfway down the block was an all-night coffee shop that

I'd walked by a few times, but only during the day. Tonight it looked like a refuge for druggies and prostitutes waiting for their connections, downing cups of lukewarm coffee, and pretending to look at the menu. We found a booth in the back away from the action.

Hippie mountain man's name was David. He didn't tell me his last name and I didn't want to know. "Do you know John Lennon lives in this neighborhood?" he asked.

"Yeah, he lives in the building across the street from me on 72nd."

"I've worked for him."

"Are you a musician?"

"No, a roadie."

"Wow! What's he like? I'd love to meet him. I'm a singer."

"I only worked for him a few times. He seemed nice but I didn't get to talk to him. Yoko's always around and she kinda guards him."

"I get that vibe."

The waitress handed us some grease-stained menus and rolled her eyes when we told her we just wanted coffee. "*Two more deadbeats taking up space,*" she was probably thinking.

"Do you live in the neighborhood?"

"No. I'm from the Island. My friend lets me crash at his place on 75th on the weekends."

I thought back to when I was spending every weekend crashing at my friends' house in South River. Maybe things could work out with David if he was in the city a lot, but then quickly nixed that idea. Even if the sex turned out to be amazing, I didn't want to put my energy into a relationship right now. Tonight was about two lonely people looking for a hook-up on a Saturday night.

"No boyfriend?" he asked without subtlety.

"No. I like the way you cut to the chase. What about you? Do you have someone?"

"I haven't had time. I've been on the road a lot," he said and grabbed my hand across the table. "Let's get out of here. Can I walk you home?"

"Sure." *Am I gonna ask a stranger up to my house at midnight?* I wondered as we got closer to my apartment.

"Do you wanna come up and watch *Saturday Night Live*?"

"Sounds like fun. I'm not ready to say goodbye, Carol."

Bruce's voice parachuted me back to reality. "I can tell you're censoring your thoughts, Carol. Just say whatever comes into your mind."

"You mean, about that night?"

"If you want to talk about it. Or anything else that pops up."

I smiled. "Pops up" was a good way to describe what happened with David that night. He "popped up" and stayed that way for hours! I couldn't decide if he was a sex addict or the best lover I'd ever had. Finally, I'd said, "I'm getting kinda tired. Are you gonna come?"

"I don't think so. I have a problem."

Oh great, what have I got myself into? I pulled the sheets over myself and wished I could smoke a cigarette.

"I can stay hard but I can't come."

"That's not fair!"

"Yeah, I keep thinking when I meet the right one, it'll be different. Some chicks use me."

"Bummer!"

"Yeah. Most of the time I feel used."

"Maybe you should see a shrink."

"I don't need a shrink. There's nothing wrong with my *head*. I need a fuckin' good lover!" He shouted. He swung out of bed, grabbed his clothes off the floor, and stomped into the hallway bathroom, muttering something under his breath. I started to shake and threw on a t-shirt just in case I had to make a mad dash out of the apartment. My hand was on the phone, ready to call the cops when the apartment door slammed shut. Still shaking,

I walked into the living room, sat on the couch, and started to cry. *Would I ever learn my lesson and stop living on the edge?* Mountain man thought he didn't need a shrink but *I* obviously *did*.

So here I was, lying on Bruce's couch and *not* saying the first thing that popped into my head. I wasn't going to tell him all the details of that night. It was too embarrassing!

Instead, I said, "I wish I had a cigarette. You're still smoking. It's not fair!"

"Who said life was fair? Just take some deep breaths and let your mind wander."

"Okay." I closed my eyes.

27
WEARY WOMEN'S BLUES

I get up with the sun to start my day.

I know there's lots of dues I've got to pay.

But when the sunlight goes away,

I get those weary women's blues.

When they call I can't refuse.

It's the sad songs that I choose to get me through the day.

Even though I felt lonely, I wasn't actively looking for love, and I'd sworn off one-night stands after my hippie mountain man fiasco.

"It's okay to feel sad about being alone," Bruce said at my Monday night session.

"Why is it so hard for me to be by myself?" I asked, staring at the water stain on the ceiling. *Yes*, I thought, *it definitely looks like a penis.*

"Most people have a hard time with it, especially women."

"Yeah, all the women's lib stuff can't keep you warm at night. I started writing a song about it this morning. "Weary Women's Blues"—How's that for a title?"

"It's good you're expressing your feelings. When you were a child, girls were conditioned to get married and be housewives."

"Yeah, we've been brain-washed."

"You've told me about situations when you were with someone and *still* felt lonely."

I winced a little as I thought back to my summer of free love in Berkeley after Joshua broke up with me. Sleeping with guys just to prove I was attractive, crying after sex, not understanding why I felt so hollow and disconnected the next morning. *How could something so intimate feel so isolating?*

"There were plenty of those," I said.

Bruce didn't say a word. As I lay there, the faces of the men I had one-night stands with flashed through my mind like a speeded-up home movie, each face grotesquely morphing into the next.

"In one session you talked about a film you saw that listed needs versus wants."

"It stuck with me," I said, grateful to be rescued from the bizarre montage of ex-lovers reeling through my head. I took a deep breath. *Oh, for a cigarette!*

"Why do you think that is?"

"I don't know! *That's* why I'm here!" I was getting frustrated and asking myself, why *was* I here? I forced myself to concentrate. "I guess, wanting a relationship is healthy, but needing one never works."

"You've got to get to the root cause of why love isn't fulfilling," Bruce said after another long pause.

"That makes sense, but I have no idea."

"In therapy, you can look at the unconscious desires that fuel some of your needs and take away their power."

"And if I do that, do you think I can find real love?"

"Only when your wants outnumber your needs." Bruce's voice softened, "You won't always be alone, Carol," he said.

I sighed and let his comforting words sink in. "You know, the only time I feel understood is when I'm here."

"But your goal in therapy is to understand *yourself.*"

"My *parents* tell me that I'm finding myself. What they *really* mean is that I'm lost and they're waiting for the day when I find the road that leads back to them."

"You've been discovering the direction you want your life to go in. Being influenced by your parents and being a reaction to them is not the same thing, Carol."

"How can I *not* rebel against them? They're always trying to control me! They're always telling me I'm being influenced by my friends. It's like I was innocently sleeping and a body snatcher turned me into one of my hippie friends!"

"You sound angry."

"I am! My parents make me feel like I couldn't *possibly* make such bad decisions on my own. Not *their* precious daughter! It's all my friends' fault. I'm a sheep just following the herd."

"You may never be able to convince them, but ultimately you and your parents want the same thing for you."

"*Right*, like what?"

"They want you to be happy."

"Yeah, sure, as long as it's *their* definition of happy."

"That's not your concern. Only *you* can know what works for you. Just take care of yourself and don't worry about what they think."

"But I feel so fucking guilty!"

"Guilt is a useless emotion. Your parents did the best that they could, but now it's time for them to let go. You're an adult, Carol, and can make your own decisions."

"Right. That's the scary part!"

I closed my eyes to clear my head, but the dream I'd had that morning came back to haunt me. "I dreamt I was on a bus from New Jersey to the city and there was a string attached from me to my parents' house," I told Bruce. "The closer I got to New York, the longer the string got."

"That's pretty obvious."

"I know! My umbilical cord is following me wherever I go and I can't break loose."

"Don't be so hard on yourself."

Bruce knew how to calm me down by saying the exact, perfect thing. Damn it! Why did he have to be my therapist? Why couldn't I have met him on the corner of 72nd or in a bar on Amsterdam?

"Carol?"

"Why does life have to be so complicated!"

"The more mud you clear from your windshield, so to speak, the clearer life will become."

"It sounds so simple."

"Believe in the process."

I wasn't sure how much I believed in the process, but one thing was true. Talking to Bruce was helping my songwriting. Back at the apartment, I felt inspired to finish "Weary Women's Blues."

Then I tell myself I must be strong.
I hear my sisters telling me to carry on.
But I haven't had a good man in oh, so long.
Just those Weary Women's Blues.
When they call I'll just refuse.
No more sad songs will I choose to get me through the day.
I know it won't be easy.
It takes a lot to please me now,
And a lot of lonely nights to push old dreams away.
But I'm gonna find a way, a way, a way.

28
ROSE MARIE McCOY

Hear me, do not fear me,
'Cause I'm believing in you.
I'm pulling you through
If you want me to.

On Friday when I went to Maxine's for my voice lesson, an attractive, middle-aged black woman was sitting in the waiting area. She was wearing a red beret and a camel hair poncho with an alligator belt cinching her waist and high-heeled brown leather boots. She looked like someone important. What surprised me was her childlike voice.

"Are you a singer?" she asked, giving me a warm smile.

"Yes, are you?" I answered.

"I used to sing a lot when I was younger, but now I concentrate on my songwriting."

"I sing and write songs, too."

"Like Carole King? You look a little like her—your wavy hair and all."

"She's one of my favorites."

"I'd like to hear your songs sometime. Here's my card."

Her card was impressive: Rose McCoy, songwriter and producer, 1650 Broadway.

Thanks, Miss McCoy! That would be incredible! I could mail you a demo."

"You can call me Rose. Why don't you make an appointment to drop it off in person?"

"That would be great! I'm Carol, Carol Marks."

Just then Maxine and a pretty, young black teenage girl walked into the hall. I stood up and Maxine introduced me. "Carol, this is Regina Simms. You'll be hearing her on the radio soon," Maxine said and winked at Rose. "It looks like you two have already met. Rose is one of the most successful songwriters in New York. She's producing Regina's new album."

I smiled, but I was speechless. *Why can't I say anything?* I asked myself. Whenever I got around famous people I clammed up. After Rose and Regina left, I asked Maxine if she knew of any artists who'd recorded Rose's songs.

"Many," Maxine paused for a moment. "Let's see, Nat King Cole, Lenny Welch, and Elvis, to name a few."

All I could say was, "Amazing!"

Rose is the real deal. She's practically a living legend! What if I blow it! I thought as Maxine began playing my warm-up exercises.

I started vocalizing but was thoroughly distracted. I was singing *La-la, La-la, La-La, La-La,* but I was thinking *Ro-sie! Ro-sie! Ro-sie!*

I read Rose's business card over and over again on the crosstown bus and was still clutching it when I walked into my apartment. Was she just being polite or was she truly interested in hearing my songs? I obsessed about her all weekend, then on Monday morning I finally got up the courage to call. Rose picked up after three rings,

"Hello?" she said in her little girl voice.

"Hi Rose, I'm Carol Marks. I don't know if you remember me," I said nervously. "We met at Maxine Adler's studio last Friday. You said I could make an appointment to show you some of my songs?"

"Sure, when would you like to come?"

"Friday's my day off, I could meet you at 3:00 after my voice lesson."

"That'll be good. You know the address?"

"You're at 1650 Broadway?" My heart was pounding so loud, I was sure Rose could hear it on the other end.

"The entrance is on 51st. Just give the guard my name and he'll let you in."

"Thanks Rose! See you then."

I hung up, feeling ecstatic. A famous songwriter was giving me a chance to play my songs for her! I thought back to when I used to ride the bus to the city through the Lincoln Tunnel. I could never stop staring at the dividing line—on one side was boring, conventional, suburban New Jersey, and on the other side was live-out-your-dreams New York City. Could this be my chance? Was meeting Rose my dividing line?

Friday finally came. I mustered up as much confidence as I could, walked into 1650 Broadway, and announced myself to the doorman. I was carrying a fake black leather briefcase bought from a street vendor near Times Square. In it were my demo tape, a practice vocal tape, lyric sheets, and a notebook. The doorman phoned Rose and motioned towards the elevator. Her office was on the eighth floor. The sign on the door read: "Do not come here without an appointment."

Rose welcomed me warmly and led me into her office. I followed her through a small front room with an old spinet piano that led to a bigger room with a couch, filing cabinets, and a large metal desk. I took a seat on the couch and stared out the windows looking onto 51st Street.

"I have to keep the door locked because people are always trying to hang out here in between appointments," Rose said, as she took a seat behind her desk. "When I don't answer, they slip their lyrics under the door.

If I stopped every time someone came, I'd never get any work done. So, what do you have for me?"

She opened her top desk drawer and took out a portable tape recorder. I handed her my demo and she put it in the machine. I'd cued the tape to one of my more bluesy songs, "I Wanted To Be Fooled" because it showed off my vocals. I didn't dare look at Rose while my demo was playing. All around the room photographs of famous singers were looking at me—Nat King Cole, Lenny Welch, and Maxine Brown among them. The demo seemed to go on forever and my insecurities came rushing back to haunt me. Rose stopped the tape in the middle of the second song. "You've got potential, Carol. You can really sing and you playing the piano is a plus! We can work on a song together."

"Thank you, Rose. I would love that." I was trying to sound professional, but in my head, I was screaming, *This is it! My lucky break!* I stared at Rose's BMI and Cash Box Music awards on the wall in front of me and for a moment I let myself imagine being at the Grammy Awards. *And the award for song of the year goes to Rose Marie McCoy and Carol Marks!*

"How is next Friday around this time? Can you bring some ideas for me then?"

"Absolutely!"

As I left the building I saw Tiny Tim walking in. Who knew how many more famous people I'd meet at 1650 Broadway? I had so much energy I walked the whole twenty blocks uptown to my apartment.

The first thing I did when I got home was to open the piano bench to look for song ideas. I found a purple loose-leaf notebook, music sheets, and a few cocktail napkins with hastily scribbled lyrics on them. I put everything from the emptied piano bench on the living room couch and went into the bedroom. Hidden in my underwear drawer under my vintage satin bathrobe lay my half-written journal. I made myself a cup of mint tea and sat on the couch searching for lyrics like a miner digging for gold. One unfinished song caught my eye.

29
LET ME BRING OUT THE ANIMAL IN YOU

The first time I looked at you
I saw another you deep in your eyes.
A wild man acting tame,
Trying hard to break through your disguise.
This is a full moon night and it's all right—
I've got a wild streak in me too.
So don't hold back, don't fight it.
You're so close and I'm so excited.
Give in and let me bring out the animal in you!

Rose had been so warm, so down-to-earth, I wasn't as nervous when we met the following Friday, but I had no clue what she'd think of my song idea.

"Where'd you come up with that title?" she asked with a chuckle. "'Let Me Bring Out the Animal in You'—it's a little bit dirty!"

"It just popped into my head. It's about people being uptight." I couldn't tell her it was really about a fantasy about seducing my shrink. I took a deep breath and waited to hear Rose's opinion. *And Song of the Year is, "Let Me Bring Out The Animal In You"!*

"Okay, let's give it a try!" she said.

Elated, I sat at the piano and sang Rose part of the melody to the unfinished lyrics I'd written. Then Rose took out a yellow-lined note pad and I sat with my notebook, trying to write down some ideas. Neither one of us said anything for about ten minutes. Then Rose asked, "Can I read you what I've got?"

I tried quickly writing down the lines she'd come up with.

"I like it! How did you come up with the lyrics so fast?"

"Songwriting is like telling a story. You don't need any poetry or fancy words. Just write from your heart and think of the situation. It's like you're telling a story. I learned that when I was writing a Coke commercial."

"You wrote a Coke commercial? That's pretty amazing!"

"Yeah, I was having a hard time with it and then I asked myself what does Coke do? It makes the situation better. With that in mind, I wrote the commercial that James Brown ended up recording."

Meeting with Rose became part of my regular Friday routine. We were making progress on the song, but even more interesting were the stories she told me about her life. She'd graduated high school and hopped on a bus to New York, leaving behind the segregated, rural town in Arkansas where she'd grown up. Her parents wanted her to go to college and become a teacher, but she wanted to follow her dream and be a singer. We had that in common!

A cousin got Rose a job ironing shirts in a Chinese laundry and a room in a Harlem boarding house. She started going to nightclubs in Harlem and singing with different bands. A booking agent heard her and got her gigs in New Jersey clubs where she had to mix with the customers and get them to order her drinks.

"Singing was fun *and* I was getting paid. I worked it out with the bartender so that when the men bought me drinks, he watered them down.

There were some rough characters, but I knew how to fight back if I had to."

"When did you start writing?"

"A friend of mine got me an audition with a small record company where I wrote my own songs. After my first record came out, another company asked me to write for one of their blues artists."

"Were you still performing?"

"I kept singing. Songwriting didn't pay much then. Lead sheets cost money, so I just told whoever did the lead sheet to put their name on the song."

"That's not fair! You should've gotten all the credit!"

"You gotta do what you gotta do."

Rose had come a long way from bartering lead sheets for songwriting credits. She and her husband James lived in Englewood Cliffs, right over the George Washington Bridge, a wealthy area where a lot of music and show business people lived.

"Did you sing mostly in New York and New Jersey?" I asked.

"I toured all over. James encouraged me to go. I opened for Moms Mabley in towns across the Midwest and drove all the way to a club in Montreal."

"That must have been lonely, being away from your husband."

"It was, but it gave me something to write about."

"When did Elvis record your songs?"

"I found out about it when I got back from my gig in Montreal. My writing partner, Charlie Singleton, called me up very excited. 'We got Elvis!'" he said. I didn't even know who Elvis was!"

"Your life is so Hollywood! They should make a movie about you!"

Rose laughed. "I'd go for that, and I'd like Lena Horne to play me!" she exclaimed, and we both started laughing.

Between stories about her life, Rose was giving me songwriting tips that I could never learn in a book. She knew a woman who'd written a book about songwriting but never had *one* song published.

"You can't learn songwriting from a book. It's a spiritual thing. You just write like you talk and then the phrasing and the melody come from that. Everything in the song has to go back to the title."

"How do you get your titles?"

"Some mornings I wake up with a song idea. That's why I keep a tape recorder and a pencil and paper next to my bed."

"Cool, I'm gonna try that."

"Sometimes I get a title from something somebody says, but I mostly write from my own experiences."

"Me, too."

"You're too *young* to have lots of experiences. Are you with anyone, Carol?"

I shook my head no. "I've had my heart broken too many times."

"Hmm, a pretty girl like you shouldn't be alone. I'm gonna keep my eyes out for someone," Rose said with a schoolgirl giggle.

I felt my face getting red. Maybe someday I'd tell Rose who I was writing our song about, but I wasn't ready for that.

"Do you need a ride uptown?"

Rose and I walked across the street to a parking lot where everyone knew who she was. I could feel my eyes getting bigger when the attendant pulled up in her shiny black Cadillac and Rose gave him a big tip. I got in the car and settled into the luxurious taupe leather car seat.

"I love your car!"

"Thanks. I buy a new one every year. Everyone should have two fortunes, Carol. One to blow and one to keep."

"I'll settle for one, Rose."

I was feeling relaxed until I glanced down at Rose's feet and saw she was driving with one foot on the gas and the other on the brake. It was a really jerky ride.

"Thanks for the ride!" I said as I got out, feeling relieved.

Before I went to bed that night, I put my notebook on the nightstand, in case I woke up with some fresh ideas for our song. When I woke up the next morning, I jotted down some lyrics for the bridge:

Don't you want to run out in the night with no destination in sight.

Let out what you're feeling, wrong or right. Bring out the animal tonight?

I reread what I'd written and smiled to myself. It was a damn good song!

I wished I could share them with Bruce. Better yet, I wished I could sing it to him and let him know my feelings. *Was it just a fantasy?* I needed *and* wanted to find out.

30
1650 BROADWAY

Lots of good times waiting just for you,
But first you must believe in what is new.
The joy is in the doing, not what's done.
Your dreams are taking shape now, life's begun.

I was learning more about the people who came through the doors at 1650 Broadway. Many of them were publishers, agents, and songwriters who'd moved their offices from the Brill Building, the birthplace of rock-n-roll. Rents were going up there and hitmakers were setting up shop at 1650, just a few blocks away. Behind every door beat the heart and soul of the music business and I could feel the heavy vibes as I walked down the hallways. I finally felt like an insider when the doorman stopped asking, "Who are you here to see?" I felt privileged to be part of the scene.

Rose introduced me to some famous people. Millie Jackson's office was right next door and once Maxine Brown stopped by looking for songs to record. One night when we were leaving, Rose stopped to talk to comedian Nipsy Russell, whom she'd worked with in Harlem years ago. Then there was Otis Blackwell, who'd written many Elvis hits like "Don't Be Cruel" and "All Shook Up," two of Elvis' best-known songs. Rose told me that at one time Carole King and Neil Diamond wrote songs in the building, too.

That blew my mind! If I'd met Rose sooner, I might have met *them*, but I'd probably be tongue-tied and blow it.

My celebrity shyness wasn't getting any better. No matter how many famous people Rose introduced me to I still could only smile and act politely. I'm sure Rose noticed how awkward I felt, but she was too cool to say anything about it. "Carol," she used to say, "If there's something about a person you want to change, just ignore it. You'll be surprised. It'll change by itself."

"I feel so nervous when I'm around famous people," I finally confessed.

"The bigger they are, the nicer they are, Carol. Just be yourself," Rose smiled. She was sitting on the couch across from the piano as I worked on the chords to "Let Me Bring Out the Animal in You."

"I hope someone big records our song."

"Don't say *hope*. Be positive. We'll make it happen, but it isn't as easy as it used to be."

"What do you mean?"

"More artists write their own songs and aren't looking for new material. There was a time when I could scribble lyrics on a piece of yellow-lined paper and walk into a publisher's office and sing him the song. Before I'd finished singing, they'd either give me money to make the demo or add it to my advance."

"Did you get paid after the song came out?"

"No. Most of the time I didn't sign a contract."

"Did you fight it?"

"It wasn't worth it. Only the big record companies paid."

"How do we get *our* song published?"

"I have someone who can do the lead sheet and we can book studio time downstairs. There's a recording studio in the basement."

"That's convenient." I was trying to sound cool and professional, but I felt like jumping up and down and screaming out the window, *I'm making it in the music business! This is actually happening to small-town, other-side-of-the-tunnel me!*

We finished the melody that afternoon and Rose asked me to sing it into her portable tape recorder. When the lead sheet was done, we'd figure out a date for the recording.

"I'll call you when I get the recording booked. Evenings okay?"

"Yeah, just let me know and I'll be there! I can't wait!"

"Do you need a ride uptown, Carol?"

"No thanks, I feel like walking today." I *did* feel like walking. And anyway, I couldn't tell Rose that the way she drove stressed me out. I'd seen how she put her foot on the gas and the other on the brake the last time she gave me a ride. It worked for her, but it freaked me out. Besides, I needed the exercise and time to digest what was happening.

Two weeks went by and I didn't hear from Rose. I was getting worried and imagining all kinds of negative scenarios. What if she changed her mind about the song or played it for someone and they didn't like it? What if she got involved in another project? Worst of all, what if she stepped on the gas when she should've stepped on the brake, and drove off the George Washington Bridge! Finally, around ten o'clock on Sunday night, the phone rang.

I knew it was Rose as soon as I picked up.

"Is it too late?" she asked. Her little girl voice sounded particularly youthful, the way it did when she was happy.

"No way!" I practically shouted.

"I got the lead sheet and booked the studio downstairs for next Tuesday night, February 13th. Can you make it?"

"You bet! I can't wait! Did you get the musicians?"

"Yeah, they're my usual, and the girl you saw me with that day at Maxine's is gonna sing the demo as a favor."

"Thanks, Rose! That sounds great! See you soon."

"Our song's gonna be a smash!" she exclaimed. "Think positive!"

I hung up the phone and stared out the window. The February snow had started to fall, covering the dirty streets and transforming the city into a blank, white sheet. Was it an omen of new beginnings, or was I reading too much into it? "Sometimes a cigar is just a cigar," Freud once said. I'd leave the over-analyzing to Bruce.

I thought back to the day I moved into my apartment and my father got the key stuck in the lock to the front door. I'd been through a lot since then and had paid some heavy dues. As I looked out the window, I gave myself permission to feel happy. I didn't even care that the day after the recording session was Valentine's Day, and I had no man to share it with. Making a professional recording of my music was way cooler than any corny holiday. There were other ways to get high, and right now music was all I cared about.

I called Nina to tell her the good news. I knew she'd still be up studying. Some days I wished she'd never moved out of the apartment to go to grad school, but she had to follow her dream, too. As long as I had music to play and good friends to talk to, I was okay with being alone on Valentine's Day. Romance could wait. I had no way of knowing that cupid had other plans.

31
VALENTINE SURPRISE

Take my hand and follow me

And we'll let the darkness be our guide.

And when we reach ecstasy,

There'll be nothing left for us to hide.

So don't hold back, don't fight it.

You're so close and I'm so excited.

Give in and let me bring out the animal in you!

I had no idea what I'd find behind the metal door with the sign that read: "Do not enter when light is on." I looked down at the leather bracelet that had been on my wrist since the night Melanie put it there to symbolize strength and sisterhood. This was my first professional recording session, and I needed all the help I could get. I took a deep breath and firmly knocked on the door. A thirty-something guy with tinted glasses and headphones around his neck opened it a crack and stuck his head out. "You here for Rose's session?" he asked.

"Yes, I'm the songwriter, Carol Marks!" I said, catching my breath. It felt good to say that out loud, *Carol Marks, songwriter.*

"Pete. Sound engineer. Rose's over there." He pointed his clipboard in the direction of the drum set on the other side of the room. The studio was the entire width of the building, half a city block, a far cry from the New Jersey basement where I'd recorded my demo tape. I blinked a few times as my eyes adjusted to the spotlights scattered throughout the ceiling. *Maybe that's why Pete's wearing tinted glasses. Or is he just stoned? Probably stoned.*

"Carol!" Rose called to me. She and the musicians were huddled around the drum set. I made my way across the room, trying to act like I'd done this before.

"This is Carol. We wrote the song together," Rose said, putting her arm around me.

The drummer nodded in my direction and went back to setting up. The bass player gave me a friendly hug and the keyboard player shook my hand. They were seasoned black musicians, in their thirties or early forties. I couldn't believe they were playing on our recording! Rose told me when she'd called about the session that they were big-time players who'd played with the greats. For them, this was just another gig, but for me, it was a big step up. I was in the inner sanctum, where songs became hits and singers became stars.

"We're waiting for the guitar player. I had to get a sub since my regular guy had a gig," Rose said as she passed out the lead sheets. "Regina's in the isolation booth. Why don't you see if she has any questions."

I walked over to a small, sectioned-off room on one side of the studio. Regina was sitting on a stool in front of a large shiny microphone that looked like it was dipped in gold. I couldn't take my eyes off it. The only other one I'd ever seen was on the cover of Frank Sinatra's *Strangers in the Night* album, at my parents' house.

Regina looked younger than I remembered. She was wearing a sweatshirt, jeans, and high-top sneakers and chewing a wad of bubble gum, which I hoped she'd take out of her mouth before she started singing.

"Hi, Regina. Do you need anything?" I asked.

"No, I'm cool. I hope this doesn't take too long, I have stuff to do," she answered as she cracked her gum. She looked like she wished she was anywhere but here.

Does she know how lucky she is? What a brat! She's seventeen with a record deal and she's already acting like a diva.

As I walked into the main recording area, I spotted the guitar player hurrying in. He was wearing a black turtleneck sweater, brown motorcycle jacket, and brown suede boots. His shoulder-length, black curly hair and medium build reminded me of pictures I'd seen of Michaelangelo's David. *Definitely my type,* I thought. I took a sip of my take-out coffee, trying to look hip.

He was clearly an outsider, I thought as I watched him tuning his guitar. Not because he was white—musicians didn't care about things like that—but because of his air of aloofness. Everything about him exuded confidence and sophistication, but it somehow came off as a stuck-up vibe, like the guy Carly Simon was singing about in "You're So Vain". *Stick to the music,* I told myself. If his guitar playing is as together as his appearance, he'll be one hell of a musician!

"The guitar player's cute," I whispered to Rose as we took our seats next to the sound engineer in the recording booth.

Rose gave him the once-over. "He *is* kinda cute. I can introduce you after the session."

We were sitting next to Pete in the control room, facing the window that looked out into the main recording area. In front of us was a large mixing board with rows and rows of dials and levers and two small monitor speakers. He gave us a pair of headphones and began explaining to me what the dials and levers did. There was a channel for each instrument with bass, treble, and mid-ranges that he could adjust during the recording. Regina would be singing a scratch vocal so that the musicians could follow the song, but after the initial recording, she'd go back and record the vocals by herself. The recorded tracks would be played through the headphones so she could go over the vocals line by line, then go back and punch in notes if needed.

I looked up from the dizzying dials and caught the guitar player staring at me through the glass. I quickly put my head down. Tonight, of all nights, I didn't need any distractions.

The drummer counted off and the band started playing. The first take was a run-through to get the sound levels and make sure all the musicians knew where their solos came in. I was astounded. They were so good! I couldn't believe they'd never heard the song before and were just following lead sheets. I wanted to tell Rose how impressed I was, but her head was down, concentrating on the music.

Right from the first take, the musicians seemed really into it. Our song was coming to life! Even Regina surprised me with her bluesy, soulful voice and the growl she added when she sang the hook, "Let me bring out the animal in you." *Maybe she isn't an ungrateful brat, after all. Rose knows what she's doing!*

The band was on their third take and their playing was getting tighter. The musicians had a good groove going and the energy was building. I couldn't sit still. I closed my eyes and let my body move to the music. Halfway through the song—*splat*! "Shit! Cut!" The engineer yelled. I felt my face go red. I'd been so into the music that I'd knocked over the half-filled coffee cup I'd precariously perched on the soundboard. I rummaged through my bag for some tissues and wiped up the spill with shaking hands, trying not to touch the dial settings. I was so embarrassed I didn't dare look at Pete, let alone the guitar player!

"It's okay," Pete said in a softer voice. "You didn't screw anything up."

"Let's go, guys! From the top! Time is money!" he said through the mic.

The bass player put out his cigarette and the band started playing.

When the song ended, Rose and I looked at each other. She had a big smile on her face. "This is it, Carol, and it's gonna be a smash!"

As the players were packing up, Rose walked over to the guitar player and waved to me. "Glad you could make the session and fill in for Billy," she told him. "You were dynamite! This is my co-writer, Carol Marks. Can you believe this little girl came up with the idea for the song?" Rose said as she turned her head and winked at me, then walked over to talk to Pete at the mixing board.

"Good song! I'm Eric."

"Thanks! You sounded great," was all I managed to say. I felt a warmth coming from him. His aloof exterior was starting to melt. *Did I read him wrong? He actually seems sweet.*

"Do you have a card? I might know some people looking for songs."

"I've been meaning to order some, but I can give you my number." *I sound so unprofessional. He probably thinks I'm an amateur.*

"Sure, write your number on the back of the music sheet. Here's my card in case you need a guitar player. Do you live in the city?"

"West 72nd."

"You're practically in my neighborhood. I'm on West 87th."

I felt so high from the session I gave Eric a big smile. The conversation just flowed. We walked out the door together, still talking, and made our way uptown. It felt good to share the most important night of my career with him, even if he was a stranger. His intensity was subtle but palpable. He had to be a Scorpio: deep, sexy, and mysterious. One of those people that you could never totally know. There'd always be a secret buried deep in their psyche and that was part of the attraction. I didn't know if my first impression was right but I knew I wanted to find out.

As we walked, he took out a cigarette from a blue package and offered me one.

"Smoke?"

"I quit a few months ago, for my voice. What brand is *that*?"

"They're French, Gaulois."

"Wow! You've been to France?"

"Yeah, I got a gig in Paris last summer with a jazz band."

"What was Paris like?"

"Amazing, but it's meant for lovers."

"I'd like to go someday. It looks so romantic!"

"Have someone in mind?"

Hmm, is he trying to find out if I'm with someone? "No, I've been concentrating on my music."

Before I knew it, we were at 72nd. I wanted to ask Eric up to my apartment but it was late and I'd sworn off one-night stands.

"This was fun. Thanks for playing on my demo."

"Au revoir, ma chérie."

I was too revved up to sleep. I took out the pint of chocolate Haagen-Dazs that I kept in the freezer for emotional emergencies and dug in. *My mother would never approve of me not using a bowl! I don't need anyone's approval! I'm an independent woman living on her own and loving it!* The phone rang and I looked down at my watch. It was exactly midnight, officially Valentine's Day. I hoped it wasn't one of Joshua's stoned-out phone calls begging me to go back to him. I hesitantly picked up the phone and was relieved to hear Nina's voice on the other end.

"How'd the recording session go?"

"Incredible! The band nailed it, the singer was perfect, and the hunky guitar player walked uptown with me."

"That sounds like an added bonus."

We talked for a few minutes while Nina filled me in on grad school and told me about the crush she had on her sociology professor. I tried to persuade her not to do anything to jeopardize her degree. But Nina did what Nina wanted to do.

As soon as I hung up, the phone rang again. "Okay, sleep with the guy, I don't care!" I said.

"Is that the way you answer the phone?" a deep voice asked, half chuckling. *Oh my God, it's Eric!*

"My face is turning bright red. I thought it was my girlfriend calling back."

"I thought about you all the way home, Carol. I know it's short notice, but I was wondering if you'd like to have dinner with me tomorrow night. You don't think it's too weird that it's Valentine's Day?"

"Not if you don't! I'd really dig that."

"Cool, I'll call you back tomorrow and we can figure out where we're going. Sleep tight!"

Now I *really* wouldn't be able to sleep. I dug my spoon into the last of the Haagen-Dazs and found some *I Love Lucy* reruns on TV. Cupid hadn't forgotten me after all!

32
ERIC

Don't you want to run out in the night,
With no destination in sight,
Let out what you're feeling, wrong or right?
Bring out the animal tonight!

Eric didn't disappoint. True to his word, he called me the next day and told me he was taking me to a French restaurant on the Upper East Side. I had no idea how he managed to get reservations on such short notice, especially on Valentine's Day, but I was too excited to ask. *Just another part of his mysterious aura,* I thought.

The only fancy dress I owned came from the same West Village thrift shop where I'd bought my 1940s satin bathrobe. It was a sleeveless black cocktail dress with three levels of fringe that looked like something from the Roaring Twenties. Over it, I wore an unclaimed skunk fur coat my grandfather had given me from his dry-cleaning store. I dabbed some patchouli oil behind my ears to hide the faint scent of mothballs.

Our reservation was for 8:00. When the phone rang at 7:45, I was afraid to answer it. For a split second, I thought, *Maybe Eric is canceling and this is too good to be true.*

"Carol, I'm running a little late. I'll get a cab and pick you up in front of your building in ten minutes."

"Okay." *Hmm, is this a pattern? He was almost late for the recording session too.* I quickly put any doubt out of my mind. I didn't want anything to ruin our evening.

Ten minutes later, we were sitting in the backseat of the cab. Eric handed me a red rose.

"This is for you. It would look pretty in your hair, behind your ear, like Billy Holiday."

All I could manage to say was "Thanks!" *This is gonna be some night! I'm glad I followed my instincts and put in my diaphragm before I left.*

Rouche's was an upscale French restaurant with white table cloths, French waiters, and entrees that I couldn't pronounce and wouldn't dare put catsup on. *He's sure trying to impress me! Thank god, I got over my phobia of eating in restaurants.* I was relieved when Eric ordered the duck and not some way-out-there dish like frog legs. I ordered something I could recognize, lamb chops. They were good but would've tasted better with catsup.

Between the expensive wine, the rich food, and the intense attraction I was feeling for Eric, I was more than a little high as we slid into the backseat of yet another cab and headed crosstown to my apartment. Eric's hand on my leg was turning me on. I couldn't wait to start peeling away his layers. Not just his clothing, but everything under his worldly musician facade. I wanted it all.

We hurried up the stairs to my apartment, flung our coats on the living room couch, and headed straight for the bedroom. Eric unzipped the back of my dress and it fell to the floor. He looked surprised when he saw my bare breasts and began gently kissing my nipples. I was trying to keep it together long enough to unzip his pants and feel his hardness behind the zipper. Tonight, there was no time for foreplay—no candlelight, no incense, no mood music. We were both beyond turned on and I couldn't wait to feel Eric inside me. Even though it was our first time, surprisingly there were no awkward moments. Everything just flowed. I worried that I couldn't sleep with Eric next to me, but I fell into a deep, dreamless sleep. I stayed in bed until noon, slipped into my satin bathrobe, and trying not to wake him, went into the kitchen to boil some water for instant coffee.

A few minutes later Eric walked in wearing just his underwear with an obvious hard-on poking through.

"I could make love to you all day, Carol, but we've got plenty more days for that," he said as he hugged me from behind.

"Want some coffee?" is all I managed to say.

"Before that, I'd like to hear you sing. Play me something."

"Okay!" I said and walked over to the piano. My hands were shaking and I couldn't look at him as he leaned on the piano in front of me and I started singing my favorite Carole King song, "Will You Still Love Me Tomorrow." As I began the second verse, I got the courage to look up at Eric. His eyes met mine and I melted. How could I not wonder if Eric would be here tomorrow? Although I'd sung it many times, this was the first time the song felt truly real.

For the second time that morning, Eric put his arms around me. "Yes, I will," he whispered in my ear. How I wanted to believe him!

I led him to the kitchen and we sat down at the café table. "All I have is instant coffee and stale granola bars that I got from my gig at the health food store," I said.

"That's cool. I'm still full from dinner. Do you have to work today?"

"No, Fridays and Sundays are my days off."

"I'd like to show you my place. It's small, but it works for me since I'm on the road a lot."

We took turns taking a shower. I wasn't ready for a mutual rub-a-dub-dub. Besides, we might've gotten carried away and never left the apartment! I quickly dressed in my uniform of bell-bottoms and a cable knit sweater. Eric put on his dress clothes from the night before. He looked handsome and sophisticated in his black dress pants and fitted satiny grey shirt.

I felt nervous as I walked up the four long flights to Eric's studio. "Wow! You have a lot of guitars!" I exclaimed as I entered, almost tripping over a speaker wire. The place looked like a music store. Four guitar cases were lined up, almost blocking the bathroom door, and amps, mic stands, and other music equipment leaned against every available surface. *Looks like we'll be spending most of our time at my place,* I thought with a sense of relief. I felt more comfortable in my own bed and didn't want to deal with any ghosts of Eric's ex-girlfriends that might be hanging around. I still had a ghost of my own to deal with, and his name was Joshua. I'd have to put an end to that!

Eric was more than happy to hang out at my apartment. We were lost in our cozy winter world. Some days we never bothered to get out of bed. In between lovemaking we ate take-out Chinese food in bed, smoked joints in bed, and when we got the munchies, fed each other Mallomar cookies in bed. Eric accepted me totally. He even loved patting my stomach, which was getting bigger from all the lying around and eating we were doing. I was hoping sex would help burn off some calories. Eric wasn't gaining weight, but I had to admit, I let him do the heavy lifting. I'd cooled it with the acrobatic Kama Sutra positions and was happy to receive whatever he was giving.

And did he have a lot to give! Just like in the *I Ching,* he was the first hexagram—*The Creative,* six straight lines meaning creative power and energy. I was the second hexagram—*The Receptive,* six broken lines meaning receptivity and openness. Direct opposites, we complemented each other perfectly, my yin to his yang—and he had *some* yang!

The next time we went out, we went to one of Eric's gigs. He was playing with a country band at an Irish bar on Second Avenue, filling in for their guitar player who had the flu. Country music wasn't my thing, but I couldn't wait to see him perform. Paddy's was small, smoky, and loud. Eric and I walked toward the cramped stage and he introduced me to the drummer as he was setting up.

"You can sit with my girlfriend Mary." He pointed to a fake blonde with ratted-up hair sitting at a table right in front of the stage. As I reluctantly made my way to the table, I glanced up at the clock above the bar.

It was 8:15 and the band didn't go on until 9:00. *Damn, I wish we hadn't got here so early. I don't feel like socializing.* Two more musicians' chicks sat down at our table. Short skirts, long hair, thick make-up, false eyelashes, typical mall chicks. As soon as I heard them talking, I ruled out Jersey and guessed they were from Long Island. Turned out they were from Staten Island and seemed very happy to spend their Saturday nights together, gossiping, drinking, smoking, and having a good old time. They proudly sat at the girlfriends' table and seemed to enjoy their "I'm with the band," status. They staked their claim to the men on stage and at the end of the night even helped carry some of the equipment.

"Who's that hunky guitar player?" the chick who'd walked in with the bass player asked Mary.

"That hunky guitar player is *my* boyfriend!" I answered a little too loudly.

"Just asking," she said.

We introduced ourselves: I'd already met Mary the drummer's girlfriend, and now loudmouthed Noreen, the bass player's, and Susie, a Joni Mitchell look-a-like who was with the rhythm guitarist. As they drank their beers and smoked their cigarettes, I felt increasingly uncomfortable.

I sipped my coke and blew Eric a kiss as he put on his guitar and walked on stage. I was proud to be with him and even prouder when he launched into his first solo. He was a mesmerizing guitar player and looked so sexy on stage that I couldn't take my eyes off him. Neither could most of the other women I noticed when I finally managed to look around the room. *Uh oh. Am I gonna have to keep tabs on him?* There was no way I was going to all his gigs. Being a groupie waiting for her man's next twenty-minute break was not how *I* envisioned myself. *I* envisioned myself on stage. That's where I belonged, not sitting at the girlfriends' table with a bunch of adoring groupies. But tonight was not the night to bring *that* up. I was there to support him, and not waste my energy trying to fit in with the band's girlfriends.

"Thanks for turning me on to country music. You sound amazing!" I shouted over the crowd as Eric and I walked outside to get some fresh air during his break.

"It's okay. Not my favorite, but the band's pretty good and they're not too much into that twangy stuff. They have a big following."

"Yeah, at least it's high energy! But I can't wait until we're together tonight."

"I know babe. It'll go fast." *Yeah, for you,* I thought. Before I could say anything, Eric walked me back into the club, kissed me, and disappeared into the crowd. Three cokes and two breaks later, he said goodbye to the band, counted his money, and sprung for a cab back to my place. Both of us were too exhausted to do more than throw our clothes on the floor, brush our teeth, and plop into bed. Besides, there was always morning sex to look forward to!

A week later, Nina managed to break through my self-imposed lover's exile on Saturday night with a perfectly timed phone call. Eric had a gig with some up-and-coming country-rock band, and I'd told him I was tired after a long day at the health food store. I did worry about some girl coming on to him, but he assured me he was not the cheating kind and I believed him. Serial monogamy, one lover at a time, was his thing, and I was hoping I'd be the last installment!

"Where have you disappeared to?" Nina asked.

"I'm in love. Eric's wonderful. I think he's the one."

"You sound like you're in La-La Land."

"What's wrong with that?"

"You've only known him a month. Slow down, Sister!"

"I know what I'm doing."

"Famous last words."

"No. This time *is* different. I've been in therapy and I'm not that trusting girl anymore."

"We'll see. Where's Eric tonight?"

"He has a gig."

"How come you didn't go?"

"I worked all day at the health food store. Besides, I don't want to be a clingy musician's chick."

"I agree. What's happening with your song?"

"I don't know. I haven't heard from Rose."

"Are you sure? You haven't been picking up the phone."

"You're right. I better call her."

"Don't let yourself get swept up by a man and forget everything else."

"Okay, enough about me, what's happening with your professor? Did you sleep with him?"

"No. He was giving me mixed signals. Besides, I don't want to take any chances of screwing up my degree."

"That's smart! I guess we're both growing up!"

"Hopefully!"

We hung up and I sat thinking for a minute. Nina had my best interest at heart. She'd seen me go off the deep end for love before. I was impressed with her decision not to sleep with her professor. She didn't want to jeopardize her career, and she was warning me not to do it either.

I picked up the phone and dialed Rose.

"Where have you been? I've been calling and calling. I was starting to get worried!" Rose said.

"I'm sorry. I'm in love! Remember the guitar player at our session? It's him! He's the best!"

"What you say? That's great news, girl! I have good news too, that's why I've been calling. I got us an appointment a week from Friday at Sky Publishers. Meet me at my office at 1:30. They want to hear our song. It came out great!"

I was stunned. I couldn't believe this was actually happening! "I'm so excited! I'll be there! Thanks, Rose!"

I almost said *I can't wait to tell Eric*, but caught myself. This was the news I needed to get back on track with my music. Even so, I still couldn't wait to tell him. The truth was, success was sweeter when you had someone to share it with.

33
MIDDLE OF THE ROAD

I'm in the center of my life, a life that isn't yet defined.

There's a fork in the road, and it's really messing up my mind.

Not too young, not too old, not too shy, not too bold,

I'm in the middle of the road.

It was March 14th, exactly one month since Eric took me to Rouche's for our Valentine's date. I walked into Bruce's office for my usual Thursday night appointment and made a beeline for the couch. Bruce stopped me before I had the chance to lie down.

"You've reached another level of therapy, Carol. It's time to leave the couch."

It happened so quickly, I didn't know what to say. I took a seat in the chair facing him, but then looked away and stared out the window at the brick walls and fire escapes. I was putting up my own walls to protect myself from Bruce's penetrating gaze.

"How do you feel about not lying on the couch?" Bruce asked.

"I don't know. I guess surprised and a little uncomfortable."

"That's understandable. It's been a while since we sat face to face."

"Does this mean I'm doing better?"

"How do *you* think you're doing?"

This was the part of therapy that was maddening when Bruce wouldn't give me a direct answer and turned my question into a question. "I think I'm doing better. I haven't had a panic attack in a while and I can eat in restaurants."

"That's because you've worked hard to examine and release unconscious fears and emotions that you were carrying around from childhood."

"Does that mean I'm done?" A sense of fear came over me. True, since I'd met Eric, I'd stopped fantasizing about Bruce and accepted that my feelings for him could be a textbook case of patient-therapist transference. But not seeing him still seemed unimaginable. Bruce was my rock, my anchor, my dock, my grounding. I could fall in love, venture out of my safe harbor, dive into tumultuous relationships, but always, somehow, find my way back to shore, to my safe haven—to him.

"The goal of therapy *is* to leave, but I believe there are still some issues that need addressing."

"Like Eric?"

"Since you did your recording, Eric is all you talk about."

"Why are you questioning my feelings for him?" *Can't he just be happy for me? Is he jealous?*

"I'm not questioning your feelings, I'm questioning how quickly you fell for someone you know very little about."

"Well, at least I know his last name: Eric Portman. That's a start!" I said to break the tension. We both started laughing. "I know that sounds funny, but the mystery is part of the attraction."

"What else *do* you know about him? Has he told you about any of his past relationships?"

"No details and I don't want to know!"

"Why not?"

I didn't want to tell Bruce the real answer. I was afraid to hear about his ex-girlfriends because of my insecurities. Eric had told me that our relationship was different and I desperately wanted to believe him.

"I don't know. I guess I want to discover Eric on my own without any preconceived ideas."

"The best predictor of the future is the past."

"I don't want to put Eric under a microscope. We all have a past. I want to focus on the present."

"Touché! What's happening with your music?"

"Actually, I have an appointment with Rose at a publisher's tomorrow. They're gonna listen to our song."

I hated to admit it, but some of Bruce's observations about my relationship with Eric were right. When I got home, I decided not to see Eric that night, so I could get ready for my music appointment the next day. I was feeling a little scared as I dialed his number.

"Hi, darling. I'm just finishing practicing. I can be over in about an hour," Eric said.

"That's what I wanted to talk to you about. Tomorrow's my appointment with Sky Publishers and I think I need some time to myself tonight to get ready. Do you mind?"

"No, but what's the big deal?"

"To *me*, it's a big deal. I just wanna make sure I get a good night's sleep. I'll make it up to you tomorrow night, I promise."

"Okay, baby, but I could make you feel nice and relaxed tonight."

"It's tempting, but I better not."

"I guess I'll see you after my gig tomorrow night? It might be kinda late."

"That's okay. Love you! Wish me luck!"

I thought Eric would be a lot cooler with me not seeing him for one night. Turned out, Eric was a Taurus, not a mysterious Scorpio. I knew Tauruses could be stubborn and set in their ways. Maybe that should've been a red flag because I'd already gotten my heart broken by two Tauruses. Michael, my first love, had left me for another woman and so had Joshua.

On the other hand, maybe Eric was protesting so much because he loved me more than I ever realized. I tried putting him out of my mind, as I searched my bedroom closet for the perfect outfit to wear for my big meeting.

Instead of sleeping better, I woke up in the middle of the night from a terrible nightmare. I dreamt I was in the basement of my parents' house, but I was much older. I'd found a cardboard box with a photo album inside. In it were yellowed newspaper clippings. One read: "Carol Marks, songwriter, makes her mark tonight at the Bitter End." Above it was a headshot taken of me from one of those walk-in studios on Eighth Avenue. At the bottom of the box was a black rectangular case with a microphone in it. The mic had red lipstick stains.

The next scene was me, middle-aged, in an elementary school classroom, sitting at a piano in front of the room wearing a tweed skirt, white blouse, sensible shoes, and wire-rimmed glasses.

I woke up in a panic. *Wire-rimmed glasses and penny loafers?* My dream felt like a *Twilight Zone* episode, showing me what life *could* be like twenty years from now if I didn't take those risks, go on that audition, practice that song, meet those people who want only the best, get to the front of the line, use my energy to get to the top before my dreams faded like the freckles on my face.

Squinting in the mirror, I was relieved to see my twenty-two-year-old self staring back, bleary-eyed. The dream was a warning. I was being pulled in both directions and I needed to make the right choices. I fumbled for the pad and pen on the nightstand that Rose had advised me to keep by the bed. "Some of my best song ideas come to me when I'm half awake. It's like the songs are being channeled through me," she'd told me.

I paused a moment, pen in hand, took a deep breath, and quickly started writing.

I'm in the middle of the road, wonderin' which way to go.

I've learned a lot, but there's still so much I don't know.

Standing on the white line, waiting for the light to turn green,

Leaving my old fears behind.

I'm at the point of no return, I've got to decide where to go.

I'm in the middle of the road.

34
MUSIC BIZ

I keep tellin' ya, I think it's gonna work out fine.
I know it's gonna work out fine.
It's got to work, to work out fine.

I woke up with a start. Eleven thirty? How did that happen? The lyrics I'd scribbled in the middle of the night were lying on the nightstand. *Middle of the Road—not bad,* I thought as I read them over. I wanted to show them to Rose, but not today. Today was all about one song—"Let Me Bring Out the Animal in You." If it went well at Sky Publishers, that would be my go-ahead sign. I'd be on the path to becoming a real songwriter, not just a wannabe. And maybe my dad would get off my back and not make me get my teaching degree!

I was too nervous to eat much. Breakfast was never my thing, anyway. I made myself my usual cup of Taster's Choice and put a Pop-Tart in the toaster. Katie wouldn't approve, but I'd run out of granola bars. Besides, I needed the sugar rush this morning.

I picked out the same lucky outfit I'd worn to my first voice lesson: knee-length denim skirt, black tights, boots, ribbed beige sweater, Dylan cap. I felt confident until I looked down at my nails. What a mess! The polish was chipped and uneven. I'd forgotten to paint them, but now it was too late. Even though I couldn't afford professional manicures, I'd always taken pride in the way my hands looked. Maybe it was a Gemini thing since Gemini ruled hands. I grabbed a bottle of pink nail polish and stuck it in the pocket of my pea coat thinking I could touch up my nails in the cab ride to our meeting.

I rushed down the stairs and was already at the curb before I realized I'd forgotten the extra lyric sheets Rose wanted me to bring. I turned around and ran back up the stairs. My face was starting to flush. *Bummer! This is starting out really bad,* I thought.

I hurried to Rose's office, almost out of breath, dodging pedestrians along the way on Central Park West. As I approached Columbus Circle, totally stressed out, Eric suddenly popped into my head. *Why didn't I hear from him?* I wondered. *Why didn't he call to wish me luck? Was he mad because we didn't spend the night together?* I pushed those negative thoughts to the back of my mind. *This is no time to let a man get in the way,* I told myself crossing Broadway. In the middle of the street, my nerves got the better of me and I could feel my legs wobbling. *No, not today. I've come too far to have an anxiety attack.* I took a deep breath and heard Bruce's voice in my head, *"You're stronger than you think, Carol."*

I flew into Rose's office ten minutes late, looking disheveled.

"Keep it together, girl!" Rose kindly said. She was wearing the same outfit she had worn the day I met her, right down to her alligator belt and brown high-heeled boots. Maybe that was her lucky outfit too.

"Sorry I'm late. I overslept. I'll have to polish my nails in the cab." I looked down at my hands and made a face.

"Music people don't care about things like that! It's all about the songs."

"Yeah, you're right. But I still want to do my nails."

Rose gave me one of her looks. "You got the lyric sheets?"

I nodded.

"Come on, then," she said, "Let's get this show on the road."

In the cab to 34th and Madison, Rose turned to me and her little girl voice took on a motherly tone. "It's positive that we got an appointment, but I don't want you to get your hopes up, Carol. It's not like the 1950s when singers needed songwriters. Back then, publishers would take anything me and my writing partners wrote."

"Yeah, it must've been so exciting!"

"It was. I'm not saying it's impossible to get a song published now. Just a lot harder."

I sunk back into my seat and let out a sigh. "You know, Rose, no matter what happens today, I'll always be happy I met you. I can't tell you how much it means that you chose me as your writing partner and you're giving me a shot."

Rose reached over and touched my arm. "You've got it, girl," she smiled. "We wrote a *great* song, and it's gonna be a smash! If this publisher doesn't like it, don't worry. One monkey don't stop no show."

We walked into the shiny, marble-floored lobby of 701 Madison Ave. at exactly 2:00. A stylishly dressed young woman at the desk in the lobby asked us who we were seeing. "We have a two o'clock at Sky Publishers," Rose confidently informed her. The receptionist made a quick call. "Mr. Deutch is expecting you. Suite 3302," she said and pointed to the elevator. Of course, she had a perfect manicure. I dug my hands deep into my coat pockets as we rode to the 33rd floor.

"Remember Carol, it's not about your damn nails!" Rose declared and we both burst out laughing. For me, it was a much-needed release.

We sat without talking in a small waiting room stocked with *Billboard* and *Rolling Stone* magazines. I futzed with my hair a little, trying to smooth it down with my hands, and calm myself. Rose had told me we'd be meeting with the son of the original publisher.

After a few minutes, a handsome, thirty-something guy wearing bell-bottom grey pants, not jeans, an electric blue tailored shirt, and a Peter Max paisley print tie came out to greet us.

"Rose! It's so good to see you!" he said, hugging her.

"Wayne, this is my new writing partner, Carol Marks. Carol, this is Wayne Deutch."

"Nice to meet you, Carol. Rose is a living legend in the publishing world. My father thought very highly of her," he said as we followed him back to his office. Wayne motioned us to a black leather couch, then sat behind a large modern desk that was strategically positioned in front of a whole wall of framed gold records. I couldn't make out the title of the songs, but the sheer number was impressive.

"What've you got for me?" Wayne asked.

"'Let Me Bring Out the Animal in You.' This little girl came up with the title." Rose loved telling people that. She handed him the demo tape and the lyrics.

Rose had warned me not to say anything while the publisher was listening to our song. It sounded impressive, coming through the expensive stereo speakers. I worked at keeping a stone face and stared down at the black and white shag rug. *Please, please like it!* I prayed.

Halfway through the song, Wayne stopped the tape recorder. I glanced at Rose, but I couldn't read her. She was still staring straight ahead with a serious look on her face.

After about a minute, that felt like an eternity, Wayne slowly smiled and said, "Hmmmm. It's different," he nodded, his eyes half-closed as if he were thinking, or maybe hearing it in his head. "I might have a movie that I could place it in. Let's give it a try."

A movie? A movie! My song could be in a movie!

I looked over at Rose again. She gave me a wink that said "We did it, girl!" To Wayne, she said, "Sounds good. But can we split the publishing?"

"I don't usually do that," Wayne said. He waited a moment and stared down at his desk. I felt myself holding my breath. Then he looked up. "Why not?" he said. "For you, Rose, anything."

We all stood up and shook hands. I tried my best to keep from looking as giddy as I felt as Wayne escorted us out. "I'll have my secretary draw up the papers as soon as possible," he said. But what I heard was, "You did it! And you're not going back to school anytime soon!"

"This is great news!" Rose declared in the elevator. "Let's go to Beefsteak Charlie's and celebrate! It's just around the corner from my office."

"Yeah!" I said. "Let's celebrate!"

Rose led me through the dimly lit dining room to a table in the back by the payphone. My eyes were still adjusting as I slid across the well-worn leather booth, and looked across at Rose. Her face was glowing. "This is where me and Charlie Singleton met every morning," she said, talking fast. "This was our corner. We'd order a cheap glass of wine and write until about the middle of the afternoon, and then things would start hopping."

"That really must've been something. I wish I'd known you then," I said.

"Yeah, I wish you coulda been there. The biggest publishers would come by to hear our songs. We'd sing our songs to them without any instruments and they'd tell us to go make a demo. Just like that, we were selling our songs! Then Charlie would say, 'You can order steak now.' Once a publisher came in and bought six songs for $80 a song. We never cared about royalties back then. We just took the advances."

"Wow! That must've been amazing!"

Rose got a bit of a far-away look. "You know those two Elvis songs 'I Beg of You' and 'Trying to Get to You'? We wrote them right here. Me and Charlie Singleton. We wrote a bunch of other hits in this booth, too. When we knew we had a good song, Charlie would roll a few pencils on the table back and forth until the publisher came up with a better offer. It worked every time!"

Sitting in the spot where so much history was made, I felt so overwhelmed I didn't know what to say. I sat there feeling the vibes, absorbing them, all the time wishing I'd known Rose back in the day. Before the red and blue patterned carpet had faded and the red leather booths were ripped. Before there were cigarette burns on the tables. When the music business was hopping—- taking chances on new talent, new sounds, new songs, and turning out hits from songwriters who kept court at the corner bar.

"Yeah, it was a gas!" Rose leaned back in the booth and smiled at me. "But you know what, Carol? This is a gas, too. It's your turn now. You've got the *new* sound."

"Let's have a glass of wine!" I said, already feeling a little high.

"What you say, girl. Today you and I have something to celebrate! It's on me!"

35
JUST GONNA THINK ABOUT TODAY

Nothing's for certain, that's for certain.
World's spinning fast some people say. That's okay.
I'm not gonna think about tomorrow, gonna keep on singing.
Just gonna think about today.

Some changes are subtle and you look forward to them, like the faint smell of spring in the air when flowers are promising to bloom. It was the last week in May and I was busy planting my own seeds. I was writing with Rose, taking voice lessons, working my day job, and seeing Bruce. At the end of the day, coming home to Eric in my bed was the icing on the cake. We'd lasted over three months, a relationship milestone for me. Eric still had his apartment, mostly to store his music equipment, but for all practical purposes, we were living together. It felt like we were putting down roots.

"Can you teach me how to sing?" Eric asked one lazy Sunday morning as we lay in bed, my head on his infuriatingly flat stomach. I sat up and straddled him.

"Cool. I'll teach you what I know," I eagerly answered, my flimsy nightgown strap falling down one shoulder. He got distracted and kissed my wayward breast.

"You're doing so well with your guitar! Why do you want to sing?" I asked.

"Never mind. Forget it. Let me teach you what *I* know!" What he knew was how to get my nightgown off in record time. Between fits of laughter, he rolled me on my back, and our lazy Sunday morning turned into a sizzling Sunday afternoon.

Later I wondered why he changed his mind about wanting me to teach him how to sing. Maybe his ego couldn't handle me doing something better than he did. In any case, if I was honest with myself, I had so much going on with *my* music that I was relieved.

I was preparing for an open call audition for a new Broadway play I'd seen listed in the *Village Voice.* They called it a "rock opera," *Jesus Christ Superstar.* I chose Mary Magdalene's "I Don't Know How to Love Him," a powerful ballad about unrequited love. Every time I sang it, it brought up the old feelings I'd had for Bruce before I'd met Eric. Now those feelings seemed like just a classic case of transference.

On the morning of the audition, I felt confident and prepared. I'd worked on my song with Maxine during my voice lessons and rehearsed it every day on my own for the last two weeks. It was unusually hot for May, so I put on a lightweight peasant blouse, a long, white gauze skirt, and sandals. By the time I got to the Mark Hellinger Theater, the line had swung around 51st Street and two blocks down Eighth Ave. I checked out the competition as I took my place in line. Some of the long-haired bearded guys really did look like Jesus, and the rest of us looked like hippies auditioning for the cast of *Hair*—a colorful collage of tie-dyed shirts, Indian beads, feathers, scarves, and peace signs.

As the line moved within one block of the theater, I studied the lyrics on my music sheet—extra insurance in case my nerves got the better of me. I could already feel my legs wobbling, so I closed my eyes and tried picturing a peaceful country scene. But my daydream was shattered by the sounds of drills and hammers coming from the construction site across the street. The midday sun was burning down and sweat started dripping off the back of my neck. Thinking I'd put my hair up, I was rummaging through my shoulder bag for an elastic band, when shouting erupted from the other side of the street. "You're nothin' but freaks! Dirty hippies! Get a real job!" Half a dozen workers had put down their tools and gathered at the edge of the construction site.

As if on cue, a lone female voice rose from the crowd, belting out the opening line from the theme song of *Hair*. As she continued to sing, strong, and clear, I found myself spontaneously joining in. Others did too, swelling the song, as the singing rose and rippled through the line in a wave of peace and understanding. The effect was exhilarating. We were all caught up in the message of harmony, but it was really a "fuck you!" to the angry guys across the street.

The louder we sang, the louder the hardhats yelled. If they crossed the street, if it turned into a mob scene, I'd be right in the middle of it. My mind flashed back to the chaos of the day I was caught up in the violence of the anti-war protest in Washington—the sickening crack as a club hit a protester's skull and the splatter of blood as he went down right in front of me. What if the hardhats started throwing bricks? We were all sitting ducks. No one was going to lose their place in line and blow their chance to be on Broadway. No one, except for—me?

It would be at least another hour before my turn to audition. Was it worth the risk? The singing had died out, and the vibes in the line were turning tense and ugly like the vibes across the street. Even if I got the part, was this what I truly wanted? I pictured myself in the cool, dark theater— walking on stage, announcing my name, singing a song that the big-shot directors had heard a hundred times. *Was it worth putting myself through that? Was it worth another hour of this tension in the brutal heat, for a job that I truly didn't want to do? No!* I walked out of the line, found the closest air-conditioned coffee shop, sat at the counter, and splurged on a hamburger and a big, icy coke.

Bruce had helped me realize that I was impulsive. Sometimes it worked in my favor, and other times not so much, like when I showed up at Robbie's commune in Virginia. But this time I knew I'd made the right decision. If *I really* wanted to be on Broadway, I'd have taken the risk and soldiered through the line. But it wasn't my dream. Being a recording artist was. Bailing out of the audition might seem flaky to someone else, but I was fine with it. I was being true to myself.

That night, I was looking forward to telling Eric about my decision and everything that had happened, but before I got the chance, he greeted me with news of his own. He walked into the apartment with a big smile on his face, gave me a bear hug, and led me to the couch.

"Carol, you know that band I've been subbing with? Well, they told me their regular guitar player is still having problems, and they want me to go on tour with them!"

My stomach sank and my heart started to race. "Really? For how long?" I managed to ask, faking a smile.

"Just three weeks. We'll be opening for some big acts! I'll be playing in Boston, Chicago, and a bunch of other cities. I didn't get the schedule yet." I was speechless. All I could think of was how lonely I was going to be.

"What's the matter, babe?" Eric asked.

Groupies. There were always groupies hanging around bands. I pictured them circling the stage door like lionesses hungry for prey.

"I'm happy for you, but three weeks is a long time."

"Don't worry. Come here. You know how I feel about you," he said, gently pulling me towards him. "I told you from the start that I was on the road a lot."

"I know, but I'm gonna miss you."

"I'm gonna miss you, too. It'll go fast."

"But what if the tour gets extended and you get tempted?"

"That's not gonna happen. You know I'm a one-woman man and you're the one."

Nothing I could say would stop Eric from going. Our relationship was getting tested and I didn't want to be the clingy chick who couldn't live without her man for a few weeks. *Work on your own music,* I told myself. *Keep it together.*

The next day I got a letter from Mona. It was like a sign from the universe. She'd called me after the bust to say she was *not* standing by her man. She was getting out of Dodge. Jeffrey Sachs was going to prison for a very long time and she was moving to Los Angeles.

"I was very impressed with your music, Carol," she wrote. "If I connect with anyone in the music business in LA, I'd like to help you."

Mona's letter was just the boost I needed. I was gonna concentrate double hard on my music. The time without Eric *would* go fast. I had a career, too. He was so wrapped up in his own music trip that he never even asked how my Broadway audition went. He'd never asked what happened with my demo either, and I hadn't brought it up. I had to make him realize *I* had some heavy-duty opportunities, too. We *both* needed to support each other's dreams. It wouldn't always be easy, a career, and a man, but I was determined to have my cake and eat it too—especially the icing!

36
STORM CLOUDS

And if the future is in question,
Won't waste my time, looking for the rain.
The sun will break through somehow.
It's shining here and now . . .

Some changes are shocking and unexpected, whether good or bad. They come out of the calm blue skies and shake you up like a windstorm, leaving you changed forever. Eric had been gone a little over a week, and just as I predicted I was feeling lonely. What I hadn't predicted was how hard it was to do my music. I asked Nina to hang out with me on Sunday, knowing she'd help get me back on track. Nina was one of the strongest women I knew. Fiercely independent, in just ten months, she'd transformed herself into a true New Yorker. She walked fast, never looked anyone in the eyes, and had the entire subway system memorized.

"Wait up, I can't go that fast!" I yelled as we practically jogged the half block to the park. It was a perfect Sunday: kids on skateboards and bikes, lovers on blankets, and the sweet smell of magnolias mixing with the pungent scent of marijuana. How could I feel depressed on a spring day like this?

"You need to catch up and get some *real* exercise!" Nina called back over her shoulder.

"Yeah? I do my favorite exercise in bed," I answered sprawling down on the nearest park bench. "I just read that a half-hour of sex burns off about 200 calories."

"Not if you're just lying there and letting him do all the work."

"You've got a point!" We both started laughing. "What's happening with *your* sex life?"

"Nothing to report. Too busy studying. But after I get my degree I'm gonna do some serious traveling."

"*Ooh*—looking for more exotic men?"

"Yeah, but I'm not going for that. I want to see the world before I commit."

"I wish I could be like you, but I miss Eric!"

Nina rolled her eyes like she always did when she thought I was going overboard about a man. Going from playful to serious, she turned to me and let loose.

"I'm gonna save you a ton of time and money. You don't need therapy and you don't need Eric. Your parents did a number on you, especially your father. They made you think that finding a man and getting married was the most important thing in life."

"Then why did they keep saying I needed to be independent?"

"I don't know, but up to now, they've been placating you about your music. They just see it as a little hobby and distraction that will go away when you meet the Right One."

"What if I've already met him?"

"Their idea of Mr. Right isn't a musician. They want you to be with a "Somebody"—a lawyer, doctor, business guy—someone rich. And the only job they want *you* to have is wife and mother. Or, if you *have* to work, teacher."

Nina knew me better than anyone, and I knew she was right. Still, it was hard to hear. I sat glued to the bench, my mouth tightly shut. She was talking so fast it was pointless to say anything until she'd finished. I tilted my head back, closed my eyes, and felt the warmth of the sun on my face. I needed time to take in Nina's words. After a minute of welcome silence, it was my turn to talk.

"You can't just wave a magic wand and tell me to change. Bruce *has* been helping me and I *am* more independent. But Eric is the real deal! I'm in love with him."

Nina jumped up from the bench. "So you're obsessed with Eric? What about your music? Why aren't you obsessed with that?"

"I don't know, Smarty Pants, why don't *you* tell *me* why I can't stop thinking about him!"

"Well, at least he's not a lawyer!" Nina joked and we both broke out laughing.

"If you mean Marvin, he's taken. He wrote to me a few weeks ago that he was in love and staying in California. If I want to keep the apartment, he'll put my name on the lease!"

"Far out! Seriously, Carol, show your parents that you *can* make it without them, or a man, or even Bruce. You can do it, you have a lot going for you."

"I know, but– "

"But you're hung-up on Eric. When are you going to realize how amazing *you* are? In less than a year, you've been writing with a famous songwriter, got your song accepted by a publisher, and now you're gonna get your very own apartment! Live your *own* dreams, Carol!"

"Boy, you really tell it like it is! But, that's why I love you," I said as I gave her a quick hug.

On the way home I stopped at the corner newsstand to buy the *Village Voice*. I wanted to check out club listings showcasing unsigned artists. *The Voice* had brought me many lucky connections: the pop-rock band in Brooklyn, my voice teacher, and what started it all, Marvin and the apartment. If I hadn't been reading *The Voice* on the corner of 72nd Street, he'd never have known I was looking for a place. Now his apartment was gonna be mine. I was on the other side of the Lincoln Tunnel and in the fast lane to becoming an official New Yorker.

That night the phone rang at 1:30, waking me from a deep sleep. I knew who it was before I picked up the receiver.

"Hi, Baby. Sorry if I woke you. Just got back to the motel. I wish you were here. I really miss you."

"Me too! How's it going?"

"It's going great! Big crowds. We're opening for Grand Funk Railroad!"

"That's so cool! Someday they'll be opening up for *you*! I can't wait to see you!"

"I'll be home in about a week and a half. I've got something I want to ask you when I get back."

"I can't wait that long! What is it? Good or bad?"

Eric chuckled. "Don't worry, Babe, it's all good! It's about our future. I'll ask you when I see you. The time will go fast."

"But can't you at least give me a hint?" I asked in my most flirtatious voice. I was starting to feel turned on.

"No," he said with a little laugh. "It's something I have to do in person," Eric teased, picking up on my sexual excitement.

His words went through me like a lightning bolt.

"Okay," I sighed. "I guess I'll have to wait. "

"You won't be sorry."

"Miss you!"

"I miss you too!"

My mind was racing so fast I couldn't fall back to sleep. Could Eric be asking The Question? The "Will you marry me, I can't live without you" question? I was feeling so many emotions—love, fear, happiness. I wanted to call Nina, but it was too late, even for her. *Thank god I'm seeing Bruce tomorrow!* I thought. *Maybe he'll calm me down.*

I felt myself blushing as I sailed into Bruce's office. I'd had two hours of sleep and a full day at the health food store, and was still flying high. He immediately picked up on my mood but waited for me to speak first.

"I've got some big news!" I announced.

"You look happy about it."

"Eric called me from Boston last night. I think he's going to propose!" I blurted out.

"What makes you think that? Did he ask you to marry him on the phone?"

"No. But he said he missed me and had something important to ask about our future. What else could it be?"

"I don't know. How would you answer if he asked? You've only known him for three months."

"My answer is *yes*! I love him!" I smiled at Bruce, but the look on his face told me he didn't approve. I was so excited about the possibility of marrying Eric, I didn't care.

"Do you really think you're ready for marriage? What about your music career?" Bruce asked, leaning toward me, looking concerned.

"Eric's a musician. He understands." Nothing Bruce said was gonna change the way I felt. I knew what I wanted and that was to be Mrs. Eric Portman. *Carol Portman, that sounded great!*

"What about your work here?" Bruce pressed on.

"Maybe I'll be so happy I won't need therapy."

"We'll see. For now, let's just take it one step at a time."

By the time I got home, I was coming down from my high and looking forward to crashing. I opened my mailbox in the entranceway, expecting nothing but bills and takeout menus. That's when I saw the elegant eggshell envelope with the LA return address from Mona. *More good news?* I wondered as I raced up the stairs. *Of course! It's May 21st!* I realized. *The sun's just gone into Gemini! This is my lucky time!* I walked into my apartment, plopped on the couch, and tore open Mona's letter. I was blown away by the stationery—Hyako Music Company, Sunset Boulevard.

Hi Carol,

Great News! I'm working for a music publishing and artist management company. We have a lot of money behind us and are interested in finding people to publish. You know how strongly I feel about your talent. I sure would like another demo tape. I've met people out here who could help you if they like it. Have you heard of Jackson Browne? His single is number eight in the nation now. . . the label is called Asylum and the manager is David Geffen.

From what I remember about your material, you have an incredible voice and talent for writing I, personally, am not interested in the money-making end of it. If I can help, that's plenty for me.

I'm living with a wonderful guy and if things keep going well, we will be married this summer or fall. If you come out here, you can stay with me until you get yourself situated.

Anyway, I guess I better go. Please send the tape as soon as it's finished and keep in touch.

Love,

Mona

I was floored! It *was* my time! "Things come in waves. When they're bad, they're really bad, but when they're good they're really good!" Bruce had once said. My life was finally coming together. I wanted to dance around the room but was too tired. I crawled into bed, put Mona's letter on the night table, and crashed.

37
I'M A WOMAN

Hello my friend, I'd like to make a confession.
I think I've given you the wrong impression of me
I'm not the girl that I pretend to be
I've not yet given up my childhood fantasy…

Eric called around eleven o'clock Sunday night from a rest stop some-where in Ohio to tell me he'd be back a day early. The band manager was saving money by traveling through the night. Eric would go back to his place, crash, and call me the next day, which was Memorial Day. The health food store would be closed and we'd have the entire day together.

I drank a cup of Sleepy Time tea and tried falling back to sleep but my mind was racing. Tomorrow could change my life forever! I tossed and turned, *Sadie, Sadie, Married Lady* running through my mind.

I thought about my strong women friends like Dani, who'd helped me write "Chained and Tamed Women's Blues." Dani was married, but she didn't let her marital status define her. She'd kept her own last name and called herself Ms., not Mrs. She was ambitious, working on her doctorate in education and teaching a women's studies class at Douglass College.

Dani had called a few weeks ago to see if we could get together for dinner when she was in town, attending a Women's Conference at NYU. I had to work at the store and told her I'd never make it downtown in time. I still wasn't able to take the subway by myself although I did manage to ride it with Eric once or twice. Dani, still her old perceptive self, picked up on my feelings of insecurity, surprising me when she said, "You're a strong woman, Carol. You can belt out a song! Someday your life will match the strength of your voice. Live your songs, Carol, live your songs!"

Dani wasn't the first person to tell me that my breathy speaking voice didn't match my blues mama belting voice. I knew my strength was expressed in my singing, but I hadn't yet figured out how to integrate it into my everyday life. I lay there thinking about all this for a long time and finally forced myself to shut my brain off. I needed to wake up refreshed. What if Eric were to see me with bags under my eyes!

The next morning I was coming out of the shower when I heard Eric's key turn in the door. I quickly put on my nightgown and glanced at the clock. Only 10:30—had he slept at all? I was so excited to see him I practically threw myself into his arms.

"*Ooh, Baby,*" he whispered in my ear as he held me close.

I bent backward, his arms still tightly holding my waist, and looked up at his sweet face. "You grew a beard and mustache! I like it! It brings out your eyes."

"Yeah, it's easier when you're on the road. I'm not gonna let it get too long. What's under that bathrobe?"

"Has it been that long?" I teased, as Eric led me into the bedroom. "If you try some new moves on me, I'm gonna wonder who taught you them!" I said, only half-joking.

"Not even tempted, *ma chérie*!"

The last thing on my mind as we made love was how many calories I was burning off. I was under and over him, head to head, head to toe. No move was off-limits until we were satisfied and we'd exhausted all possible paths to pleasure. Eric fell asleep immediately, and I tiptoed into the kitchen to get a glass of water. That's when I noticed the paper bag he'd put on the coffee table. I was dying to peek inside but didn't dare ruin the surprise. Somewhere in there must be the gift I was hoping for.

There was no telling when Eric would wake up. I tried distracting myself by opening the piano bench and going through an old notebook with lyrics I was inspired to write the morning after I lost my virginity in a seedy motel on the outskirts of Berkeley to a guy called Richard, whose last name I never knew.

I'm a woman and I need lovin
And I need someone to ease the pain
Of being a woman and needin' lovin
And the man I'm lovin's got to feel the same.

The next morning as he drove me home, Richard confessed he was engaged to a woman back East, but I didn't care. I'd crossed over to womanhood. Richard was just a means to an end. Not until later that day did I start to feel hollow and sad, wondering what it would be like to actually make love.

"I'm a Woman." That was the name of the song. It was about a woman still believing in true love and Prince Charming. I'd never sung it for anyone and I wouldn't dare sing it for Dani or Nina. I'd read Betty Friedan. I'd read Gloria Steinem. And still, I felt conflicted, sandwiched between the Women's Movement and Disney fairytales. Sexual liberation vs chastity, career vs family, sisterhood vs motherhood. Did I have to give up love to be liberated?

I've not yet given up my childhood fantasy
Of what I think my true love should be.
Cause I'm a woman and I need lovin
And the man I'm lovin's got to feel the same.

"Hey, Sexy."

I looked up and saw Eric staggering towards me, eyes half-closed, hair unbrushed, t-shirt inside out, and sexy as hell. He kissed the base of my neck and took my hand.

"Come here. I've got something for you."

"Is this the surprise you promised me?"

"It is, Babe!" Eric opened the bag and handed me a beautiful hand-painted pastel blue and yellow box. The word *Paris* was subtly painted in fancy letters on the front of it.

"Open it. It's about our future."

"It is?" I asked, praying there would be a ring inside. I opened the lid and found a plane ticket to Paris. *What? Were we eloping to Paris?* I was speechless for reasons that Eric could never figure out.

"We're going to Paris!" he shouted, drawing me into his arms. "June 10th!"

"Wow! I don't know what to say! What's happening?" I asked, wriggling out of his arms.

"The band's going on tour to Europe for four months! They said we could bring our girlfriends! Don't you see, we'll be living our dream, Carol! It's all coming together, Babe!"

For Eric, it was all coming together, but I was completely coming apart. How could I have been so naïve to think he was going to propose? What should I do now? Leave New York and put my life on hold for four months? How could I do that? But how could I say no and burst his bubble?

"Phew! June 10th. That's only two weeks from now."

"But you've got your passport, right? I remember you telling me you got one in college in case the revolution came and you had to leave the country," Eric said, half kidding, but he had a worried look. "It's our dream, babe. We're going to Paris. The most romantic place in the world! What's wrong?"

"What about all the other places you'll be touring?"

"London, Amsterdam, Rome—what's wrong with that? Don't you wanna see the world? And Paris will be our main location. We can even sublet if you want to stay!"

Eric had obviously given this a lot of thought. I should have been flattered, but I was too upset to feel anything but panic.

"What's the *matter*, Carol? I thought you'd be happy. Isn't this what we always wanted?"

"*I don't know what I want!*" I ran into the bedroom, slammed the door, and threw myself on the bed in tears. Just when things were going so well! Was it the three-month curse? I *did* love him, but was I willing to put *my* dreams on hold? What about *my* music? Did Eric just see me as his groupie?

I dialed Bruce and set up an emergency appointment. I needed him to help me sort things out. I paced up and down the bedroom and took some deep breaths until I calmed myself down, Then I fixed my make-up, combed my hair, and walked into the living room. Eric was still sitting on the couch looking serious and pale.

I sat down beside him, took both his hands in mine, and looked into his eyes. "You know I love you, but I need a few days to think about all this," I said softly.

"Don't wait too long. I've got to tell the band by the end of the week. You know how much I care about you, Carol. This could be a once-in-a-lifetime opportunity!"

He sounded hurt, and his face softened. The only other times I'd seen him looking so vulnerable was when we were making love. That night our love-making was intense and passionate—our bodies saying what we didn't dare say out loud. Eric was desperately trying to show his feelings for me, and I was desperately trying to hold onto mine.

38
PRINCE CHARMING

And now, my friend, I'm glad you took the time to listen.
Understand, for twenty years I've been conditioned to believe
That my Prince Charming really would appear—
And it's so hard to conquer twenty years of fear,
To stand alone and have my vision clear.

It didn't take a degree in psychology to figure out what had happened between me and Eric. I was dressed in all black—black sweatshirt, black jeans, and black glasses to hide my bloodshot eyes. I walked into Bruce's office, grabbed the tissue box by the side table, and began to cry.

"What's going on, Carol?" Bruce asked softly.

"Eric wants me to go on tour with him to Europe for four months," I stammered between sobs. "That's what the big surprise was. A plane ticket to Paris, not a ring."

"You must be very disappointed. What did you tell him?"

"I said I needed time to think about it, but he has to let the band know in a week. The ticket is for June 10th!"

"Could you go to Paris for a shorter visit? Four months *is* a long time."

"I don't know. He was so excited about the trip that he seemed surprised when I told him I needed to think about it," I answered, wiping my eyes.

"Have you thought about the practical details involved in taking off for four months?"

"Not really, I've been too upset."

"What's happening with your apartment? Have you heard from Marvin?"

"Yeah, he's staying in California. If I want to, I can keep the apartment."

"You *do* have a lot to consider. Give yourself credit, Carol. The fact that you didn't say yes right away shows a great deal of maturity. I don't think you would have reacted like this a year ago."

"Aren't you gonna say *I told you so?*" I asked in a bratty voice.

"No. I can see you're in a lot of pain."

"I'm sorry. I shouldn't have said that. I know you're not like that."

"I think you'll make the right decision. Let's talk about it more at your regular time on Thursday."

When I got home I called Eric and told him I needed to be alone to figure things out. He sounded down and a little angry.

"Okay Carol, but I don't get what there is to think about—Paris, love, music. It seems like a no-brainer to me."

I promised I'd see him the following night. I wanted to call Nina, but I was in such a daze that I just plopped on the bed. My mind was going in a million directions. No way was I gonna fall asleep. I spotted Mona's letter on the nightstand and picked it up. It blew my mind all over again. Someone with real connections believed in my talent and wanted to help me. I wondered what Eric would think about Mona's offer. How would *he* feel if I told him that *I* was going to LA for four months and wanted *him* to go with *me* and drop everything?

My thoughts turned to my last conversation with Rose. She'd called to suggest I join ASCAP and asked me to come to her office to sign the song contract. "It looks good, Carol. Things are starting to heat up. Promise me you won't do something foolish like running off with that cute guitar player! I've known plenty of smart women in the music business, even big stars, who did dumb things when it came to men."

Rose was teasing me and warning me at the same time. How could she have known? Was she psychic? Why did life have to be so complicated? Had Eric just been a diversion? Or a way for me to sabotage my road to success?

The next morning I called in sick. I told Katie I had a bad cold and needed at least two days to recuperate. My voice must have sounded hoarse from all the crying because she readily agreed. Over the year I'd worked at the health food store, Katie and I'd grown closer, but were not quite friends. She kept things professional, but we did share confidences. She'd recently told me her husband was pressuring her to have a baby, and he was upset because she wanted to wait. I agreed with Katie. How could she have a baby and manage a store? Or worse, quit her job and scrounge for diaper money on her husband's meager intern salary? Lately, it seemed that male-female stereotypes were upside down. Men were acting more impulsively and women were making wise decisions. If only I knew what *I* wanted!

I rolled over to Eric's side of the bed, closed my eyes, and replayed our lovemaking. I could still smell the faint scent of Herbal Essence shampoo on the pillow. I'd teased him about using a girls' brand, but he just laughed it off and said an old girlfriend had turned him on to it and he liked how it smelled. He wouldn't say anything more about her, but I pictured her with long wavy hair with flowers in it like the woman on the shampoo bottle. I was glad he didn't give me the details. I was insecure enough as it was.

I couldn't wait until evening to see Eric, so I called him after I'd showered and drunk my second cup of coffee.

"Hi Baby, are you at work?"

"No, I told Katie I had a cold. All I can think about is you and what's gonna happen with us."

"You want me to come over?"

"Yeah."

"I'll be there in an hour."

I wiggled into the tightest jeans I could find and put on my sexiest black t-shirt. I covered the black circles under my eyes with concealer and put on some light pink lipstick to make my lips look pouty. I paced around a while, then walked over to the piano. I'd just played the first chords of Carole King's *So Far Away* when Eric walked in. He looked tired and sad, the opposite of how he'd bounced into the apartment just two days ago, all excited to see me and bursting with news.

"You didn't sleep either?" I asked as he hugged me.

"Yeah, I was beyond surprised by your reaction. I thought you'd be flying high."

"What if I just went to Paris with you for a couple of weeks?"

"I don't know."

"It's just that I have a life too, and I can't just up and leave it. I'm not like those other musicians' chicks. Besides, their boyfriends are probably supporting them."

"Is that what it's about? Money?"

"No, I don't want your money, but I do have to pay the rent."

"I know Carol, but four months is an awfully long time for me to be without you or . . ."—he hesitated for a minute—"someone."

I tried to hide my shock. *Did I hear him right? Is he saying that he can't be without a woman and that she doesn't have to be me? Am I that replaceable?*

"You're saying you couldn't go without sex for four months? I *actually* thought you were going to propose to me when you got back from the tour! What a fool I've been!"

Now it was Eric's turn to be shocked. "Whoa! Now it all makes sense. *That's* why you looked so disappointed when you opened the box. You thought the ticket was gonna be a ring!"

"Obviously, I was way wrong."

"I love you, but *marriage*? I can't change my life for you, Carol. I thought we had something real and you got what I was about."

"I thought so too. And *I* thought you got what I was about."

We sat huddled on the couch for a few minutes. Then Eric turned to me and held both my hands. "I love you, Carol, but our lives are going in different directions. Let's not make this any more painful. I'll just pack up my things." He reached over and tenderly wiped away the tears from my cheeks.

"I'm sorry. I really wanted it to work," I said shakily, trying to keep it together. Eric opened his mouth as if he were going to speak, then stopped, got up, and walked into the bedroom without a word. He came out with his clothes balled up in a plastic bag and gave me one last hug. He glanced down at the table, sheepishly picked up the ticket, crammed it in his pocket, turned his back, and walked out the door.

I sat there staring at the Paris box. It was as empty as I felt. When I finally walked into the bedroom, all that remained were some tortoiseshell guitar picks Eric had left on the dresser when he'd emptied his pockets the last night we'd made love.

It was official. Eric was gone.

39
TIME FOR ME TO GO

Goodbye, my friend, it's time for me to go now.
I think it's time to bring my soul back home now.
I've said all that I could possibly say,
I'm just hopin' and prayin' for a brighter day
When all our daughters won't have to feel this way.

"You made the right decision, Carol," Bruce said with tenderness in his voice.

"I really loved Eric. I hope I didn't make a big mistake!"

"Do you still think he was the right man for you?"

"I don't know. He was selfish. He put his career first and didn't respect mine. But now I'm alone. What if I never find love?"

"You will. You've come a long way."

"I don't know if I can ever get over Eric."

"Time is on your side. You have a lot going for you."

"You mean with my music? I could move to LA. Mona would help me get settled, but I'd rather stay in New York. I'm just gonna send her a tape. I've got some things happening in New York that have taken me a long time to get." I seemed to be answering Bruce, but I was actually thinking out loud.

"Like working with Rose? What's happening with your song?"

"Rose is still waiting to hear from the publisher. He's pitching it to some sort of werewolf movie."

"That sounds promising. And think of all the other things you've accomplished in one year. It's hard to be objective but look: You have a steady job, you're supporting yourself, you stood up to your parents, and soon you'll be officially renting Marvin's apartment. Not to mention that you quit smoking."

"But I'm a big failure when it comes to relationships - Robbie, Joshua, Eric. None of them worked out."

"You learned they weren't the right ones for you. That doesn't mean you're a failure."

"I knew I'd be crying today," I said, reaching for yet another tissue.

"It hurts now, but someday you'll look back and realize how much better off you are *not* being with them." Bruce paused for a minute and gave me a look that pierced my very soul. The intensity rippled through me from head to toe. "They were too weak for you," I heard him say.

"I hope I can get through this," I sniffled, wiping the tears from under my eyes as I tried to pull myself together. "I guess I'll have a lot of material for songwriting!" I said, taking a stab at a half-hearted joke.

"You're a lot stronger than you think. I believe you have a bright future ahead of you. Don't give up now."

I knew Bruce was right, but I wasn't ready to hear it. I needed time to mourn my almost perfect life.

Three weeks went by and each day got a little easier. Before I knew it, the middle of June rolled around, and it was my birthday. I'd been dreading spending the day—and especially the night—alone, but then Nina called and offered to take me on a girls' night out. On the day of my birthday, I asked Katie if I could leave work early. She not only agreed, she gave me a box of my favorite granola bars as a present. I left the store around two o'clock, which gave me plenty of time to shower and change.

Things were looking up as I got home from work and checked out my mailbox. It was full! I rushed up to the apartment and sat down on the couch. I was curious to see who'd sent me a card. Was I actually turning twenty-three? It sounded so *old*!

I was shocked to see a postcard from Paris in between the birthday cards. I took it out of the pile and put it on the coffee table. I wasn't ready to turn over the picture of a glittering Eiffel Tower lighting up the evening Parisian skies. *I almost got to see that*, I thought.

The first card was from my college roommate Marsha in Colorado. She'd painted an abstract blue and purple watercolor and written: *Happy Birthday, Lady of The Blues*. The next card was from my parents. There were individual notes from my father and mother inserted into the card with a hundred-dollar check. My mother wrote:

Dear Carol,

What does a mother say to a daughter who is 23 years old? Can I give you all of my experience and knowledge? Can I offer you the strength of my maturity? Can I guide you along life's path? No, none of these will do, for you must travel the path of self-discovery. I know that you must do it alone, but a mother can only hope that her echo will break the sound barrier. I can only hope that a ray of light will shine into the window of your heart and mind. My echo, my ray of light.

Happy Birthday,

Love,

Mommy

My mother's words made me feel very emotional. Tears were already welling up in my eyes as I turned to my father's poem.

At 23 love will seem true,

Full of depth, beauty and storm.

It will seal your heart like glue,

And make you a starry-eyed fawn.

Then all joy may turn to tears

And pain from a broken heart,

Though this boy, this love, will disappear

From the tender embrace of life's art.

These hurts are but lessons in strength

Which bitterly test who you are.

As always in the wings we'll wait

With our love to fill your needs,

For you are our life, our Fate—

We are one, like the earth, sun, and seeds.

By the time I reached the final line, bittersweet tears were flowing down my face. The heartfelt emotion of both of my parents touched me to the core. It was good to know that they would always be there for me, but even better to know that I could stand on my own two feet. It was a strange paradox—the freer I felt from them, the closer I felt to them.

I toyed with the idea of tearing up Eric's postcard, but I was too curious. I turned it over and read:

Hi Carol,

The tour's keeping me very busy, but I remembered it was your birthday and wanted to send you birthday wishes from Paris. As you know, the life of a musician is as unpredictable as a roller coaster ride, but two musicians in love is an even more difficult journey. I will always think of you fondly, ma chérie.

Love, Eric

I still missed him terribly and it hurt to be without him, but I was all out of tears. I put his postcard on top of the pile and placed them inside the Paris box I'd left sitting on the coffee table.

Eric was right—it was time to get off the roller coaster. I wanted to grab the brass ring but take my own steadier ride. I'd had enough drama to last ten lifetimes. I'd been with cheaters, bad boys, rebels, wanderers, and dreamers. I looked around the apartment. Marvin had forwarded me the lease a few days ago and it was now officially mine! In a few months, my rented piano would be paid off, too. It wasn't anything fancy, just a used Kohler and Campbell upright, and sometimes the second G below Middle C got stuck, but it was all mine, and I knew I'd be writing a lot of new songs on it.

I showered and slipped into the tie-dyed sundress I'd splurged on a few days after Eric left and took a good look at myself in the mirror. The dress was brightly colored, with a red, blue, and green batik pattern and not a hint of black. My breasts fit into it, no need for a bra, although I'd given in and bought two of them, and I even wore them occasionally! I was putting on concealer to cover the redness around my eyes when the buzzer rang. "Hi there, Birthday Girl!" Nina brightly greeted me as I pressed down on the intercom. "Ready to have fun?" I opened the door to the sound of her footsteps bounding up the stairs.

Nina burst in and gave me a big hug. "Happy Birthday!" she exclaimed, reaching out to twirl me around. "Wow, nice dress!" Laughing, she looked around, checking out the apartment. "The place looks good too. New curtains?"

"No, I've had them for a while."

She flopped on the couch and pointed to the Paris box. "That's pretty! What's inside?"

"Nothing but memories."

"Come on, it's time to make some new ones!" Nina exclaimed. She stood up, grabbed my arm, and led me out the door.

40
EPILOGUE

The sounds we hear take us to a place we've never been, the rhythm pulls us in
A wild ride, and suddenly we're in another time, your eyes meet mine
Heart and soul, discovering a world where we belong,
Beyond the lines, beyond the rhymes, beyond the song.

For the first time in my life, I felt like I had my own home, a real home. I'd signed the lease and Marvin's apartment was officially mine. I called my parents to tell them the good news and they begrudgingly admitted that I'd kept my part of the bargain—I was supporting myself and making inroads in the music business. Going back to college could wait!

Rose and I were on a roll. The publisher said that "Let Me Bring Out the Animal in You" was still under consideration for the werewolf movie, to play at the end when the credits rolled! Regina's recording with the little growl made the final cut for her album, which was coming out in a couple of weeks. I couldn't wait to hear how the song came out and see the credits on the back of the album cover: *Music and lyrics by Carol Marks and Rose Marie McCoy*!

Rose and I were shifting gears and writing country-pop songs. I'd come up with a song idea, "Tonight Will You Love Me One Last Time," and was finding songwriting therapeutic. I was releasing all the emotions

I felt about my break-up with Eric and finding a way to explore them. My weekly voice lessons with Maxine were paying off. I was pretty close to getting up the confidence to ask Rose if I could sing on the demo of our new song.

Marvin had sold me his furniture for practically nothing, but I wanted to add a few of my own touches to help me get organized and straighten up the apartment. One weekend, I took the bus to my parents and asked if they could donate some pieces. They were more than happy to oblige. I chose a modern pole lamp with three directional lights and a white Formica desk, and my father loaded up his trusty station wagon and dutifully drove me back to New York.

Remembering how he'd got the key stuck in the door the first time he'd helped me move to the city, I wasn't taking any chances. This time *I* turned the key in the lock as he nabbed a good parking spot a few doors down from the building. We managed to lug the furniture up the stairs and into the apartment and positioned the desk between the sofa and the piano so I could easily go from one to the other when writing. Just before he left, my father gave me a big hug and handed me an envelope. Inside, again, was a hundred-dollar bill, just as when I'd first moved in. Reading his note made me teary-eyed:

> *Carol,*
>
> *Your mother and I may not always agree with your decisions, but we are proud of you. We wish you much success in your new endeavors, but remember we're here for you and you always have a home in New Jersey.*

I made myself a cup of peppermint tea and started sorting through the piles of papers I'd accumulated over the last few months. Receipts, bills, and lyrics were haphazardly scattered all over my dresser, kitchen table, and even the top of the piano. Sitting at my desk for the first time, I was methodically examining each scrap of paper when I came across an old Chinese take-out menu. *Why did I keep this?* I wondered, turning it over. And there it was: 212-247-1254. Bruce's number, right where Marvin had scribbled it before he'd left for California. Marvin had been right. Bruce was the person I'd needed to call.

I smiled, thinking back to our last therapy session. Bruce had spoken first, "How do you think you're doing?" he asked.

"Pretty good. I'm so busy with songwriting and getting ready to play at The Bitter End that I don't have much time to worry about anything else."

"How would you feel about being on your own and not seeing me for a while?"

"Are you breaking up with me?" I asked half-jokingly. We had broached the subject of ending therapy several times, but it always seemed nebulous and far away.

Bruce smiled. "I think it's time to test the waters. You've proven to yourself that you can overcome life's obstacles. You're a survivor."

Even though I'd known this day was coming and that the goal of therapy was to leave, the realization that the time had actually come left me dumbstruck. When I finally found the words to speak, I was even more stunned to hear myself agreeing with Bruce.

"I can't believe I'm saying this, but you're right. I *am* a survivor," I said. I took a long, last look around the room that had been my sanctuary, my respite, for over a year. We stood up, and then I shyly looked up at Bruce. "Still, I'm gonna miss you."

"Remember, Carol, my door is always open if you need me."

I'd walked out of Bruce's office over three months ago. There were many times I felt tempted to call him, but something always stopped me. Of course, I missed his kind, handsome face, his understanding eyes, his reassuring voice, and the way he always calmed me down. But I was making my own decisions and I felt empowered and free.

My eyes turned back to the piles on the desk. One of Eric's postcards peeked out from under some old bills. There were several others from London, Rome, and Athens, but they didn't make me feel like I was missing out. Yes, there were times when I longed to feel his arms around me, but I was right where I wanted to be—in the heart of the greatest city in the world.

The late autumn wind gusted under my woolen poncho and I wrapped it around me a little tighter and sped up my pace to The Bitter End. So much had happened since the last time I'd been there to see Melissa Manchester with Melanie a little over nine months ago. Now I was going to perform on that very stage!

The sign in the front window caught my eye as I reached the club, stopping me in my tracks.

Sunday Afternoon Singer-Songwriter Showcase at The Bitter End
Featured Artists:
Manny Armstrong
Carol Marks
October 22nd–3PM

There it was—Carol Marks! I felt like pointing to my name and yelling, "Hey, that's me!" to all the passersby. I was playing at The Bitter End, the place where legends were made and so many of my idols had started out—Joan Baez, Judy Collins, Carly Simon, even Bob Dylan. Rose said that publishers and A&R label reps still frequented the club looking for new talent. So who knew? Maybe I'd be discovered too!

I checked my reflection in the window, smoothed my hair, and walked in the door. It was bright and sunny outside, but inside it could easily have been midnight. As my eyes adjusted to the dark, smoky club, I spotted Nina sitting at the reserved table, talking to Stevie and Dani, who'd come in from Jersey to support me. As I made my way toward them, weaving through the maze of tables in the timeless atmosphere of the half-filled club, Dani stood up to greet me.

"Thanks for coming! Can you believe this?" I asked, slipping off my poncho. Dani reached out and gave me a big bear hug.

"I always believed in your music!" she said, squeezing me hard.

"Me too!" Stevie joined in. She hugged me too, then stood back and shared her unsolicited opinion of my outfit. "Nice top! It'll look dramatic when you're at the keyboard!"

"Thanks, that's what I thought," I smiled. I'd chosen a white and silver off-the-shoulder blouse with bell sleeves from an upscale boutique in my neighborhood.

"Aren't you nervous?"

"My butterflies have butterflies!"

"That's a good sign," Nina assured me. "It means you're going to give a great performance!"

Just then Melanie came rushing through the door with the new boyfriend she'd met at NYU. And yes, he was rich! She looked very happy as she introduced us. "Good Luck! Break a leg!" she whispered in my ear.

As the waitress came to take our order, the club manager signaled me over for a soundcheck while he adjusted some speakers on stage. I tried out the Fender Rhodes keyboard on the intro to my first song. It reminded me of the keyboard I'd performed on with the band back in DC, except that this one was in tune. I *one, two, three'd* into the mic, the sound guy nodded OK, and I returned to my friends.

I'd just taken my seat when a tap on my shoulder made me turn around. There was Rose, looking as sophisticated as ever in a red dress, red beret, and brown leather coat.

"Carol, you look beautiful!"

"Thanks, Rose, so do you! Hey, everybody—this is my famous songwriter friend, Rose Marie McCoy!" I proclaimed. "We're working on some songs together!"

Just before the lights dimmed, I was floored to see my voice teacher walk into the club.

"Maxine!" I rushed over to greet her. "Thank you for coming to my show!"

"Carol dear, I wouldn't miss it for the world," she said and gave me a little hug. "Remember dear, take some deep breaths right before you begin, and don't start singing until you're absolutely comfortable."

The lights dimmed further yet as the first performer took the stage. He looked like a typical folksinger as he adjusted his twelve-string guitar, his embroidered guitar strap resting across the front of his faded denim shirt. He started in on a Dylan song, still staring down at his guitar, and I made a mental note to make eye contact with the audience. I clapped politely when he finished, but it was hard to concentrate as I waited for my turn in the spotlight.

And then I heard: "Let's give a big welcome to *Carol Marks!*"

"You're gonna be great," Rose whispered and beamed me a smile. I could hardly feel my feet as I stood up, and a wave of applause pushed me onto the stage.

I took my seat at the keyboard as if in a trance. I'd pictured this moment so many times that now when I was actually here, I felt like I was dreaming. I looked out at my smiling friends around the table and felt all their love and good vibes. Then I placed my hands on the keys, adjusted the mic a little closer, looked up once more at the crowd, and started to sing. I'd rehearsed my song so many times, the words flowed out of me, transporting me to another place and time.

Colored lights, and microphones that glitter in the night.
The singer's dressed in white.
She's standing there, acting cool,
As if she doesn't care how many stare.
The band begins, their fancy notes are playing short and long,
Beyond the lines, beyond the rhymes, beyond the song.

I looked up and that's when I saw him. Bruce. Standing in the back by the door. Now I *knew* I must be dreaming! The crowd blurred, and all I could see was him. Our eyes locked and a surge of energy went through me. I smiled and kept on singing.

Beyond the heartaches and the joys,

The stillness and the noise,

The grown men and the boys,

Beyond the song. . . .

ABOUT THE AUTHOR

Singer-songwriter Carol Selick performs a repertoire of jazz, rhythm and blues, pop, and her own work, and appears as a vocalist with her husband, jazz trumpeter and vocalist Gordon James. A gifted lyricist, she partnered with Hall-of-Famer Rose Marie McCoy, a songwriter for Nat King Cole, Louis Jordan, Maxine Brown, Ike & Tina Turner, and Elvis Presley, and she co-founded and directed The New Jersey Garden State Opry and the New Jersey Children's Opry, where she wrote and performed original songs. She holds a degree in Early Childhood Education and Music from Rutgers, and taught piano and voice for many years. Her recordings, *Life is Believing in You* and *Just Gonna Think About Today,* feature a mix of standards and originals, and she performs the bluesy vocals on James's 2019 release, *Come On Down*, praised in *Blues Blast* as "piping-hot New Orleans fare, satisfying and spicy with just the right amount of sweet dessert!"

Visit her at: carolselickmusic.com

CREDITS

A LIFE TO REMEMBER
Words and music by Carol Selick and Johnny Brandon.
Copyright © 2002 Grenadier Music (BMI). All Rights Reserved. Used by
Permission.

CHAINED AND TAMED WOMAN'S BLUES
Words and music by Carol Selick and Dori Seider.
Copyright © 2021. All Rights Reserved. Used by Permission.

IT'S GONNA WORK OUT FINE
Words and music by Rose Marie McCoy and Sylvia McKinney.
Copyright © 1961 Ben-Ghazi Enterprises, Inc./Twenty Nine Black Music.
All Rights Administered by Songs of Universal, Inc. All Rights Reserved.
Reprinted by Permission of Hal Leonard, LLC

JUST GONNA THINK ABOUT TODAY
Words and music by Carol Selick and Johnny Brandon.
Copyright © 2002 Grenadier Music (BMI). All Rights Reserved. Used by
Permission.

LET ME BRING OUT THE ANIMAL IN YOU
Words and music by Carol Selick and Rose Marie McCoy
Copyright © 1989 McCoy Music (BMI). All Rights Reserved. Used by
Permission.

THE MIDDLE OF THE ROAD
Words and music by Carol Selick and Johnny Brandon.
Copyright © 2002 Grenadier Music (BMI). All Rights Reserved. Used by
Permission.